Murder of a Botoxed Blonde

A Scumble River Mystery

DENISE SWANSON

A SIGNET BOOK

SIGNET
Published by New American Library, a division of
Penguin Group (USA) Inc., 375 Hudson Street,
New York, New York 10014, USA
Penguin Group (Canada), 90 Eglinton Avenue East, Suite 700, Toronto,
Ontario M4P 2Y3, Canada (a division of Pearson Penguin Canada Inc.)
Penguin Books Ltd., 80 Strand, London WC2R 0RL, England
Penguin Ireland, 25 St. Stephen's Green, Dublin 2,
Ireland (a division of Penguin Books Ltd.)
Penguin Group (Australia), 250 Camberwell Road, Camberwell, Victoria 3124,
Australia (a division of Pearson Australia Group Pty. Ltd.)
Penguin Books India Pvt. Ltd., 11 Community Centre, Panchsheel Park,
New Delhi - 110 017, India
Penguin Group (NZ), 67 Apollo Drive, Mairangi Bay,
Auckland 1311, New Zealand (a division of Pearson New Zealand Ltd.)
Penguin Books (South Africa) (Pty.) Ltd., 24 Sturdee Avenue,
Rosebank, Johannesburg 2196, South Africa

Penguin Books Ltd., Registered Offices:
80 Strand, London WC2R 0RL, England

First published by Signet, an imprint of New American Library,
a division of Penguin Group (USA) Inc.

First Printing, April 2007
10 9 8 7 6 5 4 3 2 1

"When writers as sharp as Margaret Maron, Earlene Fowler, and Jerrilyn Farmer all rave about a colleague as convincingly as they have about Denise Swanson . . . take notice." —*Chicago Tribune*

Murder of a Real Bad Boy

"Swanson is a born storyteller." —*CrimeSpree Magazine*

"Pack your bags and don't forget your funny bone as we head out for another knee-slapping adventure in Scumble River." —The Amplifier (KY)

"Scumble River is a joy to visit. . . . Skye is an intelligent and full-figured heroine who holds on tight to her independence, the mystery is fast-paced . . . and it wraps up nicely." —*Romantic Times*

Murder of a Smart Cookie

"In her seventh novel, Denise Swanson continues her insightful look at small-town life. *Murder of a Smart Cookie* smartly spins on a solid plot and likable characters." —*South Florida Sun-Sentinel*

"[A] hilarious amateur sleuth mystery. . . . [Swanson] has a lot of surprises in store for the reader." —*Midwest Book Review*

"A hoot." —*Romantic Times* (4 stars)

Murder of a Pink Elephant

"Get the hammock strung, the lemonade poured, and settle in for the must-read book of the summer. . . . With a sharp tongue and even sharper mind, Skye once again proves herself adept at outwitting not only the bad guys, but the well-meaning good guys." —*Butler County Post* (KY)

"One of my favorite series. I look forward to all my visits to Scumble River." —*CrimeSpree Magazine*

"Current readers will appreciate the trip into Scumble River, while new readers will want to go back."

—The Best Reviews

Other Scumble River Mysteries

This one is for my mom, Marie Swanson, and her wonderful friends—Marge Broucek, Esther Knorr, Lorie Rink, and Dolores (Aunt Pooch) Swanson—or, as I affectionately call them: The Yo Yo Sisters.

Acknowledgments

Thanks to Tracey Thomas, who knew Vince and Loretta would make a great couple long before I did. Also, to Kim Puckett, a teacher who e-mailed me the quip regarding the No Child Left Behind law.

Thanks to Dave Stybr, for sparking the idea for the chapter titles and the ending.

And to Louis Graham, welcome to the family. Just remember, anything you say or do can and might be used in a future book.

Author's Note

In July of 2000, when the first book, *Murder of a Small-Town Honey*, was published in my Scumble River series, it was written in "real time." It was the year 2000 in Skye's life as well as mine, but after several books in a series, time becomes a problem. It takes me from seven months to a year to write a book, and then it is usually another year from the time I turn that book in to my editor until the reader sees it on a bookstore shelf. This can make the timeline confusing. Different authors handle this matter in different ways. After a great deal of deliberation, I decided that Skye and her friends and family will age more slowly than those of us who don't live in Scumble River. Although I made this decision while writing the fourth book in the series, *Murder of a Snake in the Grass*, I didn't realize until recently that I needed to share this information with my readers. So to catch everyone up, the following is when the books take place.

Murder of a Small-Town Honey—August 2000
Murder of a Sweet Old Lady—March 2001
Murder of a Sleeping Beauty—April 2002
Murder of a Snake in the Grass—August 2002
Murder of a Barbie and Ken—November 2002
Murder of a Pink Elephant—February 2003
Murder of a Smart Cookie—June 2003
Murder of a Real Bad Boy—September 2003
Murder of a Botoxed Blonde—November 2003

The Scumble River short story and novella take place:

"Not a Monster of a Chance"—June 2001
"Dead Blondes Tell No Tales"—March 2003

CHAPTER 1

Rubbed the Wrong Way

"Ahhhhh!" An earsplitting scream penetrated Skye Denison's deep sleep.

She fought her way to consciousness, but she was still half dozing as she lay trying to remember where she was and what had roused her.

It was the Wednesday afternoon before Thanksgiving, and she had been dreaming she was the holiday turkey. A dream brought on, no doubt, by the butterlike substance slathered over every inch of her skin, the seaweed wrapped around her, and the tinfoil covering her from neck to toes.

Of course, being stretched out on a steel table with an overhead heating element, baking her at what felt like 350°, might have added to the illusion. That, along with the timer that had just popped out, might give anyone fowl dreams.

"Ahhhhh!" Another scream surged through the louvered doors of the spa treatment room.

This one cleared the confusion from Skye's mind and brought her fully awake. She shot upright . . . or at least she tried to. But rather than sitting up and swinging her legs over the edge of the table as she intended, she found she couldn't fold in the middle. Instead, she slipped and rolled onto the floor, where she landed like a turtle stuck in the mud.

In her dream, Skye, AKA Thanksgiving dinner, had been struggling to avoid her mother, who was wielding a giant meat fork and carving knife. Remnants of that nightmare surfaced when Skye realized her arms were bound to her sides and her legs pressed together by layer upon layer of Reynolds Wrap. She was completely immobilized.

Her heart pounding and her breath coming in gulps, Skye fought a rising sense of panic. Closing her eyes, she concentrated on thinking tranquil thoughts, and once she had calmed down, she discovered she could move by rolling.

Skye had just made it to the door, and had almost convinced herself that the shrieks she had heard were part of her dream, when there was another scream, this one even louder than the first two.

Shit! Why had she ever agreed to a seaweed wrap? Heck, why had she agreed to spend her holiday weekend at Scumble River's new spa? She wasn't a spa kind of girl. Getting naked and letting perfect strangers tell her what was wrong with her body had never appealed to Skye.

Granted, the massage had been lovely, and apparently so relaxing that she fell asleep, but where was the masseuse? Or, for that matter, anyone else? What kind of spa was this? What kind of place would wrap you up so that you were helpless, then just leave you lying around like Thanksgiving leftovers? In what kind of place did screams go unchecked? Her thoughts raced as she tried to figure out how to hoist herself upright and open the door.

Finally, Skye came up with a way to use the knob like a hook to haul herself to her feet. Once erect, she used her fingernails to tear a small hole in the foil covering her hand. Using the three fingers she had been able to poke through the slit, she turned the knob and pushed the door open.

She had just made it into the hallway when another scream echoed off the marble floors. This one sounded worse than the previous ones. Was she already too late to help?

Hopping was the only form of locomotion Skye could manage with her legs bound together, and she had to go slowly since she couldn't risk falling and not being able to get up again. Soon she developed a rhythm of hopping, opening each door she came to in the hall, and looking inside.

The last scream had sounded close by, and as Skye approached the fourth door down, another shriek blasted through. Skye grabbed the knob, turned it, and flung herself into the room.

She had prepared herself for the worst, but even so, Skye came to an abrupt halt when she saw what was happening. Swaying, she fought to stay upright as a wave of hysteria threatened to overtake her. She stared at her best friend and school librarian, Trixie Frayne, lying spread eagle with a young woman seated between her thighs ripping out strips of wax covered in pubic hair.

Skye sank to the floor, her shoulders shaking, tears of laughter running down her cheeks. She had just rushed through the halls like a foil-covered tortilla in order to save her friend from the horrible, the feared, the deadly . . . Brazilian bikini wax.

"Oh, Miss, I am so sorry. Are you injured? Do you need the doctor?"

"No, Ustelle." Skye looked up at the masseuse, who had appeared in time to see her collapse. One last hysterical giggle escaped her lips as she reassured the worried young woman, "I'm fine. Really. Just laughing at my overactive imagination."

"How did you get in here, Miss?" Ustelle grasped Skye's shoulders and raised her to her feet with one effortless motion—an impressive demonstration of the woman's strength, since Skye was far from a lightweight.

"I'll explain later." Skye started hopping toward the door. "Just get this stuff off me."

"Yes, Miss." Ustelle looked back over her shoulder and fixed her younger coworker with a stern gaze. "Amber, I would be most unhappy if this incident was talked about."

Amber gave the masseuse a calculating glance. "What's it worth to you?"

Ustelle's mouth flattened as she snapped, "We'll discuss it later."

"Whatever." Amber shrugged.

Ustelle's face was red when she turned back to Skye, but she calmly guided her down the hallway and into her own treatment room. As she peeled the Reynolds Wrap from Skye, she apologized again. "I am so sorry for having left you so long. I had to make a personal call, and I did not think it would take as much time as it did."

"Sure." Once freed of the foil, Skye stepped into the corner shower. "I understand."

"Please do not tell Dr. Burnett or Miss Margot." Ustelle handed Skye a loofah. "If I lose this job, I shall be forced to return to Sweden."

"I won't tell them," Skye promised, wondering if the spa owners were really so unforgiving that they would fire an employee for so minor an infraction.

"Thank you. Anything you require for the remainder of your stay, I shall take care of it for you." Ustelle's long blond braid bobbed as she spoke and her blue eyes shone with earnestness.

"Really. It's nothing. Don't worry." Skye dried herself with the giant towel the masseuse handed her, turbaned a smaller towel around her wet hair, then slipped on the white terry robe the spa asked all its guests to wear between treatments. "I'm going to rest until dinner. We'll just forget about this whole afternoon."

Once Skye reached the room she was sharing with Trixie, she threw off the spa robe, which was too tight anyway. The label might say one size fits all, but clearly, the manufacturer had never met a woman above a size twelve.

Replacing the robe with the jeans and sweater she had worn upon her arrival that morning, Skye began to feel back in control. She unwound the towel from around her head and combed out her chestnut curls. When her hair lay like a wet poodle down her back, she looked at the clock. Two hours until dinner. If she wanted some quiet time to relax and decompress, she couldn't stay in the room.

Trixie would be back soon, wanting to discuss what had just happened.

Skye grabbed a book, and set out to find a place to sit and read while her hair dried. The old Bruefeld Mansion, now the Scumble River Spa, had recently been remodeled and enlarged by the new owners. The two wings of the main house had been converted into guest accommodations, the central building into treatment rooms and common areas, and the attic into staff lodgings. The basement had been renovated to provide an area for the mud baths and a private suite of rooms had been added to the first floor in the rear as living quarters for Margot Avanti and her husband, Creighton Burnett. In addition, VIP cottages, a gym with an indoor pool, and a hair salon had been built next to the mansion.

With the vast space available, and the limited number of guests, Skye was sure she could find a quiet spot to be alone. She wanted to gather her thoughts before word spread of her performance this afternoon. Once everyone found out what a fool she had made of herself, hopping to the rescue like Crusader Rabbit, she wouldn't find another peaceful moment for a long, long time.

During her stroll around the ground floor, Skye noted that the turret she had observed on the outside was just for decoration, although there was evidence of a recently removed circular stairway. Next, she poked her head into the dining room, now cleared of food. She briefly considered sitting in the library, but the walnut paneling, hand-carved detailing, and towering bookcases were more intimidating than relaxing.

The central courtyard, paved with cobblestones around an outdoor swimming pool, was appealing but the pool was closed for the season, and the patio furniture was stacked under plastic tarps.

Finally, like Goldilocks she found a spot that was just right. As soon as Skye entered the solarium, she felt herself relax. Sun streaming through three walls of floor-to-ceiling windows made the room toasty warm. To the left was a pleasant view of trees leading down to the river, to the right the magnificent driveway swept from the house into the woods, and straight ahead were several acres of rolling lawn interrupted only by . . . what in the heck was that dark square ruining the perfect carpet of grass?

Skye frowned and moved closer to the center window. Straining her eyes, she finally figured out what she was staring at: the Bruefeld family graveyard. Come to think of it, she had heard that the new owners had wanted to move the coffins to the town cemetery, but due to some law or maybe some restriction in the deed, they hadn't been able to, and the family burial ground remained where it had been for a hundred or so years.

She took one more look, then curled up on the floral cushions of a white wicker rocker. Opening her book, she stared at the printed pages for several minutes, sighed, and set the novel aside. Closing her eyes, she let her mind wander, trying to pinpoint the exact moment when she had been talked into spending her Thanksgiving weekend at the spa. It had all started on Halloween, when one of the spa owners had come to Skye for help . . .

Skye stood just outside the rear entrance of Scumble River Elementary School and watched the students parade around the perimeter of the parking lot dressed in their Halloween costumes, which ran the gamut from beautiful princesses to ghastly monsters.

As the school psychologist, Skye didn't have much to do on a day like Halloween. She couldn't test any students or observe in any classroom, and no one wanted to have a meeting. She'd spent the morning writing reports, but had decided to take a break from the paperwork and attend the afternoon Halloween procession.

Normally in Illinois, mothers made sure Halloween costumes were loose enough to wear over snowsuits, but this year the weather had surprised them. The sun glared down on the concrete steps and asphalt drive as if it were July. Skye huddled in the little bit of shade the overhang provided. She had dressed in khaki slacks and a short sleeve peach polo shirt, prepared for the non-air-conditioned school, but the sweat still dripped off her face and pooled under her arms.

As the last of the children completed the circuit, the teachers marched their students into their classrooms for refreshments and games. Skye was considering going to the special education classroom to see if she could help with their party when the PA system squawked, "Ms. Denison, please come to the office."

Skye felt a frisson of unease at the announcement. It was exceedingly unusual for her to be summoned via PA at the grade school. While the high school principal called for Skye's assistance at the first sign of an angry parent or sticky situation, the elementary school principal went to the other extreme, handling everything but the most severe matters on her own. Skye hurried toward the front of the school, a line of worry appearing between her eyebrows as she wondered what could have happened.

When she entered the school office, she saw a stunningly beautiful woman who seemed somewhat familiar standing at the counter.

Skye nodded to her, then said to Fern Otte, the school secretary, "You sent for me?"

"Yes." Fern clipped off the word, giving it an impatient edge. She was a tiny woman whose affinity for brown clothing enhanced her resemblance to a wren.

Skye wasn't sure what had put the ticked-off look in Fern's small black eyes, but she hoped it wasn't something she had done. Getting on Fern's bad side was a career-limiting move. Behind the secretary's mild façade, she ran the office as if it were the Department of Motor Vehicles—everyone took a number, waited their turns, and kept their mouths shut.

The silence lengthened until finally Fern said, "This"— the pause was almost imperceptible—"person insisted I summon you, and refused to give a reason."

"Oh." Skye looked toward the woman causing Fern's pique; Skye had to be careful not to appear to be taking her side against the secretary. "I'm Skye Denison. You wanted to see me?"

"I'm Margot Avanti. Is there somewhere we could speak in private?"

"Is this about one of our students?"

Margot ignored Skye's question and restated her request, "I'd prefer to speak to you alone."

Skye gave Fern an apologetic look, and said to Margot, "We can use my office, but I'm afraid it isn't air-conditioned."

"Fine."

Skye led the way to her office. The woman followed, the only sound the click of her high heels on the worn gray linoleum.

In order to break the silence, Skye attempted a small joke. "I have to apologize for my office. I'm sure you've heard about the 'No Child Left Behind' law, but what we really need is a 'No School Psychologist Stuck in a Broom Closet' law."

The woman looked at Skye blankly, then carefully studied the interior of Skye's office before stepping inside. The room contained a small desk and two metal folding chairs. It had started life as a storage room for the cafeteria, and a faint odor of sour milk still permeated the air.

Once they sat down, Skye asked, "What can I do for you, Ms. Avanti?" as she tried to edge her seat back a little. With her knees nearly touching the other woman's, Skye felt as if they were about to play patty cake.

"Please call me Margot." Despite the heat, the woman's ash blond hair remained perfectly straight, her makeup was intact, and her Yves Saint Laurent blouse and skirt were crisp and unwrinkled.

"Margot it is." Skye had a strong sense of having seen the woman previously. "We haven't met before, have we?"

"No, Ms. Denison, I don't think so, but"—Margot's smile was smug—"you've probably seen me in magazines or on TV. I was one of the top American models before I retired a few years ago."

"Ah, that explains it." Now Skye recalled seeing Margot in an ad for very expensive jewelry. She had been wearing diamonds and not much more. "By the way, please call me Skye."

"That's a beautiful name." Margot tilted her head. "Do you have sisters called Sun, Moon, and Cloud?"

"No, just a brother named Vince." Skye studied Margot, trying to decide if the woman was mocking her. Margot's face had an eerie perfection that showed little emotion, making her as hard to read as a game show host.

Finally, Skye gave up trying to guess the woman's intentions, and asked again, "Why did you want to see me?"

Margot reached into her purse and handed Skye a brochure. "My husband and I are opening a beauty spa and resort on the old Bruefeld Estate."

"Yes, I've heard a spa was coming to town. How did you happen to choose Scumble River?"

Skye's question was one that most of the townspeople were asking. Opening a spa in the rural community seemed as silly to them as trying to farm a few acres in the center of Chicago's Grant Park. Scumble River had a population of three thousand, and was located in the middle of the Illinois prairie. There was little to recommend it to the wealthy clientele most spas attracted.

"My husband, Dr. Creighton Burnett, discovered that the mud of the Scumble River, as it goes past the Bruefeld Estate, is rich in sulfur, iron, manganese, and nickel, and has a salt rate of twenty-seven percent. When our own secret ingredient is added, it is the perfect formula for smoothing and softening the skin and making it look young again."

"I see. But do you really think women will travel to the middle of nowhere just for some mud?"

"Not just some mud, Miracle Mud. Wouldn't you go out of your way to find the Fountain of Youth?"

Skye shrugged. "I guess some people might." She certainly wanted to look nice, and wasn't opposed to using moisturizers and makeup to shave off a few years, but flying hundreds or thousands of miles to bathe in mud was beyond what she was willing to do to look young. "But—"

Margot cut off Skye. "I can't understand why you people aren't thrilled to have a new business." The spa owner's sapphire eyes glinted with impatience, but her expression remained unchanged, as if she were incapable of frowning. "We're creating jobs, bringing in people who will spend money here—why is everyone so damned negative?"

Margot's attack surprised Skye, and she tried to explain, realizing she hadn't been as diplomatic as she might have been. "I can't speak for the whole town, but I'm sure their skepticism comes from a lack of understanding, and maybe doubts that people will come here for a stay, rather than anything against you or your business."

"You're probably right." Margot did an abrupt about-face, her shoulders drooping. "And I can see how you people might think that way, but we're going to succeed. My husband and I have put all our money into this project. Nothing and no one will stand in our way."

"I'm sure no one will intentionally try and make the spa fail, no matter what the town gossips say about it." Skye leaned slightly forward and patted Margot's hand, wondering why the woman was telling *her* all this.

"That's just it. Someone *is* trying to sabotage us. That's why I've come to you."

"Me? Why?"

Margot flipped back the oval clasp on her crocodile purse, reached in, and thrust a sheaf of newspaper clippings into Skye's hands. "Because you're the Scumble River Nancy Drew. Everyone tells me you're the only one who can solve the mystery."

"People exaggerate." Skye noticed the spa owner's purse was a Dolce & Gabbana, which probably retailed for five hundred a pop. Margot didn't need Skye's help; she could afford to hire the best private investigator in Chicago. "I'm a school psychologist, not a detective. You should be talking to the police."

"I have. They took my information, came out to the spa, and looked around. They said there wasn't much they could do. They only have one or two officers on duty at any one time, and I need someone twenty-four/seven if I want to catch the vandal."

"Then you need to hire a security firm, not me." Skye tried to avoid looking into the woman's desperate eyes.

"I did hire a firm. They've been on my payroll an entire month and haven't caught anyone." Margot pointed to the clippings in Skye's hand. "All these stories are about you solving murders no one else could figure out."

"The newspaper overstated my contribution." Skye flipped through the articles Margot had handed her, wishing she could convince Kathryn Steele, the owner of the *Scumble River Star*, to quit doing stories on her and go back to putting people who built houses from Popsicle sticks on the front page.

"According to the latest piece, you signed on as a consultant for the local police."

"True," Skye admitted. "But I only help as a psychological consultant, not as a detective."

"That's what we need. Someone who can talk to people and figure out why they're doing this to us," Margot pleaded. "It's nothing big, but it's all extremely annoying. Outside, they've dug holes everywhere. We've had to replace so much sod I feel like we should buy it by the truckload. Inside, they've ripped open the plaster. Tools and personal items have gone missing, doors are jammed, and at night we hear the most ungodly noises. I'm afraid if this continues once we have paying guests, the spa will fail." Margot pulled a checkbook from her open purse. "Name your fee."

Skye shook her head. "I'm not a licensed private detective. I can't accept money. Besides, I already have a job. I just don't have time to investigate. You need someone who could move in and observe everyone around the clock."

"Please, just think about it." Margot reached into her bag once more, this time producing a business card and brochure. "If we haven't found the culprit in the next three weeks, please come for the 'dry run' opening. We're offering the local women four nights at half price over the long Thanksgiving weekend, so it wouldn't look odd that you were there. Of course, your stay and a friend's would be free of charge, with all the spa treatments and amenities included."

Skye thanked the woman, and said she'd consider it. She walked Margot Avanti to the front door and waved goodbye. As she made her way back to her cramped, hot office, Skye was tempted by the spa owner's offer, then shook her head. Nothing was ever free.

CHAPTER 2

Beauty Is in the Eye
of the Beholder

"You what?" Trixie Frayne squealed, popping up from her chair and bouncing on her heels as if she were Tigger. She and Skye were in Skye's office at the high school. "Are you out of your mind? Why would you turn down a free vacation at a spa?"

Skye sat behind her desk with her feet propped on the open lower drawer, watching her friend. Trixie was the high school librarian. She also coached the cheerleading squad and cosponsored the school newspaper with Skye. Trixie's energy level made a Chihuahua look sedate.

"You can still call and change your mind, right?" Trixie gazed pleadingly at Skye.

"Sure, unless they caught the vandal last night. But why should I?"

"Because," Trixie drawled the word, making it several syllables, "you and I could catch whoever's messing around the first day, then we'd have the rest of the weekend to be pampered."

"What makes you think we could catch this trespasser so fast?"

"Didn't you see today's *Star*?" Trixie demanded.

"No. You may get yours delivered to the school library, but I need to wait until I get home. Besides, what does the town newspaper have to do with capturing the vandal?"

"There was an article about the new spa on the front page. It said that there's a hidden treasure on the Bruefeld Estate, and the house and grounds are cursed."

"You're kidding." Skye fought her curiosity.

"Nope. It said that the property was originally owned by a millionaire, who, when he lost everything in the crash of 1929, killed his wife, then committed suicide. The newspaper even dug up a story that before the crash, the wife hid a million dollars in jewels that have never been found. The estate's next several owners also either lost money or their lives, and the property has been unoccupied for the past thirty years."

"Interesting."

"So, what do you think?" Trixie asked. "Is it jinxed?"

"I doubt it. The 'curse' sounds like something the newspaper dreamed up. I've never heard of it, and considering that several of my aunts are the queens of gossip around here, I'm sure I would have." Skye considered the estate's history. "My guess is that something that old, that big, and that costly is bound to have an out-of-the-ordinary history. I'm sure the paper just didn't report the happy families that lived there."

Trixie shrugged. "Anyway, I'll bet the vandal that's been bugging the new owners is someone who already knew about the treasure and is looking for it. The holes in the ground and in the walls are obviously a result of someone searching for the jewelry, and the other vandalism is to delay the spa from opening to give the person more time to find the treasure."

"You know," Skye scratched her chin, "that's not a bad guess."

"It means we could set a trap for him or her, and catch 'em in the act without breaking a sweat."

"Maybe"—Skye's tone was stubborn—"but I'm still not going to take Margot up on her offer."

"Why not?"

"First, Mom would kill me if I missed Thanksgiving with the family."

Trixie finally sat down. "You don't have to. The spa is five minutes from your mom's house. I'll drive you myself."

"Second, this will be the first holiday I'll celebrate with Wally since we've been dating." She'd started dating Wally Boyd a little more than a month ago, after breaking up with her longtime boyfriend Simon Reid, whom she had caught cheating on her at the end of the summer.

"Again, the spa is five minutes away. You can see your precious police chief." Trixie ran her fingers through her short faun-colored hair. "What'll that take, a couple of hours? It's not as if you two are sleeping together."

Skye scowled at Trixie, got up to close her office door, and sat back down. Even though it was nearly impossible in a town of three thousand people, half of whom Skye was related to, she was trying to keep her love life private. "How do you know we're not having wild monkey sex?" She and Wally'd had a thing for each other for years, but only recently had all the circumstances finally been right for them to date. Skye was determined to take it slow and not jump into bed before they had established a solid relationship.

"Because neither of you has that glow really great sex gives you. So, either he's no good in bed, which I would have trouble believing because that man is so hot he sizzles, or you're making the poor thing wait and prove his devotion to you."

Skye chose to ignore her friend's baiting and went back to her original conversation. "Third, I really don't feel like playing Sherlock Holmes. This has been a tough fall for me, and I need a break."

Trixie shrieked, "What could be more relaxing than a spa, for heaven's sake?"

"Which brings me to the most important reason; I don't want to do it. Spas freak me out." Skye indicated her ample curves. "Why would I want to go to a place where you pay someone to criticize your weight, your hair, your skin, etc.? My mom does that for free."

Trixie choked on the mini Snickers bar she had just shoved into her mouth. After she took a sip of her Coke, and stopped coughing, she said, "No one at the spa will be negative to you about your looks, unless you ask them to be. Just don't select the fitness evaluation or sign up for time with the personal trainer." Trixie grabbed another Halloween candy bar from the dish on Skye's desk. "Sign up for massages, and facials, and manicures, and pedicures instead."

"Easy for you to say. You don't mind people seeing you naked." Skye glowered at her friend, who was still stuffing her face with chocolate. "You've been a size four since I met you our freshman year in high school. You don't exercise, you eat your weight in snack food, and you never gain an ounce. The spa people would love you."

Trixie got out of her chair, walked around the desk, and bent down to hug Skye. "No one will say anything about you, except to comment on your amazing eyes, your fantastic hair, and your beautiful skin." Trixie straightened and curled both hands into fists. "And if they do say anything that upsets you, I'll take care of them."

Skye swallowed, touched by Trixie's fierce loyalty. "I know you would, but that's not the point. I still—"

"Please, please, please, say we can go. Together we can help the new owners, plus I need you! If I'm home for Thanksgiving, I'll have to cook for Owen's entire family—all forty-eight of them. I'll have to clean the house from top to bottom, and Owen and I will get into a big fight because he'll be too busy with the farm to help me. And I swore the last time it was our turn to host the holiday, if his uncle and aunt and their five bratty kids stayed with us, I was divorcing Owen." Trixie hugged Skye. "Please save my marriage."

Skye had never noticed how little time there was between Halloween and Thanksgiving, until she woke the morning of Wednesday, November 26, and realized that the Bruefeld Mansion vandal was still at large, and Trixie had not been talked out of spending the holiday weekend at the spa with Skye, acting as Scumble River's newest Charlie's Angels.

Groaning, Skye pulled the covers up over her head. She'd been blocking this day from her thoughts for the past couple of weeks, hoping the spa owners would catch their vandal, call, and tell her they had no need for her services.

Unhappily, Margot hadn't phoned, and Trixie hadn't suddenly decided she'd rather be with her relatives for Thanksgiving. Willing or not, Skye was spending her long holiday weekend at the Scumble River Spa. On a positive note, she'd always wanted to stay in a cursed mansion with a hidden treasure. Heck, maybe she'd even meet a prince, or a duke, or at the very least an earl.

Yes, that was the attitude to take. This was an adventure. She'd just need to be firm about the spa treatments, and decline any that required nudity or stepping on a scale. She'd spend her time at the indoor swimming pool, and show up only for fun activities like facials and pedicures.

As she often told her students—occasionally, everyone had to do things they didn't want to. How you handled those situations was what defined you as a person.

Which meant, she'd better get moving. She kicked the bedclothes off and sat up. A brief phone call to her brother secured his services as a pet sitter for her cat Bingo, and after a quick shower, she ran some errands and packed. Skye was lugging her suitcase out the front door when Trixie's car roared into the driveway. It was exactly eleven forty-five, check-in was at noon, and Trixie had made it clear that she didn't want to miss a moment of her free weekend.

Skye was still fretting over what she had packed when she climbed into the passenger seat. Maybe she should have bought some of those fancy exercise outfits she'd seen in *Glamour*.

Trixie interrupted Skye's musings by waving a sheaf of newsprint in her face. "Did you see this week's paper?"

"No." Skye finished buckling her seatbelt, then grabbed the *Scumble River Star* from her friend's hand. "What's up now?"

Trixie flung the car in gear and stepped on the gas. She had sold her prized Mustang convertible to pay off a debt, and now owned a ten-year-old Honda Civic, but she still drove as if she were racing on the NASCAR circuit.

Skye shut her eyes and prayed as Trixie backed out of the driveway without even glancing in the rearview mirror.

"Quit cowering. You know I'm a good driver." Trixie

slowed to a modest sixty, then answered Skye's question. "Another article on the Bruefeld Mansion being cursed and the hidden jewels."

"Shit! Margot told me she spoke to the editor after the first piece was published and explained that if there was a treasure they would have found it during the renovations, and asked her to stop publishing those kinds of articles."

"What did Kathryn say to that?"

"She said that a cursed mansion and a hidden treasure were too good a story to pass up." Skye shook her head. "And until Margot could prove there wasn't a curse or a treasure, she was pursuing the story."

"Well, if nothing else, Kathryn is true to her word. This time there's even a riddle that's supposed to be a clue to the treasure's location."

"Great. If your theory is right and the vandal is really a treasure hunter, that'll make him or her even more determined to find the jewels before someone else does."

"Read the article. Maybe it'll give you an idea of where we should lay our trap."

Skye studied the story until Trixie pulled through massive iron gates and onto a wide paved driveway.

"Is this it?" Skye folded the paper and put it in her purse to examine later.

"According to the sign, the spa's straight ahead."

Skye had never seen the Bruefeld Estate. It was located south of town along the Scumble River and had been fenced off since the last owner had declared bankruptcy when Skye was still a toddler. Lining the lane was a row of massive oak trees. As they rounded the first curve, a huge Norman-style stone mansion appeared as if hovering above the ground on a magic carpet.

Once they grew closer, Skye could see that the mansion was actually situated on a small rise overlooking the river. Surrounding it were half a dozen cottages and several larger detached structures, also made of stone and slate with copper turret-style roofs, reminding her that the brochure Margot had given her had mentioned private VIP accommodations for those who wanted a more luxurious stay.

Traces of the recent reconstruction were still evident and several men seemed to be hurriedly cleaning up around the area. Skye shaded her eyes and peered intently at the smallest figure. After a moment she recognized him as Elvis Doozier, from a rather stunted branch of one of Scumble River's odder family trees.

A year or so ago Elvis had gotten into some trouble at the high school and Skye had reviewed his file. His IQ fell between seventy and eighty, which meant he didn't meet the criteria for a learning disability—students had to have average or above average intelligence to be considered LD. Unfortunately, he also didn't qualify for services in the mentally impaired category—there the IQ had to fall below sixty-nine. Thus he didn't qualify for any special services, but at the same time there was no way he could keep up with average students.

Elvis was one of the school system's failures. Guilt washed over Skye as she watched him hurrying to keep up with the other men. She'd heard he'd dropped out of school on his sixteenth birthday, and she'd meant to talk to his guardian about finding a vocational training program for him, but had never gotten around to it. Seeing him as a part of the construction crew made her hope that he had found a good job without her help.

As the road straightened and passed through a second set of gates, she lost sight of the workers. Once past those gates, they found themselves on a circular drive in front of an impressive set of granite stairs leading to the front entrance.

Skye hadn't known what to expect, never having been to a spa before, but the dozen or so women holding protest signs and marching in a circle at the bottom of the steps was not on her list of guesses.

Trixie slammed on the brakes and squealed to a stop inches from one of the protestors, who had apparently decided it would be a good idea to throw herself into the automobile's path.

Skye screamed, flung open her door, and jumped out of the car. "Are you okay?"

The woman was tall, athletically built, and her face was free of makeup. Brown hair hung straight down her back, brushing the waistband of her jeans as she turned her head. Hazel eyes examined Skye and clearly found her wanting. "We're closing down this temple of false beauty. Turn around and go home."

Trixie got out of the car at the same time that a second protestor, who wore her hair in a crew cut, joined the first. Trixie was barely five-foot-two, but she walked up to the group, all of whom towered over her like redwood trees over a shrub, put her hands on her hips, and demanded, "What's the problem?"

The brunette answered, "Real women don't need artificial beauty. Support the cause, sister. Turn around and go home."

While Trixie was arguing with the women, Skye read the various protest signs.

PAINT IS FOR HOUSES, NOT FACES.
REAL WOMEN HAVE CURVES.
ONLY BARBIE SHOULD LOOK LIKE BARBIE.
STOP DYEING TO BE BEAUTIFUL.
WE HAVE ENOUGH YOUTH, HOW ABOUT A FOUNTAIN OF SMART?

Trixie narrowed her eyes. "No one's getting in the way of my free weekend."

Crew Cut stepped into Trixie's personal space and snarled, "Women like you make me sick. Everything is me, me, me. You never think of the greater good."

"How can you say that? You don't know anything about her." Skye moved next to her friend and glared at the protestor. "Trixie is the most generous person on Earth."

The brunette shot the crew-cut woman a look, and then said in a conciliatory tone, "Our organization, Real Women, is trying to stop the disturbing trend of artificial beauty infiltrating every walk of life. It was bad enough when movie stars and models were having their flesh carved, starving themselves, and hiring trainers as if they were poodles competing in some dog show, but now this movement is creeping into Middle America. And we aim to stop it."

"Fine." Trixie's expression was stubborn. "I promise we're not having any surgery, we are certainly not going on any stupid diet, and the last person who tried to train me was my mother—the issue was the potty versus diapers. All I want is a few days of peace and quiet with the occasional massage, facial, manicure, and pedicure."

Crew Cut poked her finger into Trixie's shoulder. "The point is your money supports the idea that it's okay for these people to tell women they aren't beautiful unless they look like twelve-year-old boys."

"But it's not my money." Trixie stamped her foot. "They're giving us this weekend free."

Both Crew Cut and the brunette shook their heads. The latter said, "That doesn't matter. Your being here gives the wrong message."

Trixie's firm jaw was set. "Look, the average woman would rather have beauty than brains because the average man can see better than he can think. Do you really think a few cardboard signs will stop anyone from staying at this spa if they think it will make them look younger and more attractive?"

Crew Cut's gaze was unbending. "Maybe we won't be able to stop everyone, but we sure can stop you."

Skye was torn. In some ways, she agreed with the protestors. And heaven knows she would be happy to turn around and go home. But these women seemed to think their rights superseded Trixie's rights, and Skye wasn't about to put up with that. She was sick of people who thought freedom of speech meant freedom to harass anyone who didn't think the same way they did.

She took Trixie's arm and attempted to walk around the women, but the protestors formed a line, blocking the spa's entrance. They were at a standoff when another car drove into sight. Squinting into the sunlight, Skye frowned and dropped Trixie's arm. The approaching white Oldsmobile looked mighty familiar.

Trixie took one look at Skye's face, muttered something about getting their purses, and hightailed it back to the Civic.

Skye barely noticed her friend's defection as the Oldsmobile's driver got out, flung up her arms, and yelled, "Surprise!"

CHAPTER 3

Chewing the Low Fat

"What are *you* doing here?" Skye asked.

Before she answered, Skye's mother reached up and tucked a stray curl behind Skye's ear, pulled Skye's sweater down, and brushed a streak of dust off her jeans. May's own short salt-and-pepper hair never had a strand out of place, and her crisp twill pants and matching jacket looked as if they had just left the ironing board. "When Trixie mentioned you two were coming to the spa for Thanksgiving," May said, "we decided it was the perfect chance to surprise you with one of those girls only weekends they're always talking about on the TV."

Skye stowed away for later examination the fact that her mom and best friend had schemed together behind her back, and asked, "What about Thanksgiving dinner?" May had hosted the relatives from both sides of the family for as long as Skye could remember.

"Aunt Kitty agreed to have it this year. I sent our regrets."

"But there's no reason to miss it. We're nearly as close here as we are at home. Besides, I already invited Wally."

"So he said." May was a dispatcher for the Scumble River Police Department, and Wally was the chief of police. "That's another reason I decided this was a good year for you to skip. That way, next year, when you're back together with Simon, it'll be less awkward." May didn't approve of

Skye dating Wally, who was older, divorced, and not Catholic.

"Mother!" Emerald green eyes that matched May's own blazed. "I *am* going to the family Thanksgiving dinner. I *am* bringing Wally. I am *not* getting back together with Simon." Skye gritted her teeth. Why couldn't May understand? The last time she'd seen Simon was nearly two months ago, when his mother and hers had locked them together in the bowling alley basement in an attempt to force them to make up. He had refused to explain how he "forgot" to mention that the college friend he was staying with on his trip to California was a woman; and Skye had refused to trust him without an explanation. Now Skye shook her finger at her mother and snarled, "Simon is out of my life. Deal with it."

Another vehicle pulled into the driveway, saving May from responding. This one was a Mercedes with a license plate that read CRMPAYS. May grabbed Skye's arm and dragged her over to the Benz.

A six-foot-tall, well-toned woman with smooth mahogany skin and black hair worn in a coronet of braids got out of the driver's seat. May hugged her, and said to Skye, "I asked Loretta to join us. Since she and Vince are dating, I want to get to know her better."

Loretta gave Skye a hug and kiss, and said in a droll tone, "Surprise."

Loretta Steiner was Skye's sorority sister, sometimes attorney, and possibly her future sister-in-law, although Skye wasn't holding her breath about that since her brother Vince had a "love 'em and leave 'em" reputation. Skye would need to get Loretta alone to hear how May had convinced her to attend this little party.

Before Skye could begin to worry about who else might show up for the weekend, an old red Camaro roared down the lane and stopped with a loud backfire. Both Skye and her mother stood with their mouths hanging open as a long-legged, middle-aged redhead dressed in lime spandex pants, matching faux fur jacket, and stilettos emerged from the over-the-hill sports car. A solidly built teenage girl wearing fashionably faded and torn jeans, a tie-dyed tunic, and a calf-length sweater followed her. Loretta's only reaction was a raised eyebrow.

May turned to Skye. "What are The Trollop and Frannie doing here?"

Skye ignored her mother's question, and said, "This better not be another harebrained matchmaking scheme you three have cooked up. If Simon pulls into this driveway, I'm moving to Alabama."

May held up both hands in surrender. "Honest. I don't know anything about it."

Skye looked questioningly at Loretta and Trixie, who both shook their heads.

Skye's little group approached Bunny Reid, AKA The Trollop, AKA Skye's ex-boyfriend's mother.

Fighting to keep her tone neutral, Skye asked, "Bunny, Frannie, what brings you two here?" Frannie was one of Skye's favorite students. They were extremely close, and Skye was surprised the teen hadn't mentioned her plans.

Bunny enveloped Skye in an Obsession-scented hug. "Frannie wanted to write a story for the school newspaper— 'The Treasure of the Cursed Spa.' Her dad agreed to pay for her weekend as an early birthday present, but she needed an adult chaperone, so she asked me." Bunny was the manager of the local bowling alley where Frannie worked part-time. "I thought you and Trixie were the school newspaper's sponsors. How come you don't know about the story?"

"That's exactly what I want to know." Skye raised an eyebrow.

Red crept up Frannie's face, but she kept quiet. Frannie's mother had died several years ago and her father, Xavier Ryan, was Simon's assistant at the funeral home. Xavier did his best, but a teenage daughter was a challenge for him.

Skye didn't want to embarrass Frannie in front of everyone, but she did plan to speak to the girl later, alone. Instead, she asked Bunny, "What about the bowling alley?"

Bunny shrugged. "Thanksgiving weekend is slow, so I closed it down."

Skye opened her mouth to ask if Simon knew about that,

since he was the bowling alley owner, but then remembered he wasn't her concern.

"Isn't this great, Ms. D?" When it became clear that Skye wouldn't challenge her claim to be writing a newspaper story, Frannie regained her usual bouncy personality and tugged on Skye's arm. "It's just us girls. Remember our pontoon trip last summer? I'll bet this will be even more fun."

Skye remembered the outing very well. Frannie had accidentally made Skye fall into the water, then May and Trixie had refused to let her get back on the boat—grilling Skye like a toasted cheese sandwich until she revealed her thenboyfriend Simon's faults.

Trixie grinned. "Yep, I think we'll have a ball."

May linked arms with Loretta and added, "We can really bond and become good friends."

Bunny grabbed May's other arm, ignoring her effort to jerk it away. "That's right. Just us girls. We'll have the best time ever."

Skye scowled at the women. Last time, they nearly drowned her. What would they do this time? Smother her in moisturizer?

A few minutes later, Margot came out of the main building. She announced that the police had been called and the protestors would be arrested for trespassing if they didn't get off her property. After a hurried conference, the demonstrators moved to just outside the main gates. The remaining women gathered their luggage, and Margot led Skye and her group inside.

In the lobby, Margot announced, "Please leave your bags here. They will be delivered to your rooms shortly." She flashed her professional smile. "The other guests have not yet arrived. There will be twenty of you in all, unless *Spa* magazine sends someone to write about us. So far they haven't RSVPed."

"How about lunch?" May asked.

Before the spa owner could reply, everyone's attention was diverted to the front door. A tall, thin woman swept in. Oversized sunglasses hid most of her face and a silk scarf concealed her hair. She was trailed by a young man pushing a cart overflowing with luggage.

Margot murmured, "Excuse me," to Skye's group and hurried over to the new guest. "Esmé, darling, welcome."

After watching the two women exchange air kisses, Skye strained to hear their conversation. "God-forsaken" and "hick town" were the only snatches she could make out. Her guess was that the new arrival did not like having to leave civilization to come to the spa. Finally, Margot pointed to the stairway and motioned to the bellboy.

As she brushed past Margot, the woman dropped her fur coat at the spa owner's feet, and Skye clearly heard her say, "Darling, have someone bring that to my room. It's so hot in here, I can't bear wearing it for another moment."

Margot waited until the woman was out of sight, then picked up the fur, deposited it on the reception desk, and scribbled a note. Turning back to Skye's group, Margot resumed her welcome speech. "You were asking about lunch. There's a healthy buffet set out in the dining room. I'll show you all to your rooms right now, then please help yourself to the food whenever you're ready. Treatments have been arranged for you this afternoon—there's an appointment card in your room—and at six we'll regroup for a wonderful dinner."

"Will there be a choice of menu or is all the food healthy?" Skye asked. Visions of tofu and celery danced in her head. Why hadn't she considered this predicament and packed accordingly?

"There is a choice," Margot reassured Skye. "But it's all healthy."

Four days of wheat germ and alfalfa sprouts. Skye bit her tongue, nearly gagging. This was already turning into a weekend in hell. She could kill Trixie for talking her into it.

CHAPTER 4

It's to Diet For

The rest of the afternoon had gone quickly. After Margot's promised healthy lunch, everyone had separated for the spa treatments that had been planned for them. Skye had been scheduled for a seaweed wrap, during which she made a fool of herself trying to rescue Trixie, and that brought her to the present time.

Thud!

Skye's eyes flew open as her stroll down memory lane came to an abrupt end with the sound of something rattling against the solarium windows. At first she thought it was hail. The sky had darkened, and now it was difficult to see outside.

Splat!

She squinted, finally focusing as a mound of dirt clattered against the pane. Someone was throwing soil. "Stop that," she yelled, struggling to free herself from the clutches of the wicker rocker's soft cushions and sit up. When she heard the next broadside she shouted again, "Stop that! You'll break the window."

Why would anyone throw dirt at a window? Could it be the protestors?

As Skye finally managed to stand up, she heard what sounded like a shotgun blast. She leapt back, gasping as she saw one of the windows shatter, exploding inward. She froze as she was showered with splinters. It took her a few seconds to take in that it hadn't been a gunshot, just a rock thrown through the window, and she wasn't hurt. She had been far enough back that the glass had lost its momentum by the time it reached her. But as she stood immobilized, she began to feel hundreds of tiny pricks, galvanizing her into action.

At first she tried to pluck off the shards before they cut her, but she soon realized that it would be better to disrobe and shake out her clothes. She had just managed to get her sweater off without turning it inside out and was shaking the glass off it when the hair on the back of her neck rose. She stiffened; it didn't feel as if she was alone anymore.

Holding the sweater to her chest, Skye pivoted slowly. When her gaze reached the doorway, she caught her breath.

Poised just beyond the threshold stood a young woman Skye recognized as the technician who had been giving Trixie the Brazilian wax earlier that afternoon. Ustelle had called her Amber, and it was a fitting name; her strawberry blond hair and aqua eyes glowed with good health. She had changed from her spa uniform into Ralph Lauren jeans that rode low on her hips and an embellished purple satin cami with sequined straps.

They stared at each other until Skye asked, "How long have you been standing there?"

Amber shrugged, then turned to go, apparently not interested enough to even ask what was going on.

"Wait." Initially, Skye had pegged the girl's age as early twenties, but now she wondered if she were closer to eighteen or just extremely immature. "This was just thrown through the window." Skye pointed to the grapefruit-size stone laying between her and the broken pane. "Did you see anything?"

Amber shrugged again and strolled away.

Skye shook her head, hating to see such rudeness, especially in someone so young. Heaving a sigh, she put her sweater aside and carefully removed her jeans. She had just managed to ease them over her tennis shoes when once again she knew she wasn't alone.

The young woman hovering in the doorway this time seemed ethereal in comparison to the first girl. Long platinum hair veiled half her face, and loose, white crop pants and a white silk halter top hung on her emaciated frame. Double rows of ruffles cascaded down her chest, delineating her nonexistent cleavage.

Her skin was oddly translucent, and for a moment Skye was sure she was seeing a ghost.

The wraith looked Skye up and down, giggled, and sauntered away.

Skye's cheeks reddened, and she was relieved that the solarium was isolated from the rest of the house. All she would have needed would be Margot's snooty friend Esmé seeing her half naked and hopping around. Come to think of it, she was lucky that most of the guests were getting ready for dinner, or she might have had a larger audience for her striptease act.

Putting the two unpleasant encounters behind her, Skye focused on finding out who had thrown the stone. Trying to avoid getting cut, she picked her way over to one of the unbroken windows, cupped her hands around her face, and peered through the glass. As she suspected, it was too dark outside to see anything.

Looking around the solarium, she noticed a telephone. Next to it was a card that explained this was a house phone and she could dial zero for the front desk or a room number to reach a guest. Skye dialed zero and asked to be connected to Margot. Skye described what had happened, and the spa owner promised to have someone look into it immediately.

Skye redressed, then walked back to her room thinking about the wraith. Which guest could she have been? Margot had given her a list when they checked in that afternoon. There were a dozen or so women from the local area, most of whom Skye had a nodding acquaintance with, as well as Margot's ex-model friend Esmé Gates, and Esmé's stepdaughter, whom Margot said was arriving late that afternoon. The wraith must have been the stepdaughter. What *was* her name?

*   .*   *

"Whitney, this is Skye Denison, our town's school psychologist. Skye, this is Whitney Quinn, Esmé's stepdaughter." Margot finished the introductions.

Although there wasn't assigned seating, Margot had met Trixie and Skye at the dining room entrance and subtly steered them to her table, where Dr. Creighton Burnett already sat along with Esmé Gates and Whitney.

While Esmé and Margot looked enough alike to be sisters, Margot's beauty had a serene quality, while the best word to describe Esmé was severe. Lipstick, eyeliner, and eyebrows were all drawn on in precise strokes. Her dinner dress was an Armani; the gray-taupe of the chiffon skirt lay in a perfect row of ruffles, while the matching brocade jacket skimmed her torso without a crease.

Esmé's blue eyes were hard—she had barely acknowledged the introductions—and now she stared at each of her tablemates, daring anyone to tick her off. She reminded Skye of a Komodo dragon she had seen on a nature special—regal and cold. When she had nodded a greeting to Skye and Trixie, Skye felt a shiver run up her spine. There was an eerie hunger in her smile.

Esmé's gaze reached her stepdaughter, and she pointed to Skye, and asked, "Was this the woman you said was doing some kind of dance, waving her jeans in the air?" She flicked Skye a glance the same way a lizard zaps a fly. "The one you said looked like a frog in a blender?"

Skye's nostrils flared, but she bit her tongue and didn't respond.

When the girl didn't reply either, Margot, her voice knife-edged, said, "Esmé, darling, how often must I tell you, if you can't be kind, at least have the decency to be vague."

Before Esmé could react to Margot's chiding, Trixie asked, "Skye, what happened?"

"Someone threw a rock through one of the windows in the solarium. Unfortunately, I was near enough to be showered with glass." Skye shot Whitney a stare that made the young woman slump in her chair. "I was shaking the shards from my pants when Whitney stopped by, but I must have frightened her. She ran away before we could chat. Before

Whitney's appearance, Amber popped in, but she ran off, too." Skye forced a laugh. "I had no idea the sight of me in my underwear was so scary."

Everyone laughed, then Margot said, "Amber shouldn't have been in that area. Was she with you, Whitney?"

"No." Whitney sounded bored. "Why would she be with me?"

"Because you know her from school, don't you? She mentioned that when I interviewed her." Margot turned to Skye and Trixie and explained, "Whitney and Amber went to high school together, but when Amber's parents divorced, she moved from the area and they lost touch."

Skye and Trixie nodded and murmured, "I see."

Margot looked back at Whitney. "Didn't you get back in contact with Amber recently?"

"Sort of. We're both old movie buffs and joined the same chat room online," Whitney answered.

Margot remarked, "I believe Amber said it was around the time of her stepmother's funeral?"

"I guess." Whitney shrugged. "We just e-mailed. We can't really be friend, friends. Her dad cut her off without a penny when he remarried, so she's too poor to hang around with anymore."

Skye bit her tongue, trying to keep from lecturing Whitney on the subject of true friendship.

Luckily, Margot stepped in and scolded the young woman about her behavior that afternoon. "It's too bad you two distracted Skye from the broken window, Whitney. By the time she called me, and Creighton went out to check, there was no one outside, although he did find the ground disturbed next to that wall."

"Dr. Burnett," Skye asked, "did it look as if someone was digging, trying to find something, or only wanted the dirt to throw at the window?"

"Definitely looking for something." Creighton Burnett fingered his silver mustache. "We've had several such holes dug around the property. The groundskeepers are having trouble keeping them filled and resodded."

Trixie smoothed her napkin in her lap. "The treasure, of course."

Esmé looked up from the small mirror she was using to refresh her lipstick. "Treasure? What treasure?" Her bored expression had changed instantly to one of avid interest.

Margot sighed. "There are some silly rumors going around that the original owner's wife hid her jewelry somewhere, either in the mansion or on the grounds, when the stock market crashed in 1929. He killed her and then himself before she could tell anyone where her jewelry was." Margot gestured vaguely to her right. "The man who bought the estate after the murder/suicide took place published a book about the whole affair. There's a copy in the solarium if you're interested."

Whitney had been taking a drink of water and she muttered into her glass, "The only book *she's* interested in is my father's checkbook."

No one at the table spoke, pretending not to have heard her.

Finally, as the silence grew uncomfortable, Skye said, "Maybe it was the protesters trying to disrupt things and just pretending to be searching for the treasure. They seemed pretty intent on closing down the spa."

"They'll never convince the women coming here that they'd be just as happy growing old and looking ugly." Margot waved away Skye's suggestion. "What a silly idea."

"I think they have a point." Skye looked Margot in the eye and refused to be the first one to blink.

"You would, my dear." Esmé's smile was like the gaze of a cobra—scary enough to freeze her prey until she was ready to devour it. "You're one of them."

"Excuse me?" Skye knew where the ex-model was heading, but wanted to see if she would say it to her face.

"The imperfect." Esmé narrowed her eyes. "Although you aren't hopeless. If you lost all that extra weight and did something with that hair, you could probably marry well and move uptown."

"I don't think the protesters protest because they want to be beautiful and aren't," Skye countered.

Esmé's laugh was hard. "Right. And people aren't more violently opposed to fur than leather because it's safer to harass rich women than motorcycle gangs."

Dr. Burnett cleared his throat, then stood, lifted a bottle of wine from the bucket where it had been chilling, uncorked it, and began to pour. "Even if the jewelry was hidden here back then, that was over seventy years ago, and someone would have found it by now. Margot told that to that silly newspaper woman, but she insists on publishing those lies anyway."

"Creighton's right." Margot lifted her glass. "To a peaceful, serene, and youth-restoring weekend."

Trixie's eyes met Skye's, her thoughts written across her face. The odds of this weekend being any of the three were about a hundred to one.

After they sipped the wine, two waitresses began to serve the food. Skye recognized them as recent Scumble River High School graduates, both pretty girls but with little interest in academics or careers. She couldn't quite read their name tags, but she knew she'd eventually remember who they were.

Skye had also identified the housekeeping and grounds staff as locals. It looked as if the only employees Margot and Creighton had brought in from out of town were the professional spa staff. In their initial conversation, Margot had said if the spa was a success it would provide several jobs for the surrounding area, and it looked as if she had been telling the truth.

Dinner was everything Skye had feared—tiny, tasteless, and tiresome. When the waitress slid Skye's plate in front of her, at first she thought it was a joke. At the ten o'clock position were three baby carrots, a half dozen peas, and a water chestnut snuggled into a nest of bean sprouts. A postage stamp size piece of fish lay in the center. And at four o'clock a half circle of what looked like a strange breed of malformed brown rice clung to the china.

Skye waited until everyone had been served, then asked hopefully, "Are there any rolls?"

Esmé froze, her fork and knife poised above a baby carrot. Whitney snickered, and Margot shuddered. No one spoke.

Finally, Dr. Burnett answered in a gentle tone, as if addressing someone mentally ill. "My dear, one of the issues our spa will help you with is your addiction to carbohydrates."

"Oh." Skye shot Trixie a withering look.

"Yes," Esmé testified. "I haven't had a piece of bread or a strand of pasta in six months." She patted Dr. Burnett's arm. "Creighton saved me. When I retired from modeling and married Rex, I lost control and ballooned up to a hundred and twenty pounds. Rex was threatening to divorce me. If Creighton hadn't gotten me on his Fountain of Youth diet, I would have lost my husband, and who knows how fat I might have gotten. And now that I'm trying to get pregnant, he's already designed a diet that guarantees I'll gain no more than ten pounds during the pregnancy."

Margot nodded. "Botox can get rid of the wrinkles, but you need Creighton's diet and our Miracle Mud to completely defeat Father Time."

Botox. Finally Skye understood why neither Margot's nor Esmé's faces showed any expression. Happy to solve that mystery, but not giving up getting something edible for supper, Skye asked, "I thought Margot said there would be some choices at mealtimes."

"Why, of course, regular, vegetarian, and vegan," Dr. Burnett said. "Would you prefer one of the others?"

"No, but, um, I'm not really here for your diet, so couldn't I have a normal meal?"

"I'm afraid not." Margot bared her teeth in a not so subtle message to shut up. "Didn't you read your brochure? We all follow the Burnett Diet. It's too hard on those participating to have others eating forbidden food in front of them."

"Room service?"

"No." Margot's voice had lost a bit of its smoothness. "Nowhere in the spa. Even the staff eats according to our diet. It's helped them all. Our masseuse dropped the five pounds she'd struggled with all her life, Amber's diabetes is under control, and Frisco, our fitness trainer, finally got his cholesterol below two hundred." Margot regained her even tone and asked, "Now that that's settled, would you like what's on your plate or vegetarian or vegan?"

"What I have." Skye forked a bite of fish into her mouth and forced herself to chew and swallow the bland morsel. "Just call me a carnivore." This was bad enough. Skye was afraid to see what the vegan meal might be like.

The horrible meal finally came to an end and Margot stood. "Herbal tea and dessert will be served in the parlor."

Dessert? Skye's mind was immediately lost in a chocolate dream, but the rest of Margot's statement penetrated her fantasy.

"I'm thrilled to announce that tonight you'll be entertained by world famous soprano, Elyse Piven, singing selections from Wagner."

Skye shuddered and prayed that dessert was a chocolate fountain she could drown herself in.

May's little band of merry women was also not pleased with their dinners or the prospect of the evening's entertainment. They circled Skye like hyenas around a ripe carcass as soon as she set foot in the parlor.

Loretta grabbed Skye's arm and hissed into her ear, "Do you have any idea how boring this performance will be?" Ever the suave attorney, she kept a smile on her face and nodded pleasantly to the other guests passing by them.

Skye nodded, but before she could respond verbally, her mother took her other arm and whispered, "That was awful. I thought we were supposed to bathe in this Miracle Mud, not be forced to eat it."

Bunny, ex-Las Vegas dancer, was not as discreet as Skye's mom, and didn't attempt to lower her voice. "I've seen anorexics eat more food than what they just served us."

Skye shoved her hands in her pockets. "Maybe you all should check out." She studied the toes of her shoes. "According to the owners, this is the world-famous Burnett Diet, and it's all we're going to get for the entire weekend."

"Are you and Trixie staying?" May asked.

"Yes."

"Why?" May narrowed her eyes. "You two hate diets. What aren't you telling us?"

"Nothing." Skye crossed her fingers and lied. "We've just decided to give it a try."

Frannie, who had been silently taking in the adults' discussion, put her hands on her hips and said, "There's something going on here, and I'm not leaving until I get my story."

Trixie joined them in time to hear Frannie's vow. "You seem pretty sure Ms. D. and I will okay your piece for the school newspaper."

"Ms. Steele said if you two don't use it for the *Scoop*, she'll use it in the *Star*."

Trixie and Skye looked at each other. They shrugged. Frannie had trumped them.

"No one is going anywhere except, maybe to bed." May shook her head. "An opera singer. What in heaven's name were the owners thinking? They should've gotten a gal from the Grand Ole Opry."

May herded everyone through the large parlor to the back corner. The room was decorated in cream and gold, with a white marble fireplace. Satin draperies the color of expensive whiskey pooled on the white marble floor. Tobacco-colored leather couches and chairs provided intimate seating for groups of four, six, and eight. Wrought iron and glass tables showcased crystal vases full of chrysanthemums and asters, while brass lamps glowed invitingly.

Skye's gang claimed a couple of sofas and two armchairs that had been arranged in a square. Almost as soon as they were settled, waitresses from the dining room wheeled in the dessert cart and Skye turned her attention to not drooling.

Finally, the cart arrived, and one of the servers asked, "Apple tart or brownie?"

Everyone made their selections, all except Loretta and Frannie choosing the brownie. Before anyone could take a bite, the tea arrived. The choices were all herbal, and to Skye, tasted like dishwater, especially when she compared it to her favorite, Earl Grey.

At last, they were all served, and Skye picked up her fork.

She broke off a tiny corner and placed the piece in her mouth, determined to savor the dessert rather than devour it. Yuck! It took all her self-control not to spit it right back out. The brownie was a fake. It didn't taste of rich chocolate or sweet sugar or moist cake. Instead it tasted like . . . like a mouthful of cardboard.

Skye scanned the others. May, Trixie, and Bunny had identical horrified looks on their faces. Loretta and Frannie's expressions were more puzzled as they poked the bits of apple and pastry.

Skye finally managed to swallow the bite she had taken, and choke out, "How's the tart?"

Loretta wrinkled her nose. "It tastes like mulch."

Frannie added, "Even the apples don't have a flavor."

Bunny, Trixie, and May joined in with their complaints, and Skye finally said, "Guess we'll have to raid the kitchen, if this is all they're going to serve."

"Why don't you just put on your tinfoil suit and save us by producing a big juicy ham?" May's tone was querulous. "Trixie told us how you rescued her from the terrible Brazilian Waxing Monster."

The others joined in and Skye shot Trixie a how-could-you look. Her friend's gaze slipped from Skye's, and she slumped down staring at her feet.

Skye tuned out the rest of the teasing while wondering if this evening would ever end. Right now she'd even welcome an appearance of the spa vandal.

CHAPTER 5

Wash That Vandal Right out of My Hair

The trespasser didn't appear, but Margot did. Walking to the grand piano on the opposite side of the room, she announced, "I hope everyone has finished their deliciously healthy desserts. Both the tart and brownie were made without sugar or trans fats. Carob was substituted for chocolate in the brownie and the apples were organically grown. After all, you are what you eat."

Trixie nudged Skye with her elbow. "If that's true, I'm cheap, fast, and easy."

Skye rolled her eyes.

The room was buzzing with everyone's reaction to the spa owner's statement, so Margot cleared her throat, then said at the top of her voice, "If I could have everyone's attention, please. Madam Piven is ready to start her concert. She asks that no one speak during her performance. Now, for your enjoyment, selections from *Der Ring des Nibelungen*."

Skye flinched. Opera reminded her of Simon. This particular four-opera cycle reminded her of a never-ending evening she had sat through with him several months ago, before he went to California and spent the week with his college friend, Spike, before she found out that Spike was female.

A scatter of polite applause welcomed the singer.

Skye was pretty sure those clapping did not realize what they were about to hear. Looking around to make sure no one was paying attention to her, Skye tore the corners off her paper napkin, and stuffed them into her ears.

Forty minutes later Skye squirmed and checked her watch. The makeshift earplugs weren't working. It seemed as if the soprano had been singing for hours. She glanced around; the rest of the guests looked as bored as she felt.

Scooting down, Skye rested her head on the back of the sofa, closed her eyes, and allowed her thoughts to drift. She wondered what all the men were doing while their women were spending Thanksgiving weekend at the spa. Her father, Jed, would be the worst off. He didn't cook, and had only a nodding acquaintance with most household appliances. Owen, Trixie's husband, knew how to use a microwave, but the dishwasher was beyond his comprehension.

Frannie's dad Xavier, Bunny's son Simon, and Skye's brother Vince would most likely consider this a break and take advantage of their womenfolk being gone. Skye winced; she hoped her brother wouldn't take *too* much advantage of Loretta's absence.

Which left Skye's recent significant other, chief of police Walter Boyd. Wally hadn't been happy to hear Skye would be occupied for the four-day vacation. Clearly, he'd been hoping to take their relationship to the next level during their days off, and maybe it was time.

Skye and Wally had a long, emotionally charged history. Although they hadn't started dating until recently, there had been chemistry between them since she was a teenager and he was a rookie cop. Nothing had happened when she was underage, or even when she returned to Scumble River as an adult, because by then he was married, and when his wife left him, Skye had been involved with Simon.

Finally, at the end of September, both Skye and Wally were free and over twenty-one. Their dates had gone well, and the sexual attraction was an eleven on a ten-point scale, but Skye had been determined to take things slowly. Now, maybe it was time to let nature take its course. It was getting harder and harder to end their evenings with a good-night kiss.

Too bad Skye had already promised to help Margot. Still, Wally was picking her up Thursday around noon. Skye's plan was that they'd go for Thanksgiving dinner at her aunt's, spend a couple of hours socializing with the family, then go back to his house for dessert—a dessert she'd been denying them both for too long. Wally was in for a pleasant surprise.

Skye's lips turned up slightly in a Mona Lisa smile, which quickly melted away when she noticed a commotion at the door. Barb, the girl who had been working behind the reception desk, stood on the parlor threshold, gesturing wildly to Margot.

The spa owner frowned and shook her head, but the clerk insisted. With an apologetic murmur, Margot stood and edged out of the room. Skye followed, both out of curiosity and as a way to escape having to listen to one more aria.

Margot and Barb were moving quickly, but Skye kept them in sight. She almost gave herself away when Margot abruptly stopped a few steps before the lobby's entrance. Just in time, Skye ducked behind a large sculpture. She peered around the carving, blinked, and looked again.

What was Elvis Doozier doing with Amber? To begin with, he was at least five years younger than the girl; second, she had at least thirty IQ points on him; and last, Amber appeared to like expensive trinkets, while Elvis's idea of haute couture was the blue-light special at Kmart.

When Skye peeked again, Barb had continued on into the lobby, but Margot, Amber, and Elvis were standing in a tight triangle, and the two women were arguing. What were they saying? Skye edged closer, carefully keeping in the shadows.

She heard Margot's voice first. "How many times must I tell you, Amber, spa employees are not allowed to 'see' each other on spa grounds?" She didn't give the girl a chance to respond, but continued, "I warned you when I caught you and Frisco together that I was only giving you one more chance."

"I am not screwing this, this dork." The girl swished her ponytail, emphasizing each word. "He's stalking me."

Margot turned to Elvis. "Young man, you are not allowed in the building unless you are working on something with your construction crew. And you are to stay at least two hundred and fifty feet from Miss Ferguson. Is that clear?"

"Yes, ma'am." Elvis's shoulders drooped and he muttered, "But I ain't stalkin' her. Alls I was doing was asking her for a date."

"Regardless," Margot jabbed him in the chest with her index finger, "keep away from her and keep out of the mansion."

Margot swiveled on her high heels and marched into the lobby. Amber passed Skye without seeming to notice her, and Elvis stomped off the other way. Once she was sure her path was clear, Skye followed Margot, who was approaching a slim woman standing at the reception desk.

Before the woman could speak, Margot gushed, "Ms. Kimbrough, may I call you Nancy? I'm so happy you were able to fit us into your schedule. *Spa* magazine said they didn't think you'd be able to make the opening."

Ah, the magazine critic Margot had mentioned.

Skye tried to slip away without being noticed, but Margot spotted her and called her back. "Skye, come meet Nancy Kimbrough. She's a writer for *Spa* magazine. Nancy, this is one of our guests, Skye Denison."

While they shook hands Skye covertly examined the reviewer. Nancy's delicate features were a blend of Asian and European, making her age difficult to guess. She could be anywhere from twenty-five to over thirty.

Margot put a hand on Skye's back. "Skye can tell you how wonderful everything has been going so far."

Skye quickly sorted through her experiences—she'd been deserted by her masseuse, showered in glass, made to eat Styrofoam disguised as food, and bored nearly to death by a soprano. What part of that did Margot want her to share?

Her silence must have clued the magazine writer in on the

problem because Nancy took Skye's arm and said, "Let's talk in my room." Turning to Margot, her tone slightly challenging, she added, "I assume it's ready?"

By the time they walked up the stairs and Nancy opened the door, Skye had finally come up with some positive statements to make about the spa. The mansion was beautiful, the staff friendly, and she'd enjoyed her massage. Nancy seemed to want Skye to stick around and chat, which would have been fine because the writer was really nice and Skye could feel their personalities clicking, but she decided she'd better go find Trixie. They needed to go over their plan for catching the vandal that night.

"As Groucho Marx said, 'I've had a perfectly wonderful evening. But this wasn't it,'" Loretta remarked, sitting cross-legged on the sofa in Skye and Trixie's room.

She had knocked on their door a few minutes earlier wearing red satin pajamas and bearing gifts of food.

"How in the world did Mom persuade you to come this weekend?" Skye lay on her stomach across the bed, savoring a cheese-topped cracker.

"Well"—for once the self-possessed attorney looked uncertain—"the thing is"—she took a sip of her champagne—"I was amazed at how happy your parents were about me dating Vince. I . . . ah . . . thought they'd either be openly negative or fake nice, but they weren't."

"Yeah, I have to admit, Mom surprised me, too."

Trixie polished off a candy bar. "I knew May would be thrilled." She licked the chocolate off her fingers. "After all, Loretta is healthy, successful, and of child-bearing years."

"That's true." Skye reached for another cracker. "And, for once, Vince actually seems serious. As long as you want children, you're in like Flynn."

Loretta held up her hand, palm out. "Chill. We've only been seeing each other a couple of months." She opened a bag of potato chips. "No offense, Skye, but your brother would have to really prove to me he's straightened up before I'd even consider getting serious. So let's not go planning the wedding yet."

"It's not me you have to worry about." Skye giggled. "But Mom's probably already decorating the nursery."

Trixie started to hum "Rock-a-bye Baby" and Loretta threw a pillow at her.

"Hey, you never really answered my question. Surely, you didn't give up your Thanksgiving just because my parents were nicer than you expected."

"Sort of. I just thought it'd be good to spend some time with May. Maybe bond a little as friends rather than prospective daughter- and mother-in-law."

"And?" Skye prodded.

"And your mom pointed out it was either this, or dinner with fifty of your closest relatives probing me like they were aliens and I was their abductee."

"Now, that's a reason I believe." Skye toasted Loretta with her can of Diet Coke. "So, how did you know to bring all these supplies?" She pointed to the food and drink covering the coffee table.

"Girl." Loretta shifted position and hugged her satin clad knees. "My law firm had a meeting at a spa a few years ago, and I darned near starved."

"Isn't that the point—to cleanse the body and get healthy?" Trixie asked.

Skye looked at her sharply. "Trixie, honey, you drive way too fast to worry about cholesterol. Besides, who eats all the candy from my jar at school?"

"That doesn't count." Trixie wrinkled her nose. "Chocolate is the catnip of the female world."

"I see." Sometimes Trixie's logic was beyond Skye, so she turned to Loretta. "Anyway thank you for sharing your stash." Skye jerked her thumb at Trixie. "She was having such withdrawal pains, I thought she was going to eat my fudge-colored eye shadow."

"Me?" Trixie grabbed another Hershey bar and peeled off the wrapper. "You should talk. You have such a love/hate relationship with chocolate you should be dating it."

Before Skye could retaliate, Loretta demanded, "Now, tell me the real reason you two are here."

Skye looked at Trixie, who shrugged. "Okay, but don't tell Mom or the others."

"Deal."

"Margot contacted me about a month ago about some problems they were having with the spa." Skye recounted Margot's conversation, the newspaper stories, and Trixie's cajoling, then ended with, "Which is why we're here."

"Do you two have a plan?"

"As a matter of fact, we do." Skye swung her legs off the bed. "Our theory is that the vandal is really a treasure hunter and is one of the staff."

"Makes sense." Loretta nodded. "Could be one of the locals Margot and the good doctor hired for the nonprofessional positions, since they'd be most likely to know about the rumor of the secreted jewelry even before the newspaper ran the story."

"Right." Trixie picked up where Skye had left off. "And since today's paper has a riddle which is supposed to be a clue to the treasure's location, we figure the treasure hunter should be out tonight."

"You two solved the riddle?" Loretta frowned.

"No. Unfortunately, the only one I know who is good at riddles is Simon, and I can't ask him." Skye frowned. "But we figure that if we sort of hang around outside in the shadows, we have a good chance of seeing anyone who tries to dig something up."

"What if the treasure is inside the mansion?" The lawyer in Loretta's voice was loud and clear.

"We figure that if the treasure is inside the building, the treasure hunter will have to wait until it's emptier—which would mean after the guests leave on Sunday," Skye answered, not sounding overly convinced herself.

"I see." Loretta gathered the leftover goodies and packed them into her tote bag, then got up and went to the door. "When are you planning on beginning your surveillance?"

"Midnight," Skye answered. "We figure whoever it is will wait until everyone is in their room and most people are asleep."

"Midnight?" Loretta smirked. "You, Miss Thing, are staying up past ten o'clock? I'll bet the last time you were up that late was when the Kappas pulled the panty raid on our sorority house."

"Hey, I've chaperoned my share of overnighters at the high school. Midnight and I are well acquainted."

"You may be well acquainted, but I bet you aren't friends."

After Loretta's departure, Trixie said to Skye, "She doesn't think our plan will work."

"I'm not too sure of it myself."

"Wake up."

Skye rolled onto her stomach and pulled the covers over her head.

"It's nearly midnight." Trixie pulled the blanket and sheets down and held a glass of water threateningly over her friend's head. "Get up, or get wet."

Skye whimpered, but crawled out of bed. She stood looking around the room, trying to remember where she was and why Trixie was dressed like Batgirl. "Where did you get the cape?"

"It's my swimsuit cover-up."

"Oh." Skye wondered why Trixie might need it to catch a treasure hunter, but it was too late at night for her to really care. She stumbled into the bathroom and splashed water on her face, then pulled on a pair of black sweatpants and sweatshirt.

After stuffing her hair under a baseball cap, she tied her tennis shoes, and buckled on her fanny pack.

When she came out of the bathroom, Trixie said, "Are you finally ready?"

"As ready as I'll ever be at this time of night without caffeine."

"What's in your fanny pack?" Trixie ignored Skye's whining and followed her to the door.

"Stun gun, mace, flashlight, and plastic fasteners."

"I get the stun gun and flashlight, but why the ties? Are we going to empty the trash cans?" Trixie asked.

"Very funny," Skye whispered. "They're the ones that once you close them can only be opened with scissors or a knife. I brought them to secure the perpetrator's hands or feet. I saw the cops use them on *Law and Order.*"

"Well, that explains it."

"Now, I'm going to open the door, so be quiet."

The passageway was silent and dark, the only illumination coming from night-lights plugged into the electrical outlets. Skye shivered. There was something eerie about this time of night. They reached the outside exit and pushed the bar. The cold November air smelled of burnt leaves and a hint of snow.

They emerged on a side patio with steps leading down to the river. Skye stopped suddenly, and Trixie plowed into her.

Skye whispered, "Any indication someone's following us?"

Trixie shook her head.

Skye took the stairs slowly, listening for any hint of a footstep or breathing. Nothing. Once they reached the shore, Skye paused, not sure whether to go down to the river or stick close to the mansion.

Trixie took Skye's arm and whispered, "I think I figured out the riddle. I'm pretty sure it's a lifeboat, which means we should go to the boathouse."

Skye hesitated, replaying the riddle in her mind: THE MAN WHO INVENTED ME DOESN'T WANT ME. THE MAN WHO BUYS ME DOESN'T NEED ME. THE MAN WHO NEEDS ME DOESN'T KNOW IT. She could see Trixie's logic, so she nodded and started down the steps.

Once they were on the shore they edged toward the boathouse and peeked inside. It appeared to be empty so they stepped inside. Almost immediately they heard footsteps and positioned themselves on either side of the entrance. Skye took out her stun gun and Trixie whipped off her cape. A moment later someone came through the doorway. Trixie wafted her cape as if it were a net and threw it over the figure's head and shoulders.

Skye leapt on the intruder, bringing him to the ground

and putting the stun gun against his shoulder. "Move and I fry you like a mosquito caught in a bug zapper."

Before the bundled figure could react, Trixie yelled, "Incoming," just as another person ran into the boathouse.

CHAPTER 6

Stick in the Mud Bath

By the time the last person entered the boathouse, there were five staff members lined up against the wall. Once Trixie and Skye made it clear they were working for Margot, looking for whoever was hunting for the treasure and in the process messing up the running of the spa, the treasure hunters were eager to explain themselves.

Ruth, one of the three housekeepers, Bryan the bellboy, Barb the reception clerk, Rudy the groundskeeper, and Earlene the cook had shown up for the festivities. All claimed that they were not the ones digging holes or committing any other acts of vandalism.

Earlene clarified what had happened. "The *Scumble River Star* was delivered this afternoon and left in the lobby. I read it after I finished cooking lunch and I had a couple of ideas as to where the riddle might lead. Then, later I noticed Barb and Bryan had the paper and a map of the grounds spread out on the reception desk so I decided to follow them."

Ruth took up the story from there. "When I was cleaning, I noticed the *Star* in the trash along with a crumpled ball of paper that had the riddle printed on it along with several possible answers. I recognized Earlene's handwriting so I decided to follow her."

Barb chimed in, "Bryan and I couldn't figure out the riddle, but Bryan overheard Rudy on the phone to his wife saying he thought he knew the answer, so we followed him."

All eyes turned to Rudy, who had freed himself from Trixie's bathing suit cover-up, and was keeping an eye on Skye's stun gun. "Sorry, everyone, I just told the old lady I was hunting for the treasure so I could stay out late and play cards with my buddies. I lost tonight and needed my emergency money, which I keep hidden here in the boathouse." In an annoyed tone, he added, "Not that I'll keep it here now that I know you lot are hunting around."

Skye and Trixie looked at each other, shrugged, and told everyone they could go.

Next, they reported the results of their detection to Margot, who said she would inform the staff that any further treasure hunting on their part would result in a termination of their employment.

Once Skye and Trixie were back in their room, and had gotten into bed, Skye asked, "So, do we have a Plan B?"

Trixie's answer was a soft snore.

Snuggling down into her pillow, Skye tried to think of how pleasant Thanksgiving dinner with Wally would be later that day, but instead the memory of the failed treasure hunter pursuit kept intruding.

On the bright side, maybe Margot would fire them once she had time to think about the debacle in the boathouse. Skye turned over and punched her pillow. Dang. Why wasn't she going to sleep? Because she didn't like feeling dumb, and she had no idea how to catch the treasure hunter.

The only plan she could think of was to get rid of the intruder's motivation, which meant solving the riddle and finding the jewelry. Unless, of course, the treasure hunter was really a vandal trying to sabotage the spa, in which case she was really off track.

She scooted into a sitting position, grabbed her tote bag, and pulled the newspaper from the bottom. According to the article, when Mr. Bruefeld told his wife they had lost all their money, she hid the jewelry so it wouldn't be taken by the bill collectors. The story reported that Mrs. Bruefeld had been found shot to death by her husband. He'd killed her just prior to his own suicide, supposedly to "save" her from a life of poverty. And when the coroner examined her, he found a riddle clutched in her hand. Her maid claimed that her mistress had told her that the riddle was a clue to where the jewelry was hidden.

The newspaper story ended by saying the riddle was thought to have been solved several times after the Bruefelds died, but the treasure was never found.

Skye yawned and looked at the clock. Three in the morning. She lay back down and tried to make a mental list of what she knew so far, but her theories had as many holes in them as the lace on her bra.

Still trying to make sense of the past twelve hours, she fell into an uneasy sleep. Four hours later, papers being slid under the door woke her up. They were computer printouts, one with her name on it and one with Trixie's. The schedules indicated mealtimes, all the available activities, and reminders of the individual treatments they had signed up for when they checked in yesterday.

This morning she had an appointment for a Miracle Mud bath at nine thirty. It was supposed to take away all aches and pains, as well as cleanse the impurities from the skin, and subtract ten years from one's age. Wouldn't Wally be surprised when he picked her up at noon to find her looking twenty-three?

Skye's stomach growled, reminding her that breakfast began in less than an hour, and unlike home, she was sharing a bathroom. After showering, she put on a pink velour jogging suit and French braided her hair, then woke Trixie.

Trixie sat up in bed with her eyes scrunched closed and mumbled, "Breakfast? What's the point? The food'll be awful."

"Probably, but surely, there'll at least be some form of caffeine."

Trixie slid back down, muttering, "Wanna bet?" She pulled a pillow over her head and was snoring before Skye made it out the door.

As Skye approached the dining room, Esmé rushed past her without acknowledging they had ever met. Skye closed her mouth, swallowing the "good morning" she was about to utter.

A buffet was set up against the wall opposite the fireplace, and she helped herself to slices of melon and pineapple and a cup of blueberries. A hot plate held egg white omelets, but the sign indicated the filling was cottage cheese and cod, so Skye passed. She couldn't find any type of toast, muffin, or Danish. Finally, she settled for a container of unsweetened plain yogurt.

Her biggest disappointment was no coffee, only herbal tea. While she sipped a glass of low-sugar, low-carb, low-calorie cranberry juice, she took a pad of paper from her tote and started making a list of supplies she needed to bring back with her this evening. Earl Grey tea bags, chocolate, Diet Coke, and bread topped the column.

As Skye tried to decide whether she could get away with smuggling in a toaster, Margot glided gracefully into the chair opposite her. She was dressed in a sapphire blue linen pantsuit, and looked as if she had just enjoyed the services of the spa's hair stylist and makeup artist.

Skye made an attempt to smooth her French braid as Margot said, "I'm disappointed you didn't catch anyone last night."

"Technically, we caught too many people," Skye joked.

"What's your next plan?"

Skye shrugged. "The only thing I can think of is to solve the riddle and find the darn treasure." She popped a grape in her mouth. "I'll be seeing the police chief this afternoon. Maybe he can point me in another direction."

"What?" Margot swallowed wrong and started to choke. "This is a girls-only weekend. The police chief can't come here."

"He's picking me up out front. Remember when I agreed to do this, I told you I had to be gone Thanksgiving afternoon?"

"Sort of." Margot's collagen-enhanced lips thinned. "I thought since you failed last night, maybe you'd cancel your fun."

"Sorry. This is a family thing." Skye added to herself: not

to mention a "new boyfriend thing" she didn't want to mess up. "Trixie will still be here investigating."

"Investigating what?" Nancy Kimbrough pulled out a chair. "Mind if I join you two?" The *Spa* magazine writer was dressed in black yoga pants and a white tank top, her long black hair held back with a coated rubber band.

"Not at all." Margot popped up from her seat. "Can I get you something to eat? Maybe a cup of herbal tea?"

"No, thanks, I already had coffee and muffins in my room." Nancy waved the spa owner back into her chair.

"Coffee! Muffins! Where did you get those? We follow a strict no caffeine or carbs diet here."

"I always travel with my own coffee pot and I happened to buy some muffins yesterday from a wonderful bakery in town." Nancy narrowed her eyes. "Is that a problem?"

"No. Of course not." Margot blinked, perhaps remembering who she was talking to, and added soothingly, "It's just that my husband designed the diet himself. The program is based on a thousand calories per day. Our aim is for our guests to leave us stress free and with a head start on a healthy eating plan."

"Surely, since I'm not really here for that reason, you don't mind if I supplement your menu for my own tastes?"

Margot shook her head. "But do please be discreet."

"Discretion is my middle name." Nancy pulled her chair closer to Skye's. "Now tell me about the investigation you mentioned earlier."

Skye looked at Margot, unsure how to answer.

Margot shook her head once, and said, "Yes, Skye, what investigation are you talking about?"

"The treasure."

Three pairs of eyes—blue, green, and brown—all turned toward Whitney, who had just spoken. This morning the young woman wore a white mini skirt that rode low on her hips with a white cami that ended just above her pierced belly button.

She handed Nancy a section of the *Scumble River Star* and pointed to the bottom of the page. "Look what that cute bellboy showed me this morning."

Both Skye and Margot tried to talk, but the writer shushed them. "Let me read this first."

Margot glared at Whitney, who stared back innocently.

Skye decided now was a good time to make her escape. She tried to stand, but Margot grabbed the leg of her chair and wouldn't let her scoot back.

Fortunately, Nancy was a fast reader, and few minutes later she put down the newspaper. "Interesting." She turned to Skye. "So you and the friend you mentioned last night are trying to find the treasure."

Skye and Margot answered yes, at the same time Whitney said no.

Nancy cocked her head. "Which is it?"

"It's yes and no," Whitney blurted out. "Yes, they're trying to find the treasure, but no, that's not what they're investigating."

"Thanks, Whitney," Skye said, "but since this is my story, you don't mind if I tell it, do you?"

The young woman huffed, swishing her ponytail from side to side, but gestured with her hand for Skye to continue.

Skye forced herself to give Nancy a relaxed smile. "In a small town everything gets blown out of proportion."

"Sure."

Skye searched her mind for a plausible story.

"I'm guessing everyone wants to find the treasure," Nancy said to Skye after she'd been silent for a while.

"Yes, and one particular one was bothering Margot, someone digging up the estate and so on, so my friend Trixie and I thought maybe we could find out who it was and put a stop to his or her messing around."

"Except," Whitney broke in, "they didn't catch just one treasure hunter, they caught lots of them, and now they're back to square one."

"Right." Skye nodded. "Which is why, while I spend Thanksgiving with my family this afternoon, Trixie will continue to investigate."

"Maybe I can help," Nancy offered.

"Well . . . sure." Skye tried to figure out whether that would cause problems, but couldn't think of any. "Now, if you'll excuse me, I have an appointment for a Miracle Mud bath in half an hour."

Everyone walked off in different directions, and Skye returned to her room, where she read the instructions for the treatment. She was supposed to shower, and wearing only the spa robe, arrive at the treatment room five minutes early, where an attendant would work a deep conditioner into her wet hair. No makeup or jewelry was allowed. The guest was asked to consult with Dr. Burnett prior to the treatment if they wanted Botox injections while they had the mud bath.

Skye showered, and despite instructions to wear nothing underneath the spa robe, put on an old one-piece swimsuit. After twisting her wet hair into a towel and slipping on flip-flops, she headed to the Miracle Mud bath area of the spa, following the small map that had been included with the appointment's instructions.

In order to reach the special suite Margot and Dr. Burnett had had constructed from the mansion's basement, Skye was directed down a flight of stairs and through a tiled hallway. According to her directions, at the end of this passage was a room that contained two uniquely designed ceramic vats that heated the Miracle Mud and kept it at a constant temperature.

Skye emerged from the corridor and saw a pair of large windows with a river view. In fact, it almost looked as if the water was flowing straight into the spa. How had they done that? Skye summoned a picture of the mansion and realized it had been built into a hill, allowing for the back to be level with the shore, and making it easy to pipe in the Miracle Mud.

Finally, tearing her gaze from the view, Skye saw a small desk and chair near a doorway. The chair was empty and there was no sign of the attendant, but Skye could hear loud music coming from the treatment room beyond.

She hesitated, thinking maybe the woman was settling another guest into the bath, since the brochure indicated two tubs were available.

As she stood there, unsure of what to do, Skye looked around. Besides the desk and chair next to the door leading into the mud bath room, there was a wall with several shower heads attached and drains along the floor, nearby a rolling cabinet of the special silvery colored towels that were the spa's trademark, and a small alcove with a shampoo sink and chair.

Shoot. She hated waiting, but she didn't want to have to walk all the way back to the main reception area. She tried calling out, "Miss, Miss. I'm here for my nine-thirty appointment." Could the attendant hear her over the loud music? She moved closer to the closed treatment room door and raised her voice. "Anybody there?"

Still no answer.

She should turn on her heels and get Margot. No, that was silly. She'd just take a little peek. If the attendant was busy she'd wait; if no one was there, she'd leave.

Her flip-flops made a soft flapping sound as she crossed the small space. She nearly stepped on a wadded towel stained with greenish-brown steaks laying on the floor near the door. She reached for the knob, but hesitated before grabbing it because there were greenish-brown smears similar to those on the towel, coating the brass surface. She bent over and sniffed. It smelled herbal.

Taking a tissue from her robe pocket, she used it to release the door without getting her hands dirty, then laughed at herself for being so fastidious when in a few minutes her whole body would be covered in mud. She eased open the door and called out, "It's now or never if you don't want me to come in!"

Skye counted to ten, then swung the door wide, but didn't cross the threshold. The room was a twelve by twelve tiled room with a mud vat on either side of the doorway. The music was even louder in here and Skye spotted a hot pink portable CD player on a shelf next to various bottles, bath brushes, and silvery towels. The song sounded familiar, and Skye caught herself humming, but she couldn't quite come up with the words.

At first the room appeared empty, but then she noticed a pink and black silk kimono hanging from a hook near the door, and on the floor underneath matching satin slippers lay on their sides. Skye stepped back, ready to close the door, when something stopped her. Where was the robe's owner? Surely, no one would leave such an expensive garment and walk away nude.

Before she could talk herself out of it, she walked over to the vat on the right. It was about thigh high and there were steps to help get in and out. The contents radiated heat, and smelled soothing.

As Skye crossed over to the other side of the room, she turned off the CD player. The loud music grated on her nerves and seemed somehow wrong under the circumstances. Nearing the other bath, she noticed evidence that this one had already been used. There were greenish brown smears on the rim of the vat and on the steps. The odor seemed different, too. Skye leaned closer to sniff. Yech. Along with the smell of herbs, there was a stench of fresh feces.

Skye gagged and moved back, but not before she spotted the outline of a hand just beneath the mud's surface. Had the Miracle Mud been transformed from the Fountain of Youth to the Cauldron of Death?

CHAPTER 7

Whole New Ball
of Wax

Wait a minute. Skye stopped in midstep and turned back. Maybe whoever was in the mud bath wasn't dead. Suddenly the training she'd received when she was hired as a consultant to the Scumble River Police Department kicked in. Her primary concern was the victim's welfare, which meant getting the person out of the mud bath and clearing the nose and mouth so Skye could do CPR.

Skye shrugged out of her robe—thankful she had ignored the instructions to wear nothing under it—and climbed up the steps. Plunging her arms into the mud, she felt around until she found the victim's shoulders, then worked her hands underneath the arms and clasped them over the upper chest.

With a mighty heave, Skye tugged the person into a sitting position. Once free of the sludge, it was clear the victim was female, but Skye couldn't identify her since the mud obscured her features.

Grunting with effort, Skye tried to move the woman over the edge of the vat, but for every inch she pulled, the mud sucked the victim back two. As Skye took a deep breath, trying to figure out another way to get the person completely out of the tub, she heard a scream behind her. Her head shot around like a snapped rubber band, and she saw Kipp Gardner, the spa's hairstylist, in the doorway.

"Kipp, thank God. Help me get her out of the tub," Skye ordered, but the hairstylist kept screaming.

"Kipp. Pull yourself together." Skye felt like screaming herself. "This could be a matter of life or death."

He shook his head and sank to the ground, his screams turning into whimpers.

Giving up on his help, Skye's thoughts raced. What to do? She propped the woman against the back of the bath and draped her arms over the side, hoping this would keep her above mud level. Once Skye released her, she felt for a pulse in the woman's throat and her wrist. Nothing.

As she leaned forward to check for breathing, she heard a familiar accented voice, then a slap, and finally Kipp stopped sniveling. Ustelle stepped past the hairdresser, now kneeling silently in the doorway, and asked, stone-faced, "What's wrong with Ms. Gates?"

"This is Esmé?"

"Ya. I think so. I put her in the bath half an hour ago."

"Help me get her out," Skye commanded. "I found her under the mud."

Ustelle hurried forward and between her and Skye they lifted Esmé out and onto the floor. Skye checked again for a pulse or breathing, and found none.

"When you put her into the bath, did you get mud on your hands?" Skye asked Ustelle.

"No." Ustelle bit her lip. "She said she didn't need any help, she'd get in after I closed the door."

"Did you stay in the next room for any length of time or leave right away? How long have you been gone?"

"I left as soon as Ms. Gates was settled." Ustelle looked stricken. "The baths are a half hour, and I knew you'd be coming at nine thirty. I needed to make a quick call, and I didn't want to be late for you again."

"Are you supposed to stay while the guests are in the bath?" Skye asked.

"Yes," Ustelle whispered. "Please don't tell Ms. Margot or the doctor."

"I won't tell them directly." Skye grimaced. "But you will

need to tell the police, so Margot and the doctor will probably find out."

"The police!" Ustelle squealed.

"Yes, and right now." Skye was sorry she had started asking the masseuse questions. She should have left that until
later, but she had wanted to make sure of her theory before
she said anything, and Ustelle's absence had made her de-
duction more viable. "Go to the reception desk in the lobby.
Call 911. Tell them someone's dead, probably murdered,
and we need the police." Skye paused, thinking. "Oh, and
don't touch anything here or on your way to the lobby. Take
Kipp with you, and stay there. I need to secure the scene."

As soon as the masseuse and the hairstylist left, Skye
took off the towel she had wrapped around her hair, intend-
ing to use it to cover poor Esmé, but stopped when she realized it was important not to contaminate the victim with
transference. Instead she used the towel to wipe the worst of
the mud from her arms and upper body, before putting on
her robe and stepping out of the room.

She stationed herself in front of the stairway, determined
not to let anyone else taint the scene. Unfortunately, news of
the death traveled faster than the police, and Skye had to
turn away several staff and guests who felt entitled to see the
body.

Dr. Burnett was among the first to arrive. He was doing a
type of run-walk the principals at Skye's schools had per-
fected. It was meant to convey the message, that, yes, there
is an emergency, but it's being handled and everyone else
should go back to work.

Skye crossed her arms and maintained her position. As
soon as he was in earshot she asked, "Have the police been
called?"

"Yes, Ustelle phoned them before informing me. You
shouldn't have told her to do that. You should have sent for
me. After all, I am a doctor."

Skye noticed the medical bag in his hand and shook her
head. "Listen, I know Esmé was your friend and I'm sorry,
but she's dead. No doctor can help her now."

"How can you be sure?" Dr. Burnett challenged. "You need to let me examine her."

Self-doubt nudged Skye. Could Esmé still be alive? Could Skye have missed a faint pulse? While she second-guessed herself, Trixie and May arrived, and Skye made a split-second decision.

But before she acted on it, she made a general announcement. "It looks like Esmé has been murdered. The police are on the way. Trixie, go to the lobby and make sure the police are coming. When they get here, bring them to this stairway."

Trixie opened her mouth, then perhaps reading Skye's "don't mess with me" expression closed it, and trotted off.

"Mom, your job is to keep everyone from going past this point until the police arrive."

May nodded, stepped next to Skye, and asked, "Where will you be?"

"I'll be escorting Dr. Burnett to the victim so he can examine her, in case I'm wrong about her being dead."

May nodded again, and took up a feet-apart, hands-on-hips stance at the top of the stairway.

Skye dipped her head at the doctor. "Do you have gloves in that bag?"

"Yes."

"Good. Put on a pair and follow me." Skye put her own hands in the robe's pockets and led the way back to where she'd left Esmé.

Skye moved at a fast pace, but the doctor's long legs allowed him to keep up with her. They were both silent. At the door to the mud bath treatment room, she paused. She had the weirdest feeling that she would walk through the door and find Esmé gone. Skye shook her head and focused. Evidently, she'd been reading too many mysteries; maybe it was time to switch to romances or science fiction.

Stepping across the threshold, she wasn't sure what she felt: relief she wasn't cracking up, or disappointment someone was actually dead. Ignoring both emotions, she pointed at the body. "She was submerged under the mud. Ustelle and

I lifted her out of the tub and laid her on the ground. I checked for a pulse and breathing."

Dr. Burnett knelt next to Esmé, and wiped her face off with a towel before Skye could object. Now that the mud was gone, Skye could see that Esmé's expression was one of puzzlement.

Using a stethoscope, Dr. Burnett listened for a heartbeat, then raised her eyelids with a gloved thumb.

Skye always wondered why doctors did that. Someday she'd need to ask.

He stood in one smooth movement with no hesitation or creaking, an impressive display for a man who had to be in his sixties, maybe older.

Skye asked, "So?"

"She's dead." He busied himself brushing off his khaki pants and straightening his powder blue cashmere sweater, not meeting Skye's eyes.

"Then let's get back and wait for the police." Skye didn't bother demanding that the doctor admit she had been right. Asking that of him would have been like asking an oyster to open itself and hand over its pearl without a struggle.

As they retraced their steps, Dr. Burnett blurted out, "When I heard Ustelle on the phone with the police dispatcher, at first I thought the victim was Margot."

"Why?"

"I know you all think the problems we've been having remodeling and starting up are due to someone looking for the hidden jewels, but what if it's someone trying to stop us from opening, trying to put the spa out of business? If that's the case, then Margot would have been a logical target." He gripped Skye's arm. "That's why I had to see the body."

"I understand." Skye knew this was as close to an apology as she would get.

"Esmé was a shallow, vain woman, but she didn't deserve to die that way," Dr. Burnett murmured almost to himself.

Skye was surprised by his comment. She would have thought most of the women who came to the spa would be shallow and vain. But the last part of his statement was even more interesting. "What do you mean by 'die that way'? Do you know what caused her death?"

"No." He looked startled. "I suppose I don't. Though I didn't see any injury or trauma when I examined her so I assume she drowned in the mud." He paused. "However, my examination was superficial; I was only looking for signs of life. I could easily have missed something subtle."

When they reached the top of the stairway, Skye wasn't surprised to see that a crowd had gathered. Loretta had joined May in keeping anyone from slipping by. The two worked well together, even under these appalling circumstances.

Most of the throng was milling in the hall, but Margot was nose-to-nose with May, trying to argue her way past the older woman. "I own this spa. I can go anywhere I damn well please."

"No." May's short, calm answer belied the look in her eye. Skye knew that Margot was extremely close to pushing May into an explosion.

"Darling." Margot caught sight of Dr. Burnett as he emerged from the stairwell and threw herself into his arms. "I've been so worried. What happened?"

The doctor opened his mouth, but Skye jumped in with, "It appears Esmé is dead. Other than that, it's best not to discuss the details until the police have a chance to talk to everyone individually."

Skye spied Frannie and Bunny in the pack and edged her way over to them. She grabbed an arm of each and whispered in their ears, "Try to herd this group into the lobby and keep them from talking. Circulate and listen to what the ones who won't shut up are saying."

Bunny nodded, and turned to go, then came back and asked, "She was in that Miracle Mud, right?" Today the redhead was dressed in tangerine, skintight French terry jogging pants that rode low on her hips, and a matching crop tank. A gold ring was fastened to her navel.

Skye nodded, wondering when fifty-something Bunny had had her belly button pierced.

"So, when you got her out, did she look younger?"

Bunny's brown eyes were hopeful as she absently smoothed the wrinkles at their corners with her index finger.

"No." Skye closed her eyes and shook her head. "She just looked dead."

Skye was never so happy to hear anyone's voice as she was to hear Wally's. Bunny and Frannie had managed to move most of the crowd to the lobby, but Skye, May, and Loretta had stuck around to watch the stragglers and make sure no one slipped back and tried to get a peek at the body. It had been a long twenty minutes.

Wally was talking to a woman dressed in a tailored navy pantsuit with an unfamiliar-looking badge clipped to the breast pocket. Her dark brown hair was tightly drawn back and fastened at the nape of her neck, and black rimmed glasses both magnified and blurred her hazel eyes. When she laughed at something Wally said, giving his arm a little pat, Skye noticed her nails were long and painted a pale pink, which didn't go with the rest of her appearance.

As soon as Wally saw Skye, he hurried toward her, leaving the woman with her hand hanging in midair and her mouth open. Catching Skye's eye a second before Wally took her hand and pulled her around a corner, the woman shot her a look so full of jealousy and resentment that it stole Skye's breath away.

Once they were out of the crowd's sight Wally enveloped Skye in a hug. "Sweetheart." He cupped her face, his strong hands cradling her cheeks and his concerned brown eyes locked on to hers. "Are you all right?"

Wally had turned forty the previous winter, but the silver in his black hair, and the lines around his eyes made him more handsome, not less. He radiated a strength that drew Skye like sugar water did a hummingbird.

"I'm fine." Skye intended to give him a quick kiss, but it threatened to linger, and she reluctantly pulled herself out of his arms. She still wasn't used to how demonstrative Wally was compared to Simon, but she found that she liked it. Gathering her thoughts she asked, "Where are the paramedics?"

"They're not coming." A line formed between Wally's eyebrows. "We were told the victim was dead. Isn't she?"

"Yes. In fact, Dr. Burnett, one of the spa owners, confirmed it."

"Then no EMTs." Wally gave her hand a little squeeze. "Tell me why you think she was murdered."

Skye explained about the attendant not entering the mud bath room and not staying at her post in the waiting room. She also told him about the greenish-brown stains on the doorknob, towel, and rim of the tub, concluding with, "So, it seemed to me that if Esmé got in the tub herself, she wouldn't have smeared the mud all over. But if someone held her under, her thrashing would explain the mud around the tub and on the steps, as well as on the murderer. He or she must have walked into the waiting room, closed the treatment room door once he was out, and then grabbed a towel to clean up.

"Heck, the killer could even have bathed; the shower's right there. Someone walking around in a wet swimsuit or spa robe wouldn't arouse any suspicion."

"Sounds logical to me." Wally had released her hand to take notes. "Where's this mud room?"

Skye stepped back into the main corridor and pointed. "It's down those stairs, and at the end of the hall." For the first time since she had found Esmé's body, Skye felt safe, and she was reluctant to lose that sensation by letting Wally out of her sight. "Shall I show you?"

"I'll find it. It would be better if you stay here and talk to Special Agent Vail."

"Special Agent?" Skye had never heard that title before.

"Yeah. She's from the state police. Considering our circumstances, I called them to borrow their crime scene specialists, rather than the county's unit."

Skye nodded, knowing Wally was referring to the fact that the county sheriff was under investigation—an investigation in which Skye had played an integral part in instigating.

"So, about ten minutes after I called for the forensic unit, Special Agent Vail shows up at the police department. Seems she was visiting relatives in town, and her boss asked her to come by and see if I needed assistance."

"I see."

"And with Quirk on medical leave and so many of my part-timers away for the holiday, I grabbed the chance to get some help. I'll introduce you two." Wally motioned to the woman who had been sending Skye death ray looks from across the hall. As she approached, Wally said, "Ronnie, this is Skye Denison, the psychological consultant for the Scumble River Police Department. Skye, this is Veronica Vail, a special agent with the state police."

Skye held out her hand. "Nice to meet you."

Special Agent Vail nodded to Skye, ignoring her hand, and turned to Wally. "Where's the vic?"

Wally pointed to the stairs, repeating Skye's directions, then said, "I'll go take a look at the body. Ronnie, you can take Skye's statement and help her with the witnesses while we wait for the forensic people to show up."

The special agent pushed up her glasses. "I'm coming with you. I want to get a good picture of the crime scene."

"Perhaps I didn't make myself clear when I talked to your boss." Wally drew himself up to his full six feet and looked down at the woman, who came up only to his shoulder. "The key word here is *help*, but I remain in charge of the investigation."

"But—"

"Skye needs assistance with the witnesses. There are too many for her to handle alone. Since it's Thanksgiving Day, I've only got a skeleton staff on duty. I've called in my other officers, but it will take a while for most of them to get back from wherever they're celebrating the holiday."

"This isn't the best use of my time." She flicked Skye a dismissive look. "The witnesses are already contaminated. *She* should have isolated them as soon as she found the body."

"Excuse me?" Skye was offended by both the condescending tone and accusation. "I isolated the crime scene and kept the witnesses together where someone not involved in the crime could monitor them, and that's not enough for you?"

The woman turned her back on Skye and said to Wally,

"I want to see the body since we only have *her* word that it's murder. I sure hope she didn't drag us all out for an accident."

"Skye has explained her reasoning and I agree the circumstances are suspicious." Wally's nostrils flared. "Either you stay here and follow my orders, or we call your boss right now."

Skye saw something flicker in the agent's eyes. Perhaps she was afraid her superior wouldn't take her side.

Once she got herself under control, Ronnie Vail said, "Fine. We'll do it your way."

Wally nodded, then spoke over his shoulder to Skye as he headed down the stairs. "Send Simon down when he gets here."

Shit! Simon, her lying, cheating ex-boyfriend, was the coroner. How could she have forgotten he would have to be called? So far this holiday weekend there'd been humiliation and murder. Now Simon. What was next? An earthquake? Flood? Tornado?

CHAPTER 8

What Did the Client Say to the Acupuncturist? Stop Needling Me!

Skye wasn't surprised that Special Agent Vail took over, completely ignoring Skye. Truth be told, she was exhausted both physically and mentally, and happy to sit quietly in a chair and watch. Nevertheless, after a few minutes of rest, it dawned on her that she was wearing a robe that barely fit over a mud-covered swimsuit and she probably smelled like a dirty diaper. No way was she greeting Simon dressed like that. She needed to shower, and put on some real clothes.

Reluctantly, she abandoned her comfortable haven and made her way over to where, at Wally's request, May and Loretta were still blocking the staircase until additional officers arrived to secure the scene.

Edging her mother a few steps from Loretta, Skye whispered in May's ear, "I'm going to my room for a few minutes. I'll be right back. Wally said that when Simon gets here, send him right down."

May tugged on Skye's elbow and motioned her even farther away from Loretta. "What's up with that one over there?"

She cut her eyes to Ronnie Vail.

Skye explained Wally's call to the state police for help and how Special Agent Vail had happened to be in town.

"Something about her bothers me. I know I've seen her

somewhere." May shook her head. "And why is she wearing so much makeup? It almost looks like a mask, it's so thick."

"Well, if she has relatives in Scumble River you may have seen her when she was visiting, and as for her makeup, she *was* off duty, or maybe she has a scar she's covering up." Skye tried to be fair to the woman, but she couldn't help adding, "She's certainly taken an instant dislike to me."

"I noticed." May pursed her lips. "I would have sworn it was because she was sweet on Wally, until they had that dust up a minute ago."

"I'll be right back. Keep an eye on her, Mom," Skye directed as she made her escape.

She had just reached for the knob of her door when she heard Ronnie Vail's harsh voice in her ear. "What do you think you're doing?"

Skye turned and stared at the special agent. "Going into my room to clean up and put on some clothes. Not that it's any of your business. Why aren't you with the witnesses Wally told you to watch?"

"I saw you sneak off and wanted to see where you were going." The special agent crossed her arms. "And since a couple of Scumble River officers finally arrived, I was free to do something more important than babysit."

"Now that we've both satisfied our curiosity, if you'll excuse me, there's a hot shower with my name on it on the other side of this door."

"I don't think so." Special Agent Vail grabbed Skye's arm. "The forensic team will want to take trace evidence from you first."

"Can't I just put my swimsuit and robe in here?" Skye held out the plastic bag with the towel she'd used to clean herself up. She'd almost forgotten she'd been holding it the whole time.

"Sorry." Special Agent Vail smiled meanly. "Not my call. We'll have to wait until forensics gets here to see what they want to do. But since Wally has ordered me to preserve the evidence, you'll need to stay with me until they arrive."

Skye was ninety-nine percent sure the other woman was doing this to make her uncomfortable and as a power play against Wally, but she shrugged, and allowed the agent to escort her back to the holding area in the lobby.

As Special Agent Vail had claimed, several of the part-time officers from Scumble River's police force who had arrived were keeping an eye on the people gathered in the lobby. Others were rounding up the rest of the spa guests and employees.

Trixie, Frannie, and Bunny were sitting together talking to Jeff, one of the more experienced part-timers. Skye smiled when she saw Frannie whip out a notebook and start to read it to the police officer. The teenager must have taken her assignment seriously and recorded what the other guests had talked about.

Skye had a nodding acquaintance with all of the officers, and she could see that Special Agent Vail was displeased with the friendly way they greeted Skye, treating her as one of their own.

Skye ignored the woman's glower and said to the part-timer who liked her best, "Anthony, do you know if the coroner is here yet?" Skye had helped get Anthony's little sister the special instruction she needed in school, and he and his family had been grateful.

"Yep, a few minutes ago." The good-looking officer nodded toward the hall. "He went right down to the crime scene. Do you need to talk to Mr. Reid?"

"No, not at all." For the first time since she had set foot on the Bruefeld Estate luck was with Skye, and she wasn't about to blow it. "Any instructions from the chief?"

"Nope. Far as I know we're just rounding people up and keeping an eye on them for now."

"Any ETA on the state crime scene techs?" Skye gestured to her robe. "Special Agent Vail won't let me change until they okay it."

Anthony frowned at the other woman. "The chief wouldn't like her treating you that way."

"Probably not, but he's busy and it isn't that important." Skye pointed to the front door. "Anyway, I think the crime techs just walked in."

"Good. I'll make sure they know the special agent wants you processed ASAP." Anthony gave Skye a conspiratorial wink before joining the new arrivals.

Skye let him go, hoping he wouldn't get in trouble for helping her, but pretty sure Special Agent Vail had little power with the Scumble River PD.

Anthony had nabbed one of the techs and walked him over to where Skye was standing. A split second later, Special Agent Vail noticed the other crime technicians who were still standing by the door, and went to greet them. Skye's attention was split between both scenes. It looked as if the agent was introducing herself to the men. That was odd. If they all worked for the state police, shouldn't they know her?

Skye shrugged inwardly. Maybe the special agent was new or had worked in a different part of the state. She brought her attention back to the important matter at hand, the man standing in front of her.

She introduced herself to the tech, explained she worked for the Scumble River PD, described finding the body, and told him about Ronnie's order regarding her clothes.

When he nodded his understanding, she asked, "So, I really want to shower, and get into clean dry clothes. What do we need to do to make that happen?"

The tech scratched his head, looked back at where Ronnie stood, and said, "Excuse me, ma'am. I'll be right back."

Dang. Skye frowned. She had hoped to go over the special agent's head, but the tech was too well trained.

He was back a minute later with Ronnie in tow. "All we really need is your clothing," he said. "Special Agent Vail here will go with you to your room to collect them." He handed her a folded plastic bag with a twist tie taped to the side.

"Can we do it right now?" Skye asked.

"Yes. Let's get it over with." Ronnie marched toward the main staircase without looking to see if Skye was following.

Skye hurried to keep up with the other woman.

Once they were inside Skye's room, Ronnie pulled off the twist tie, and shook open the bag, then ordered Skye, "Put everything you're wearing in here."

Skye tried to take the bag from the woman's hand, but Ronnie jerked it away. "I need to see you put the clothing in the bag."

"I have to get naked in front of you?" Skye could feel a massive dose of mortification about to be administered.

Ronnie surprised her. "None of us has a perfect body. Just strip."

Skye looked at the special agent. Now that she mentioned it, Ronnie was no size eight either. Still, she was a couple of sizes smaller than Skye. "Could you close your eyes?"

"Come on. You have a terrific life—a great job, loyal friends, loving relatives, and a wonderful and handsome guy who clearly adores you, since you're all he can talk about. The police chief must think your body looks pretty hot. Why don't you?"

Skye didn't have an answer to that. She thought she had overcome her need to be thin to feel beautiful, but this hostile stranger had more understanding about what really mattered in life than Skye herself did.

After handing over her robe and swimsuit, and the plastic bag with the towel, Skye escaped into the bathroom. When she finished her long awaited shower, and peeked into the bedroom, Special Agent Vail was gone and Skye could dress in peace.

Choosing what to put on was another matter. She hadn't packed much, since she was planning to be in either her swimsuit or sweats for most of the weekend, but this situation called for a more formal appearance. That pretty much left the three dresses she had packed to wear for the dinners, or the outfit she had intended to change into for Thanksgiving with her family. Other than that, all she had was the jeans and top she'd been wearing when she arrived.

The Thanksgiving outfit seemed the most reasonable choice, since it was obvious that no one would be leaving the spa anytime soon, which meant Skye would be a no-show for the holiday meal.

As she slipped into a mocha knit skirt and matching shell, she sighed—not so much because she would miss seeing her family, but because instead of eating the fabulous, home-cooked dinner of turkey, sweet potatoes, and green bean casserole, she'd be dining on two celery sticks and a tofu turkey leg. She didn't even want to think about what diet pumpkin pie would taste like.

On a good day her thick wavy hair took half an hour to dry and style. Since this wasn't a good day, she had two options—a French braid or a ponytail. She chose a form of the latter, gathering it all on the crown of her head with a covered rubber band and forming it into a topknot of loose curls. A quick brush of bronzer and a coat of mascara and she was nearly dressed.

Brown kitten-heeled slides, a waist-length jacket of swirled cocoa, bittersweet, and ginger, and chunky gold earrings completed the outfit. Taking a deep breath, she exited the safe haven of her room, ready to face the music even if it was a dirge.

She was surprised to find the lobby empty except for Barb, the receptionist on duty behind the desk.

Skye greeted her and asked, "Where'd everyone go?"

"That yummy police chief had all the guests and the live-in staff escorted to their rooms. The day staff and Ms. Margot and Dr. Burnett are in the parlor. Everyone has to be interviewed by an officer before they can be released."

"I'll bet they talked to you first so you could handle the phones, right?"

"Right. No outgoing allowed, and all incoming directed to the answering machine. Hey, are you Skye Denison?"

"Yes."

"Chief Boyd asked me to give you this." The young woman handed over an envelope with the spa's return address in the corner.

Skye slit the top with her fingernail and pulled out a sheet of paper. Wally's note said that Simon had declared Esmé dead, the crime techs had processed the body, and

Simon had taken it to the hospital in Laurel for the Medical Examiner to perform the autopsy. Wally also asked Skye to find him when she was free so she could help with the interviews.

"Do you know where Chief Boyd is?" Skye asked the clerk.

She consulted a list. "Each officer took a different treatment room. The chief is in the waxing room. Do you know where that is?"

"Yes." Skye nodded, memories of her hopping to Trixie's rescue reddening her cheeks. "Thanks for your help."

As she hurried toward the waxing room, Skye found her mother walking down the hall with Rudy, the groundskeeper, trailing her.

Skye stopped her. "Aren't you supposed to be in your room?"

May shook her head. "Wally and the other cops interviewed me, Trixie, and Loretta first so we could escort the others to and from their interrogations."

"How about Bunny and Frannie?"

"They're waiting their turn with the rest of the guests." May gestured to Skye. "How about you?"

"I have orders to report to Wally, then help with the questioning."

"So, this police consultant job is real, eh?" May raised an eyebrow. "I just thought it was something Wally made up to get into your pants."

"Mother!" Skye's face flamed as she caught the smirk on Rudy's face.

May would pay for that remark. Skye wasn't sure how or when, but it wouldn't be forgotten or forgiven. Skye stalked away from her mother.

When she arrived, she knocked on the waxing room door and said, "It's me, Skye."

Wally called, "Come in," and when she did, she found him sitting on the waxer's rolling stool facing Margot, who was perched on the waxee's reclining chair. The ex-model and current spa owner sat erect, both feet on the floor. She was expressionless and seemed calm, but Skye could tell it was an uncomfortable position to maintain.

"Sorry to interrupt, Chief, but I got your note and am reporting for duty."

Wally smiled at her. "Great. We can use the help. Between the guests and the staff, we've got over thirty people to interview."

"Where would you like me to set up?"

"The room next door is free, but wait here while I finish with Ms. Avanti. I want to go over a few things with you before you start."

Skye nodded and leaned against the door to listen.

Wally turned back to the spa owner. "You were telling me that Ms. Gates was a newlywed. Was this her first marriage?"

"Good heavens, no."

"How many times had she been married?"

"Mmm." Margot tipped her head, then counted on her fingers. "Let's see, there were the Bulgari yellow diamonds, the Bickham sapphires, and Pequot emeralds."

Wally scratched his head. "Which means?"

"Why, three previous marriages, of course." Margot's eyes twinkled with amusement. "After all, husbands come and go, but jewelry lasts forever."

Wally managed a slight smile, then asked, "How long had Ms. Gates been married to her present husband?"

"Not quite a year. Rex's divorce from Christine took forever."

"Christine was his first wife?" Wally clarified.

"Yes, and their divorce was really messy. When Rex's daughter Whitney expressed an interest in coming to the spa, Rex jumped at the chance for her and Esmé to spend a weekend together. He was hoping they would bond if they were away from all the reminders of the bad times."

"Was that working?"

Margot crossed her legs. "They'd only been here twenty-four hours. I'm sure they would have worked things out if they'd had more time."

Wally made a note, then asked, "You and Ms. Gates were friends back from your modeling days, right?"

Margot nodded.

"Then you probably know who her other friends were?"

Margot appeared fascinated with the shoe dangling from her toe. Finally, she said, "Friends come and go, enemies accumulate."

CHAPTER 9

Leave No Stone Massage Unturned

As soon as Wally finished questioning the spa owner, and he and Skye were alone, Skye said, "When Margot mentioned enemies, it reminded me of something. Did anyone tell you about the protestors?"

"No." Wally stood up. "What in blue blazes are they protesting?"

"When Trixie and I arrived yesterday afternoon, the spa's entrance was blocked by a group who called themselves Real Women. They believe that the spa is another example of women being told they can't be beautiful unless they fit into a certain mold." Skye repeated what she could remember of the Real Women's doctrine. "Margot got them to leave the property by saying she had called the police, but I don't know if she really did telephone."

"She must have been bluffing. There wasn't anything about a protest march in yesterday's report." Wally scratched his head. "And no sign of them today."

"That would mean either they gave up really easily, although they didn't strike me as quitters, or they're staying somewhere nearby waiting for their next chance to cause trouble."

"That narrows it down to the campgrounds over in Brooklyn or the Up A Lazy River Motor Court here." Wally made a note on his pad. "I'll have someone check into it as soon as I can shake an officer loose."

"Good." Skye searched for anything else she should tell him. "Let's see, you know about the spa vandal and/or treasure hunter, and that Trixie and I were trying to find the nuisance maker—no luck on that by the way. But did anyone mention the rock someone tossed through the window yesterday?"

When Wally shook his head, Skye described the incident, concluding with, "I think the dirt splattering against the window must have been caused by someone digging for that darned treasure. I must have scared whoever it was, and they threw the rock to give themselves time to get away before I could look outside."

Wally nodded slowly, then asked, "Anything else you can think of I should know?"

"Let me see." Skye chewed her lip. "No. The food's terrible, last night we were forced to listen to Wagner arias, and some sadist thinks it's possible to start the day without caffeine."

Wally chuckled. "Sounds awful."

"It is," Skye agreed, then said, "Sorry, I didn't think of the protestors and the broken window sooner."

"Sweetheart, you've done a great job." He put his hands on her waist and drew her to him. "You did everything right. Even the crime techs were impressed with how wide a perimeter you were able to provide when you sealed the scene."

"Really? That's so good to hear." Skye felt herself relax a little.

"Really." His lips brushed hers as he spoke. "The second smartest thing I ever did was to hire you as a police consultant."

His kiss left her mouth burning, but she managed to ask, "What was the first smartest thing you ever did?"

He tightened his arms around her. "I'll tell you later."

"Mmm. I can hardly wait." Skye snuggled against him for another minute, then reluctantly said, "Special Agent

Vail seemed to think everything I did was wrong, and I was beginning to believe her."

"There's something odd about that woman. When I have a minute, I need to call her superior and ask him for the scoop."

"Good idea. I'm getting weird vibes from her, too." Skye smiled, relieved that she and Wally were in agreement. "Do you have a list of who you want me to interview?"

"Yes." Wally tore a page from the back of his notepad. "And here's a list of questions, too, but feel free to add any that you think might be important."

"Okay." Skye glanced at the paper and nodded to herself. "Next door, right?"

"Right." Wally put his hand on the knob but before he turned it, he said, "I've asked Dr. Burnett and Ms. Avanti to keep the spa open. I think we'll have a better chance of catching the killer if everyone stays here, rather than scattering. I'll have a police officer here twenty-four/seven to protect the guests and staff, but my gut tells me no one else is in danger. Esmé's murder just doesn't fit the pattern of a random killer."

"That's good to hear." Skye walked out the door Wally held open, then turned back. "You know, Margot and Esmé look a lot alike, especially from the back."

"I'll keep that in mind." Wally stepped back into his room.

When Skye entered the room next door, she was relieved to see it had two normal chairs and a desk. Judging by the posters and the huge scale in the corner, she surmised that it must be where the body analysis took place. She was staring at what appeared to be a pair of giant pointy tongs hanging from a hook on the wall, trying to figure out their use, when a knock interrupted her.

Immediately she sat down, positioned the pad and pen Wally had given her on the desktop, and called out, "Come in."

The door was flung open and an olive-skinned man with a mane of blue-black hair swept into the room. He wore tight knit jogging shorts that emphasized his muscular thighs and slim hips, and a tank top that strained to cover his powerful chest.

He tipped his head in a slight bow. "Frisco Indelicato, personal trainer, at your service."

Skye made a note on her pad. This was the guy Margot had reprimanded Amber about dating. "Hi. I'm Skye Denison, psychological consultant to the Scumble River Police Department. Have a seat." Just her luck, she was the one assigned to interrogate the trainer. His job required him to be the most judgmental member of the staff. Nervously she pulled down her skirt and adjusted her jacket, only narrowly resisting the urge to suck in her stomach and thrust out her chest. She refused to even contemplate what he must think of her less-than-perfect body.

"Why haven't I seen you at any of my classes yet this weekend?" he demanded, straddling the chair opposite Skye.

"I prefer to work out on my own."

"Where?"

"In the privacy of my own imagination."

He gave her a startled look and his mouth opened, but before he could think of a response, she seized control of the interview, starting with the standard questions. "So, Mr. Indelicato, where were you from eight thirty until nine thirty this morning?"

"I was supposed to be leading a water aerobics class, but no one but Whitney showed up." His dark eyes flashed. "These people do not seem to realize that my time is valuable. I told Margot not to offer a cut-priced weekend, that the peasants would never appreciate what they were being given."

Skye kept her face expressionless even as he insulted her and her town. "Have you known Margot long?"

"Yes, I have been the personal trainer for many of the top models of the past twenty years."

Interesting. Skye would have guessed him to be in his thirties, but he must be older. "Were you Esmé's trainer, as well?"

"For a while." He sniffed. "But her boyfriend became

jealous and didn't want her to be alone with such a handsome man as myself."

"Oh, I see." Skye had to bite the inside of her cheek not to giggle at Frisco's egotistical view of the world. "Who was this boyfriend?"

"Rex Quinn."

"Her current husband?"

When Frisco nodded, Skye jotted down that information, making sure the trainer didn't see how surprised she was. "That must have made you angry, losing a client that way."

"Why would it? The waiting list for my services is thicker than the Chicago phone book." Frisco made a gesture as if he were shooing away a fly. "Models come and go; someone with Frisco's talent is always in demand."

After a few more routine questions, Skye said, "That's all for now, Mr. Indelicato. Please don't discuss anything we've talked about with anyone else."

He bounded to his feet, but didn't head toward the door. Towering over Skye, he said, "I understand the spa will remain open for the weekend."

"So I've been told."

"You should make an appointment with me. You have such a pretty face. It's a shame to see it wasted on such an overweight body."

It took Skye a moment to control all the different emotions that raced through her, but finally she could answer him without bursting out crying or slugging him. "I am not overweight, I am a nutritional overachiever." With that she got up, stalked to the door, and threw it open. "Now, get out."

After he left, she sank back into her seat, and barely had time to recover before there was another knock on the door. This one was impatient.

Skye had barely said, "Come in," when Amber marched over the threshold, not stopping until she was nearly stepping on Skye's feet. There was a petulant expression on her beautiful face and a querulous line between her perfectly plucked eyebrows. Today she wore another pair of designer jeans and a Roberto Cavalli blouse. She stood silently scowling until Skye said, "State your full name please."

"Don't you have a list?" The girl blew out a puff of exasperation. "Amber Ferguson."

Skye ignored the taunt. "Take a seat. I'm Ms. Denison, the psychological consultant for the police." This would be a tough one. It was hard enough interviewing strangers, let alone someone who had seen you masquerading as a foil wrapped taco *and* in your underwear shaking your sweater as if it were a tambourine.

"Could you hurry this up?" Amber threw herself in the chair across from Skye's and crossed her arms. "Bernard's picking me up for dinner in an hour and I've been waiting forever."

"Who is Bernard?"

"My father. Don't you people know anything?"

Skye ground her teeth, determined to ignore the girl's rudeness. "Please describe your job."

"I'm the makeup artist, but we all do other things, too. Like manicures, pedicures, and waxing."

Skye cringed inwardly. If Amber was going to mention Skye's previous embarrassing performances, this was the time she would bring it up. When she didn't, Skye realized that the girl was so focused on herself, the waxing and underwear incidents had barely registered with her.

After a moment, Skye asked, "Where were you this morning between eight thirty and nine thirty?"

"I was sleeping. I did Margot's makeup at seven. I have to do her makeup every morning," Amber grumbled. "Then I go back to bed."

"Alone?"

The young woman blew a bubble with the gum she was chewing, then said, "Margot's rule number five hundred and twenty-seven—thou shalt not have sex on spa grounds."

"Bummer." Skye continued to ignore the girl's ill temper. "But you don't always follow that rule, do you? Last night I overheard Margot lecturing you about sleeping with Frisco."

"That's ancient history. And the spa wasn't even open

yet. Who knew we had to follow Margot's stupid rules when there weren't even guests present."

"So, now you're hooking up with Elvis Doozier?"

"That freak? Please." Amber tossed her head. "Like I told Margot, he's stalking me."

Skye shook her head. If Elvis was really stalking Amber, he'd do it with a shotgun or a bear trap. Amber just didn't recognize the Doozier courting ritual. Skye opened her mouth to enlighten the young woman, then realized the futility of trying to explain the Dooziers to an outsider, and instead asked, "Did you know Esmé Gates before she arrived at the spa?"

"Not really."

"What does that mean?"

Amber's expression was hard to read. "I didn't like know her, know her. Just what Whitney mentioned in her e-mails."

"How do you know Whitney?" Skye remembered Margot's explanation from dinner the previous night, but wanted to see if Amber's account matched.

"We went to the same schools and our mothers hung out together."

Skye hadn't known about the mothers being friends and it took her a moment to process the information and come up with her next question. "Your mom was a friend of Esmé's?"

"Duh. Esmé was Whitney's stepmother. Her real mother, Christine, and my real mother, Pamela, were friends back when Whitney and I were in school, before both our fathers traded in our mothers for newer models."

"Oh." Skye was trying to keep Amber's history straight. "How long ago did your parents get a divorce, and your father remarry?"

Amber's aqua blue eyes clouded and she twisted her strawberry blond hair into a ponytail that she immediately released. "Four years ago."

"But Whitney's dad remarried just a year ago, right?" There was something important here, but Skye wasn't quite grasping it.

"Right. Whitney's lucky. At least she was finished with

college when her father didn't renew her mother's option."
Amber's mouth formed a bitter line. "Bernard left us when
I was a senior in high school. I went from being treated like
his princess to Cinderella without the fairy godmother."

"Your father left you as well as your mother?" Skye
struggled to understand.

"Yes. It wasn't too bad at first, but then his new wife,
Sheila, got pregnant last year and suddenly I didn't exist to
Bernard anymore."

Skye finally put two and two together. "He cut you off
without a penny, and since you were over eighteen, you suddenly had to support yourself. That's why you're working
here." Skye frowned, remembering Amber's earlier statement. "But didn't you just say your dad was picking you up
for dinner?"

"Yes." Amber gave an irritated shrug. "Now that my
wicked stepmother is out of the picture, I'm auditioning for
the role of princess again."

"What about her baby?"

"Sheila died before giving birth."

Skye paused to process what she had learned, then asked,
"So, if you're the princess again, why are you working
here?"

"Two reasons. So far, I haven't quite regained the rank of
princess—Bernard gives me expensive presents, but I
haven't talked him into the trust fund yet. And because I
never, ever want to have to depend on someone else for
money again." Amber stared at the ceiling. Finally, she
looked Skye in the eye. "What part of this do you find so
hard to believe?"

"Unfortunately, none of it." Skye's tone was gentle. "Did
the same thing happen to Whitney?"

"No. Not yet. I've been telling her to make every effort to
stay in her father's good graces. But with Esmé trying to get
pregnant, the game was probably over. Whitney wouldn't
have a chance to stay daddy's little girl if Esmé had a baby."

After Amber left, Skye thought about the young woman.
It would be awful to be thrust completely unprepared into
the workaday world. It was nice of Margot to give her a job

at the spa. Had Esmé asked her friend to give Whitney's pal a chance?

Next, Skye talked to one of the waitresses, an assistant groundskeeper, and one of the housekeepers. Since it was after breakfast, the waitress was off duty, and had been sitting in her car listening to music, the assistant groundskeeper had been alone filling in more holes that had appeared overnight, and the housekeeper had been in her room lying down with a headache.

Skye finished her interview list around five. Her stomach was growling and she was feeling light-headed from lack of food. Hurrying out of the treatment room, she ran smack into Wally, who was talking on his cell. After steadying her, he drew her to his side, said good-bye to whoever he was talking to, and asked Skye, "Anything?"

"Only one alibi, but nothing that I can see at this point that would have anything to do with the murder." Skye leaned back to look into his eyes. "How about you?"

He shook his head. "The only good piece of news is that Quirk's doctor released him to come back to work, and he's taking the midnight shift."

"That's great." Quirk was Wally's best officer and he depended on him.

"Let's see if the others found out anything."

As they walked back to the lobby, Wally explained that he had assigned Jeff and Anthony to interview the Scumble River women who were staying at the spa, including Bunny and Frannie, figuring that that group would probably have the least reason to kill Esmé, and that those officers would most likely have at least some knowledge of the women and their backgrounds.

He had assigned Ronnie Vail to interrogate the magazine critic, the second waitress, the other two housekeepers, the bellboy, and the cook.

Wally had talked to May, Trixie, Loretta, and Barb, the reception clerk, before starting the serious interviews. His list had consisted of Dr. Burnett, Whitney, Kipp, Ustelle, and, of course, Margot.

By the time they reached the lobby, Jeff, Anthony, and Ronnie Vail were waiting for them.

Wally asked, "How many of the people you interviewed had an alibi?"

"All the Scumble River women, except for Mrs. Denison, Mrs. Frayne, Ms. Steiner, Mrs. Reid, and Frannie Ryan, were together taking the self-guided hike through the grounds," Anthony reported. "They met for breakfast at eight and then walked together from eight thirty until nearly ten."

"Excellent. I was hoping we could cross them off the list." Wally turned to Agent Vail. "How about your group, Ronnie?"

"The waitress and cook were on duty at the breakfast buffet and alibi each other. The two housekeepers were working together cleaning guest rooms and never out of each other's sight for more than five or ten minutes at a time. And the bellboy claims that he was in the lobby with the reception clerk."

Wally nodded. "That matches the statement she gave. How about the magazine woman?"

"She stated that she was with Skye and Margot from about eight to eight thirty, but by herself for the rest of the crucial time."

"So she's still a suspect," Skye said. "As are all the people I talked to except Frisco Indelicato."

Wally told Anthony and Jeff about the protestors. He finished by saying, "Check the motor lodge and the campground to see if you can find them."

The men nodded and left.

"Ronnie, I want you to continue calling Rex Quinn. He's supposedly out of the country, but his daughter gave me his cell number. Right now it's going into voice mail, but try again every hour or so." Wally handed the woman a slip of paper. "I've promised the spa owners that if they keep the place open, I'd have an officer here twenty-four/seven. So if you're staying on this case, I'd like you to remain here until midnight. After that, I have an officer available for the next shift."

"Fine." Ronnie's voice was controlled and her eyes cold. "Where will you be?"

"You can reach me on my cell."

Skye noticed Wally didn't answer the woman, but instead headed toward the door, pulling Skye after him without giving her a chance to say anything.

Outside, Skye dug in her heels and stopped him. "Where are we going?"

"To get something to eat." Wally let go of her hand. "Unless you'd rather stay here and see what Margot's cook is serving for Thanksgiving dinner."

"No, thanks."

Wally opened the door of the squad car for Skye. "Coming?"

She nodded and joined him at the bottom of the stairs, sliding into the passenger seat. He closed the door and walked around to his own side.

After he buckled his seat belt, she asked, "But where can we find something to eat this late on a holiday?"

"My place."

CHAPTER 10

Getting Steamed

Skye's nervousness kept her silent on the ten-minute ride to Wally's house. She had been there only once before, and it hadn't been an enjoyable visit. As Wally turned the squad car into his driveway, she glanced at the dashboard clock. It was close to six o'clock, and she had a raging headache brought on by hunger and stress.

Wally opening her car door interrupted her thoughts, and she smiled stiffly at him as he took her hand and helped her out. Once she was standing, he rested his palm on the small of her back and guided her to the house's rear entrance—a small enclosed back porch containing a washer, dryer, and an ironing board.

Straight ahead, a soft glow from the oven beckoned them into the kitchen. Before she even reached the threshold, a heavenly smell of turkey and dinner rolls greeted her.

Wally flicked on the overhead light, and Skye could see that the table was set with a white cloth and bright flower-patterned dishes. She pointed in admiration to the table and the pumpkin pie on the counter. "How did you do all this?"

"When I finished my interviews, I called my housekeeper and explained the situation." He shrugged off his navy nylon jacket embroidered with SCUMBLE RIVER POLICE, and underneath, CHIEF BOYD in gold over the right breast pocket.

"Once she heard our plight, she agreed to bring us the left-overs from her family's dinner."

"You have a housekeeper?" How could Skye not have known that?

"About a year ago I hired Dorothy Snyder to come in and clean a couple of days a week, and do the shopping and laundry and stuff like that."

Dorothy was one of her mother's best friends. Why hadn't May mentioned that Dorothy was working for Wally? "Did Dorothy quit the factory job she took last year?"

"Yes." Wally unbuckled his utility belt and laid it across the back of one of the kitchen chairs. "She said she liked keeping house better than making phone books. She works for a couple of other guys, too."

Did Wally realize that Dorothy was probably reporting their every move to May? Skye opened her mouth, then closed it. It wasn't an issue she was ready to bring up just then. Instead she stepped over to the oven. "Let's see what Dorothy's family had for Thanksgiving."

"Whatever it is, I'm sure it will be good." Wally yawned and rubbed the back of his neck. "She's a great cook."

All of a sudden, Skye noticed how tired Wally looked. "How long have you been on duty?"

"I covered Quirk's midnights. My original plan was to work until eleven, then have Anthony come in for the rest of the day shift and cover afternoons as well."

Skye did the arithmetic in her head. "So you haven't been to bed since Tuesday night?"

"It's not quite that bad. I slept a few hours yesterday before going in to the station last night."

"Still, you must be exhausted."

"I'll be fine." Wally yawned again. "I just need a shower and a cup of coffee."

"Mmmm." Skye could almost taste the caffeine after being deprived for the past twenty-four hours. "Why don't you take your shower and I'll put on a pot of coffee? By the time you're finished, I'll have everything on the table."

"You've got a deal." He kissed her on the cheek and started unbuttoning his shirt as he walked out of the kitchen.

Wally's tiny house, built in the nineteen-thirties, had two bedrooms on one side and the kitchen and living room on the other. She could hear him humming and moving around in one of the bedrooms, then the shower came on.

As she listened to the water, she found coffee in the freezer, and filters in a cupboard. The coffeemaker was a simple model, easy to figure out. As it dripped, Skye examined the fridge. There was a strawberry-pretzel JELL-O salad and a Tupperware bowl full of whipped cream for the pie. She took both out, setting the salad on the table.

Next, she investigated the oven. Wrapped in foil was a quarter of a turkey. A white CorningWare dish held stuffing, and a divided Pyrex bowl had half sweet potato and half green bean casserole. Skye put on oven mitts and started transferring everything to the table.

She could still smell dinner rolls, but couldn't find them. Where were they? The kitchen was bright and clean, with uncrowded countertops, and she finally located the rolls in the toaster oven. She set the temperature control knob on WARM and the timer for five minutes.

Wally appeared just as the bell dinged and she transferred the rolls from oven to table. He had changed into worn jeans that molded the muscles of his legs and cupped the tight curve of his derrière. A loose Hawaiian shirt didn't hide the powerful set of his shoulders or his well-developed chest. He wore flip-flops on his bare feet.

Skye felt faint, and not just from hunger. She licked her lips and his fudge brown eyes followed the movement. He gave her a devilish grin.

Skye was torn between the food and the man. Would he mind if she spread the pumpkin pie all over his torso and licked it off? She gave herself a mental slap and ordered herself to follow her original plan: dinner, then dessert.

It was time to move the relationship to the next level, but not on an empty stomach, and maybe not even tonight. It certainly wasn't the best circumstance for their first time together. They were both exhausted and preoccupied with Esmé's murder.

Suddenly Skye's libido receded and she felt a sense of

sadness. Granted, Skye hadn't found Esmé very likable, but no one had the right to take her life. By murdering her, the killer had taken Esmé's chance to grow, to become a better person. Who knows, maybe if she had gotten pregnant, having a baby would have changed her.

Skye straightened. Well, whoever killed Esmé would be sorry. They had picked the wrong place to commit the crime. Scumble River may seem like a hick town, but it had a terrific police department and a darn good psychological consultant. Between the two of them, they'd bring the murderer to justice.

Skye pushed away the depression that had seized her and asked, "Shall we eat?" She grabbed the coffeepot and gestured toward a cup. "You take it black, don't you?"

"Yes." Wally sank into a chair. "There's that vanilla creamer you like in the fridge, and Sweet'N Low in the sugar dish."

"Great." Skye was touched he remembered exactly how she liked her coffee. "Dorothy did you proud. Don't wait for me. Dig in."

She watched him from the corner of her eye as she poured the creamer and dumped in the two packets of sweetener. He was gorgeous. He literally took her breath away. That he was sweet and funny and a good person helped, too.

They ate in silence for a while, both starving. Finally after the initial edge had been taken from their hunger, Skye commented, "These are beautiful dishes. Royal Winton's Summertime, right?"

"Right." Wally beamed at her and ran a caressing finger along the rim of the saucer. "They were my grandmother's. Darleen hated them, said they were old fashioned, so they've been in storage. I got them out last week."

Darleen was Wally's ex-wife, a topic Skye wasn't ready to talk about, especially since it might lead to Simon, an issue she definitely wanted to avoid. Searching for another subject, she decided this was a good time to find out a little about Wally's parents. "Were the dishes from your mom's mother or your dad's?"

"My maternal grandmother. Dad gave them to me when my mom passed away."

"How long ago was that?" Skye lay her hand briefly over his. "You never talk about your family, which makes me feel like I don't know you very well."

Skye could see the war in Wally's eyes. They went from warm to cold to vulnerable. Finally, he said, "There's not much to say. Mom died the year I graduated from college. My father and I were never close, and with her gone it seemed as if there was nothing for us to say to each other."

"You must keep in touch, though." Skye buttered a piece of roll. "You told me he bought you that wonderful car for your birthday." Last September, on their first date, Skye had been surprised when Wally had picked her up in a brand new Thunderbird convertible.

"I call him once a month and we exchange birthday and Christmas cards." Wally took a gulp of coffee. "When I decided to go to the police academy instead of graduate school, he pretty much lost interest in me."

"But the car?"

"I have no idea why he suddenly decided to buy me a car." Wally looked down at his plate and mumbled, "Hell, I have no idea why I accepted it."

Skye knew she had pushed him as far as she could, probably farther than she should have when both of them were worn out and preoccupied. After a moment she asked, "Ready for some pie?"

Wally looked at her questioningly, then gave her a relieved smile. "I'm stuffed. How about taking our coffee into the living room and letting dinner digest, then we can really enjoy dessert?"

"Sounds good." Skye got to her feet. "Why don't you go ahead while I clean up a little?"

"Dorothy will do that in the morning."

"I know. I'm just going to put away the leftovers and rinse the dishes—these shouldn't go in the dishwasher."

Wally pushed back from the table and got up. "I should do that, not you. It's my house."

"Yep, and next time I'll expect you to." Skye waved him

away. "But just this once we'll pretend it's nineteen-fifty and I'll let you rest."

"Okay." Wally picked up both their coffee cups and headed toward the living room. "But I warn you. I could get used to this."

His goofy grin as he disappeared through the door made up for the dishpan hands Skye had just let herself in for.

Fifteen minutes later the leftovers were wrapped and in the fridge, the dishes washed and draining on the counter, and the tablecloth shaken and replaced. Skye had found a tray in the cupboard and loaded it with a thermal coffee pot, cups, and two slices of pie with whipped cream.

Carrying the tray into the living room, she was stunned at how much better it looked now than it had when she'd seen it before. On her previous visit it'd had a neglected air, but the shag carpeting had been traded for hardwood flooring and the tweed sofa and chair were replaced by cream leather furniture. The walls had been painted a deep taupe, and a mushroom, cream, and rust area rug occupied the center of the room. Arts and Crafts style bookcases and tables took the place of the fake Early American ones that Skye remembered.

"Wow! You've redecorated since the last time I was here." Skye put the tray down on the coffee table. "It looks wonderful."

"Thanks. When Darleen left and took everything, I just bought some second-hand stuff. Then after she tried to get back together, I finally realized it was time to move on, I didn't have to live like a poor college student." Wally patted the sofa cushion next to him. "Have a seat. The couch is really comfortable." Wally clicked the TV off as Skye sat down. He gestured to the set and said, "Nothing on the local news so far, but I'm guessing our luck won't hold for long. Not with our victim being a famous model."

"Mmm. This *is* nice." Skye wiggled into the buttery soft leather. "You're probably right about the media. Even though Esmé's an ex-model, once you're in the limelight, it seems as if you're never a private citizen again—especially if you're either the victim or perpetrator of a juicy crime."

"I hate cases where celebrities are involved. So far we've only dealt with minor ones—local TV stars—but Esmé Gates was on magazine covers around the world."

"Hopefully we can solve the case before the buzzards get a whiff of it." Skye turned sideways on the sofa so she could look at Wally without straining her neck. "Do you want to talk about the interviews, or are you too tired?"

For an instant a wistful expression stole across his face, but then he took a deep breath and said, "I'm fine, and it's probably better if we go over things while they're fresh in both our minds."

"Okay. Let me get my notes."

"I'll grab mine too."

Soon they were both resettled on the couch, one on each end with their backs against the opposite armrests and their legs intertwined. The soft denim of his jeans against her bare skin was curiously sensual.

Skye took a deep breath, ordered herself to focus, then said to him, "You go first. You had the most likely suspects."

Wally raised an eyebrow but flipped open his notepad and said, "I saw Dr. Burnett first. He claimed to be working on his book, *Even You Can Be Beautiful*, and had no alibi. He said he only knew Esmé through Margot. When they were together, they mostly talked about her diet and beauty regime."

"I can believe that. She seemed extremely narcissistic the couple of times I saw her." Skye tapped her fingers on her legal pad. "We should check out Dr. Burnett. There's something about him I don't trust. Maybe he killed Esmé by accident—you know, some youth injection gone wrong—then made it look like she drowned in the mud."

"I agree we should check him out, but would he really make it look like his own spa was at fault?"

"Good point." Skye chewed on the cap of her pen. "Okay, how about Margot? Any alibi or motive for her?"

"No to both. She was alone during the crucial eight thirty to nine thirty time period, but she and Esmé appear to have been good friends for many years and she doesn't gain anything by her death. It's not as if they were both competing for the same modeling jobs anymore."

"How about Kipp Gardner? Why was he even at the mud bath treatment room?"

"He's the hairdresser, right?" Wally flipped through his notes. "He was there to rinse out the deep conditioner Esmé had put on just before taking the bath. And as for an alibi, he was in and out of the hair salon restocking supplies, so it's hard to account for him, but he claims to have never met Esmé before this weekend."

"Mmm." Skye curled a piece of hair around her finger. "We should check into Kipp's background and I'll make an appointment to have my hair done. Maybe I can get him to chat and trip him up somehow." Skye made a note. "Which brings us to Ustelle, who never seems to be around when she's needed."

"What do you mean?"

Skye gave Wally a slightly modified version of her attempt to save Trixie.

"Trixie mentioned that, although," Wally hid his grin, "her account was much more detailed. Something about foil and you looking like a giant hot dog hopping to the rescue."

"Trixie exaggerates. You should know better than to believe everything she says."

"Of course, my little frankfurter. I knew you wouldn't relish the thought of that story getting out. Too many people would roll with it."

Skye threw a pillow at Wally. "That's not funny and I don't want to hear anything more about it." She picked up the plate with the pie on it and held it threateningly. "Understand?" When he nodded, still fighting a smile, she asked, "So, how about Ustelle and her disappearing acts?"

"Since she claims she was on the phone, I've got the dispatcher checking the phone company records. She also says she didn't know Esmé."

"Another background check we should run. I'm not getting another seaweed wrap, but I guess I could get a facial. I'll tell Ustelle that I'm afraid to be alone because of the murder, and ask her to stay with me and get her to chat."

"What if she's the murderer and tries her luck with a second victim?" Wally wrinkled his brow in concern.

"I'll get Trixie or Loretta to watch from the other room or take some other precaution." Skye studied her notes. "How about the stepdaughter?"

"Whitney. Is she some kind of nut job or what?"

"Probably." Skye related her encounter in the solarium with the young woman. "I still have no idea why she ran away. Me in my underwear can't be that scary."

"Maybe we should test that out." Wally gave her a lecherous look. "You could take off all your clothes and I'll see if I'm afraid."

"Right." Skye snickered, then got back to business. "There certainly didn't seem to be any love lost between Whitney and her stepmother."

"True, but if that were a motive for murder, half the blended families would be minus a parent."

"Any alibi?" Skye asked.

"She claims to have been swimming. Said the personal trainer saw her there."

"Frisco said the same thing."

"So they alibi each other." Wally jotted down a note. "Now go over your interviews with me."

Skye complied, finishing with, "Amber doesn't have an alibi, and Frisco did admit to knowing Esmé before this weekend, saying that her new husband is the jealous type."

"Interesting."

"Amber is a school friend of Whitney's and said their moms knew each other. Also she claims Elvis Doozier is stalking her." Skye shook her head. "We should probably talk to him about that."

"Probably." Wally picked up one of Skye's feet, running a fingertip along the smooth peach polish on her toenails. "But unless we find some indication that he was involved with the murder I think we should let sleeping Dooziers lie."

Skye nodded absently, intent on the feeling of his strong hands massaging her foot.

"We have a lot to look into in the morning. It's going to

be a busy day." His voice deepened. "But it's too late to do anything about the murder now."

"Yes, nine o'clock on Thanksgiving night might be a difficult time to reach most people," Skye agreed, then sighed with pleasure as Wally's thumb pressed into the ball of her foot.

"It's a good thing I can think of something to do to keep us from getting bored until then." Wally's talented fingers moved up and started kneading her calf. "If that's okay with you?"

"Ah, yes. That feels wonderful." Skye relaxed into the soft sofa. So far, what Wally was doing felt much better than any treatment she'd had at the spa. His hands were far more talented than those of any professional masseuse.

She sighed with pleasure. She just needed to stop him before they went too far. She wanted their first time to be special, not when they were both tired and with a murder to solve hanging over their heads.

"How does this feel?" Wally's hand had moved up under her skirt and was caressing her inner thigh.

"Mmm." Then again, maybe it was already too late to stop.

CHAPTER 11

Waxing and Waning

Unlike Whitney, Wally certainly didn't seem frightened as he gazed at Skye wearing only lace panties. Unless, of course, the uneven breathing she felt on her cheek as she lay draped across him was caused by fear. However, since he was holding her close and caressing her, she didn't think so.

His shirt and jeans were layered among her skirt, shell, and jacket. Her peach bra looked almost like a bow on top of the stack. A series of slow, shivery kisses had accompanied the removal of each garment, smothering any resistance she attempted to muster. And now Skye could feel her defenses weakening even further as his lips seared a path down her neck to her shoulder.

His palms explored the hollows of her back, and her skin tingled where he touched her. She knew she should prevent him from going any farther. Another of his hungry kisses and she'd forget her resolve to wait for a better time. The heady sensation of his lips pressing kisses down her body set her aflame and when his mouth brushed first one breast, then the other, she suddenly couldn't remember why she had wanted to stop him.

Somehow her peach panties and his white Jockeys were added to the clothing pile and Wally took her hands, encouraging her to explore. Her fingertips skimmed his shoulders, his chest, down his stomach, then even lower. His body was so smooth and hard, so perfect.

Perfect. She froze. Her own body was far from perfect. This was the first time he had seen so much of it without clothing. What must he think?

As if reading her mind, Wally paused to kiss her, whispering his love for each part of her in between each brush of their lips. He continued to kiss her as his hands searched for her pleasure points.

She was hypnotized by his touch and purring her approval of his actions. Why had she ever thought they should wait? This was amazing. Wally was amazing.

When he lowered his body over hers, her senses reeled as if short-circuited, and then they were one.

Skye struggled to recognize the annoying noise intruding on her consciousness. A split second later, she felt Wally jerk awake, and she sighed. Neither one of them could ignore a ringing doorbell.

He growled into her neck, "That was incredible," then gently moved her off his body and onto the sofa cushions. As he zipped up his jeans, he said, "Don't move. I'll be right back."

As soon as he disappeared into the foyer, Skye grabbed her underwear and pulled it on. She yanked her skirt up and popped her shell over her head. She was brushing her hair when he came back a few minutes later.

His tone was accusatory. "You moved."

"Uh. Well. You see . . ." Skye felt her face redden. "It's just that . . ."

"You're still not completely comfortable with me."

"No, it's not you. It's me. I'm not comfortable with being naked."

Wally's expression was thoughtful. "We'll have to work on that."

"I'd like that." Skye looked up at him through her lashes. "That was the most amazing experience I've ever had. I didn't know it could be like that."

"Me, either." He took her in his arms, cuddling her into

his embrace. "I've waited years for you, and it was worth every second."

"Thank you." She kissed the underside of his jaw. "You are the sweetest man ever."

He harrumphed, but held her tighter, smoothing her hair, his breathing coming in a contented cadence.

After a moment, Skye sighed. The mood was broken and she had to ask, "Who was at the door?"

"Jeff. I told him and Anthony not to use the radio—I'm hoping we can avoid tipping off the media for a while longer. He said he tried my cell phone but couldn't get a signal."

"I swear, there are more dead zones in Scumble River than in the cemetery." Skye resisted spending the money on a cell for just that reason. "Why didn't he call your home phone?"

"Said he couldn't remember the number and thought it would be quicker to stop by, but I think someone put him up to coming over here to see what we were up to."

"Gee. I wonder who that could be." Skye ran her fingers over the muscles on his chest, loving the way they felt. "I'm putting my money on May."

He caught her hands in his. "If you want to stay dressed, stop that."

"Sorry." Her cheeks reddened even more. She couldn't seem to keep her hands off him. "Of course, Trixie is also high on the list of nosey people."

"We do seem to attract a lot of interest in this town. At least the Bunco Woman didn't show up with her camera." They both laughed at Wally's reference to their first date, when the mother of one of Skye's former students was taking bets on the progress of their relationship.

Skye had another idea of who might be snooping on them—Veronica Vail—but kept that one to herself. Instead she asked, "So what did Jeff want?"

Wally kissed Skye on the nose and let her go. "They found the protestors staying at the Up A Lazy River Motor Court, and the leader confessed to the murder."

Skye was speechless as Wally headed into his bedroom

and added over his shoulder, "They brought her to the station, so I've got to get over there."

As Wally put on his uniform, Skye found her jacket and shoes and applied a fresh coat of lipstick. By the time he was ready, she was standing by the door with her purse in hand. "I know you usually call in a female correctional officer from the county when you need to interrogate a woman. Do you want me to sit in since we're on the outs with the sheriff's office?"

"Sounds like a plan." Wally locked the door behind them and led Skye to the squad car. As they drove toward the police station, he said, "The more I think about it, the more I like it. It really does fit into the job description we wrote for the position when we hired you as a consultant."

"Right."

"Of course, we'd only use you for serious cases, murder, rape, assault." Wally winked, and added, "We couldn't afford your services for every little traffic violation and misdemeanor."

Skye rolled her eyes. She could make more flipping burgers at McDonald's than what they paid her to consult, but it wouldn't be as much fun.

Wally made a left, and the Scumble River police station came into view. The department was housed in a two-story redbrick structure bisected by a massive double-deep three-door garage. Accessible from two streets, the police department occupied half the main floor, with the jail and the chief's office above. The city hall took up the other side of the building and the town library the second floor of that half. The space was too small for the growing town, but no one wanted to spend the money to expand.

When Skye and Wally arrived, shortly after nine thirty, the city hall/library part of the building was dark. A white Buick Regal, an old Dodge pickup, a blue Chevy Cavalier, and a shiny black Miata were the only vehicles in the parking lot. Skye knew that the dented Cavalier belonged to Thea Jones, the police dispatcher, and she suspected the Regal and the truck belonged to the part-time officers, which left the Miata. She wondered who owned it. Surely, the protestor hadn't been allowed to drive her own car to the station.

Wally and Skye headed directly for the coffee/interrogation area. Anthony and the leader of the Real Women sat at a long rectangular table, staring at each other in silence.

As soon as Wally entered, Anthony jumped to his feet, not quite saluting. "Chief."

Wally tipped his head at the officer, then asked, "Has she been read her rights?"

"Yes, sir."

"Did she sign the acknowledgment form?"

"Yes, sir."

He turned to the woman. "Do you wish to have a lawyer present during questioning?"

"No."

"Okay. I'm Chief Boyd. What's your name, ma'am?"

She flicked a glance at Skye. "What's she doing here?"

Wally introduced Skye and explained her status as consultant, adding, "Ms. Denison will be sitting in on your interview."

"Gee, I hope she doesn't have to miss her manicure because of little old me."

Skye opened her mouth but closed it, realizing there was nothing she could say to convince this woman she wasn't one of them—the Botoxed beauties whom the protester associated with spas.

Wally ignored the woman's dig, and asked again, "What's your name?"

She looked down at the table and mumbled something.

"What?" Wally's voice reflected his growing impatience and when she mumbled again, he snapped, "Anthony, what's her name?"

The young officer snickered, then blushed under Wally's censorious glare. He attempted to answer, but another guffaw escaped his lips. Finally, he reached into the manila packet he'd been holding and took out a black wallet. He flipped it open, withdrew a driver's license, and handed it to Wally, who read it and silently handed it over to Skye.

Skye glanced at the laminated rectangle, then rechecked

what she had read. Yes, the woman's name really was Rose Blossom. Skye bit the inside of her cheek to stop a giggle. She handed the license back to Wally without meeting his eyes.

He cleared his throat, told Anthony he could leave, and pulled out a chair, then said, "Now that we've established your identity, Ms. Blossom, let's hear how you killed Esmé Gates."

"I drowned her in a mud bath."

"How did you manage to get into the spa without being seen?" Wally asked.

There was a slight hesitation, then she answered, "I dressed as a delivery person. No one ever questions you if you're in a UPS uniform."

Wally raised an eyebrow at Skye, who shrugged. It sounded like something that would work. After all, the spa wasn't a prison, and they weren't on lockdown.

"Why did you kill her?"

"She represented the type of woman that is ruining it for the rest of us." Rose's face turned a splotchy red. "Do you have any idea how hard it is to be taken seriously in a board-room if the other women in the company are all tarted up like hookers, wearing miniskirts and stilettos?" Rose's eyes slitted. "Nearly all the work of the women's liberation movement in the seventies has been eroded. The young girls now don't know how it was and don't seem to see that they're destroying what little equality we've accomplished. Last Friday, one of my so-called associates actually obeyed her boss's order to get him coffee."

This time when Wally looked to Skye she nodded. She could understand the rage that an experience like that day after day could produce.

"But Esmé Gates had never done anything to you?" Wally clarified.

"No. I didn't even know her name. I first saw her when she checked in wearing that dead animal on her back and with enough luggage to clothe an entire African village."

Wally made a note, then asked, "You didn't know she was an ex-model?"

"No. But I'm not surprised. She had that useless vacant look."

Wally asked several more questions, but Rose stuck to her story. She had killed Esmé Gates because of what she represented.

Finally, he got up and said to Skye, "Time for a break." He motioned her through the door and called for Anthony to sit with the prisoner.

Silently they climbed the stairs to his office. Only after they were seated with the door closed did Skye ask, "Do you think she really did it?"

"My gut says no, but why would she admit to a murder she didn't commit? Is she protecting someone?"

"I doubt it. My guess is she wants the publicity for her cause, and her one phone call went to the media." Skye paused. "She's just using this opportunity to get air and ink time."

"I can see that. And it would be relatively easy for her to have heard about the mud bath. We haven't released that information, but I'm sure everyone at the spa knows that detail." Wally rubbed the stubble on his jaw. "I stopped all outgoing calls and tried to collect all cell phones, but no doubt several people didn't turn their phones in, and someone told someone else, and somehow the protestor heard that Esmé was drowned in a mud bath."

"You're probably right," Skye agreed. "Not to mention all of the people who were at the spa after the murder—the EMTs, the nonresidential workers, the crime techs." Skye narrowed her eyes. "But I do know a way to test Ms. Rose Blossom, which none of those people would know."

"Ask her to describe the treatment room?"

"That, and tell us what was playing on the CD player."

"Brilliant." Wally had been sitting on the edge of his desk facing Skye, who was sitting in the visitor's chair. Now, he leaned forward and kissed her. "Only you and the murderer know that fact." He got up and started for the door. "What was playing?"

"It was familiar, but I can't think of the title," Skye admitted. "But the CD should still be in the player so we can find out."

"Right, and if Rose doesn't know those details, she's lying about killing Esmé." Wally hesitated, then said, "But if that's the case, we're not telling anyone that Rose is innocent. We'll let everyone think the killer's been caught. That way the spa will go back to normal and we'll have three days to find the real killer before all the guests go home."

CHAPTER 12

Don't Cry Over
a Spilled Milk Bath

There was no one in the lobby when Skye entered the spa. As she passed the reception desk, she noticed that all the lines were lit up and the light on the answering machine was blinking like a string of short-circuited Christmas tree lights. No doubt, all the messages were reporters trying to get the story.

Rose had confirmed Skye's guess that her one call had been to WGN, a Chicago TV station, not to an attorney, but when Wally had asked her to describe the mud bath treatment room and name the song that had been playing she had remained silent.

Both her refusal to describe the murder scene and the fact that she had called a television station rather than a lawyer had convinced Wally and Skye that Rose's confession was a fake.

Wally cautioned Skye not to confide their doubts to anyone, however. Even his own officers might slip and say something to a family member or friend. Scumble River was too small for that kind of information to be kept secret. He had already contacted Special Agent Vail and Margot and told them about the confession, informing Vail she could go home and Margot that the need for twenty-four-hour police presence at the spa no longer existed.

Skye hadn't asked what the spa owner's or the special

agent's responses were, just nodded as Wally mentioned his call. He had continued to explain his plan to Skye as he drove her back to the spa. He would covertly investigate— do background checks, study the autopsy results and the trace evidence gathered—and Skye would try to get the spa staff and guests to talk and keep an eye out for anything unusual.

She had agreed to his plan, except for one part. She had to tell Trixie that Rose wasn't really the killer. After some arguing, Wally had grudgingly agreed Skye could tell Trixie their suspicions, but no one else.

Now, equipped with the police radio and a can of mace Wally had provided, as well as the bag of contraband food Skye had gathered when they made a quick stop at her house, she crept up the main staircase. As she reached the top, a grandfather clock started to sound, making Skye jump. The bongs were still sounding when she reached her room. On the twelfth bong, Skye pulled the key card out of the lock and the tiny light flashed green.

She took one last look down either side of the hallway, afraid the spa's food police would catch her smuggling the forbidden groceries and confiscate her goodies, then slipped inside. She felt like Cinderella, but hoped she hadn't left any clues on the stairs.

From the sound of the soft snores coming from the other bed, Skye figured Trixie was deeply asleep. Not wanting to wake her, Skye eased into the bathroom to change into her pajamas and prepare for bed.

Back in the room, she opened the drawer of the bedside table and took out her fanny pack, which already contained her stun gun. After adding the equipment Wally had given her, she returned the pack and shut the drawer. With a tired sigh, she slid between the sheets.

Just as she snuggled underneath the blanket, there was a knock on the door and a teenage voice said in a stage whisper, "Ms. D. It's Frannie. Are you there?"

Hoping to shush Frannie before she woke Trixie, Skye threw back the covers, and said quietly, "Just a minute." She located her robe and put it on before opening the door. "Is something wrong?"

"Well, I'm starving and Ms. Bunny snores like a semi going uphill, but that's not why I'm here." Frannie had a pencil behind her ear and was clutching a yellow legal pad. "I didn't get a chance to talk to you after you found the body, and I wanted to get your impressions of the murder scene while they're still fresh."

"How about we have breakfast together and talk then." Skye wrapped her arms around herself and shivered. The hallway was cold.

"You've been ignoring me since we got here." Frannie thrust out her bottom lip. "Xenia said you'd be different when you were with adults."

"You know that's not true," Skye denied, alarmed that Frannie was quoting Xenia Craughwell. Xenia had moved to Scumble River last summer, fleeing from the mess she had caused at her previous school. She was a deeply troubled girl, but smart and charismatic, and Skye worried about her influence on Frannie.

"Yes, it is true." A tear clung to Frannie's round cheek. "You and Mrs. Frayne are leaving me out."

"Frannie, you know we wouldn't do that." Skye caved, although she knew she shouldn't. Frannie didn't usually have trust issues. This wasn't like her at all, and Skye was alarmed. Then it dawned on her—low blood sugar could cause acute mood swings, and it had been at least thirty-six hours since the teen had eaten any real food.

The girl's shoulders slumped and she turned to leave, but Skye stopped her with a hand on her arm. "Do you know where the solarium is?" Frannie nodded. "Let me get something from my room, and I'll meet you there in five minutes. Okay?"

Frannie sniffed, and then nodded.

"Why don't you put on some slippers or socks? Your feet must be freezing on these marble floors."

"Thanks, Ms. D." Frannie smiled, wiping away the tears.

Skye eased back into the room, intent on gathering some

food for Frannie. "What in the heck was that all about?" Trixie asked, appearing wide awake.

"Frannie is having an attack of the 'nobody loves me blues,' which I think is being exacerbated by low blood sugar." Since Trixie was up, Skye flipped on a light and started to sort through the food she had brought. "What did you all have for Thanksgiving dinner?"

"It was awful." Trixie stuck her finger down her throat and made a retching sound. "Tofu turkey, black soybean casserole, and a green sugar-free JELL-O salad."

"Ew. No wonder Frannie is in a state." Skye put the food in a tote bag and laid a towel on top to camouflage it. "Did Loretta share her stash with you afterward?"

"No. Your brother showed up and took her for a ride." Trixie got out of bed and put on her robe. "Do you have enough there for me?"

"Yep." Skye nodded. "And I left Wally with a list of provisions to bring tomorrow."

"Then let's go." Trixie had her hand on the knob. "I'm famished."

On their way to the solarium, Skye briefed Trixie on the protestor's false confession, call to the media, and Wally's plan to trap the real killer. Trixie swore on her husband's life not to tell a soul.

Frannie was already curled up on a wicker settee when Skye and Trixie arrived. They each drew up matching chairs, forming a U-shaped arrangement with a low table in the middle. The broken window had been boarded up, which gave the room a more cozy feeling than the marble perfection of the rest of the mansion.

As Skye started pulling out potato chips, dip, cold cuts, cheese, bread, Oreos, and a six-pack of Diet Coke from her insulated tote bag, Frannie's petulant expression brightened, but she asked, "Isn't outside food against the rules, Ms. D?"

Skye bit her lip and looked to Trixie for help. She hadn't thought of how Frannie would react to seeing the adults go against spa policy. Trixie was too busy filling her mouth with potato chips to respond.

"Of course breaking real rules is bad," Skye said after a

moment, "but there are a lot of people in the world who think they can make rules for others to live by, when they have no authority to do so. We came to the spa to have fun and relax. Did either of you tell anyone you were here to lose weight?" Both Trixie and Frannie shook their heads. "There was nothing in their literature that mentioned a *mandatory* diet, and no reason to enforce a diet unless the client has signed up to lose weight. Thus, I don't feel the need to follow the no-outside-food rule."

"Besides, rules are for fools." Bunny minced through the door trailing orange marabou feathers from her high heeled slippers, and flung herself next to Frannie on the settee. She peered at the food and beverage selection, and asked, "Where's the booze?"

"Sorry." Skye ignored Bunny's comment about rules, hoping Frannie would, too. She already feared she was setting a bad example for the teen. "Frannie said you were asleep."

"I was, but my stomach growled so loud it woke me up." Without asking, Bunny snagged a slice of bread and started making a sandwich.

"You better dig in, Frannie, before it's all gone." Skye gestured to the two women stuffing their faces as fast as they could.

The girl grinned at Skye, and followed her suggestion. "Thanks, Ms. D."

Skye was still full from her dinner with Wally, but she was thirsty. She grabbed a can of Diet Coke, popped the top, and took a long drink before saying, "So, what happened around here while I was gone?"

"Not much." Trixie twisted an Oreo apart. "They finally fed us their version of dinner, but Margot, Dr. Burnett, and Whitney never showed."

Bunny swallowed and added, "Someone said they were too distraught by Esmé's death and were eating in their rooms, but I bet they secretly ordered a pizza."

"Yeah." Trixie licked the cream center from her Oreo. "I've been noticing that the staff seems awfully perky to be existing on a thousand-calorie diet. I'll bet they're getting real food somewhere."

Bunny and Frannie nodded in agreement.

"What did you all do after dinner?" Skye asked.

"We all sat around the parlor with that woman officer since everyone was too afraid to go off alone." Trixie popped the chocolate cookie into her mouth and spoke around it. "Then when we got the word that the killer had confessed, we all went to bed."

"You know"—Frannie, who had seemed lost in her own thoughts, spoke almost to herself—"Whitney is pretty smart."

"Really?" She hadn't struck Skye as any rival to Albert Einstein.

"Well, not book smart." Frannie popped a chip in her mouth and chewed reflectively. "Maybe not magazine smart either." She furrowed her brow, then took a sip of soda. "Okay, probably not even back-of-the-cereal-box smart. But she really knows how to take care of herself."

"Do you mean street smart?" Trixie asked.

"Only if the street is Michigan Avenue." Frannie paused. "No, I mean she's good at finding out things and using them to her advantage. What's the word for that?"

"Blackmail?" Trixie suggested.

"Noooo." Frannie drew out the single syllable, indicating her annoyance.

"Shrewd?" Skye offered.

"Yes." Frannie nodded, satisfied. "Whitney is shrewd, and she's got her father wrapped around her little finger."

"How do you know that?" Trixie asked.

"'Cause I overheard her on the phone. Whitney was giving her dad a list of stuff to buy for her—expensive things."

"So, she said," Skye questioned, "'Hi Dad, Esmé's dead. Oh, by the way, could you pick me up a bottle of perfume, a pair of shoes, and a scarf?'"

When Frannie nodded, Skye asked, "Did he agree?"

"Yes. The phone Whitney was using was weird. I could hear both sides of the conversation. And Whitney's dad was like, 'Sure, baby. Anything you want. Let me write this down.'"

Bunny had been silent while Frannie talked, but suddenly she said, "Speaking of wrapped around someone's finger, don't you all find it odd that Margot seems to wear the pants in the family?"

"I think that's because she's used to being in the limelight," Skye offered.

"Maybe so, but most doctors I've known have egos bigger than their Cadillacs, and are used to running the show," Bunny argued.

"Bunny's right," Trixie added. "It does seem odd the way he allows her to order him around. He sure doesn't act that way with the staff. I saw him yelling at one of the housekeepers, about a missing cuff link or something, and he didn't stop even after she was in tears."

"Speaking of something missing, I can't find my new watch," Bunny added. "And one of the other guests mentioned missing earrings."

Skye frowned. Was there a thief as well as a murderer on the loose, or were they one and the same?

"That reminds me." Frannie consulted her notes. "When I overheard Whitney on the phone with her dad, she was complaining that she had to borrow Margot's cell because hers was missing."

"Could you tell where Whitney's dad was calling from?"

"Paris, and since this is the busiest travel weekend of the year, he doesn't know how long it will take to get home. He told her he had spoken to Margot, and she was willing to have Whitney stay here until he arrives."

Skye took another sip of soda. "Well, if he's in Europe, he has a pretty good alibi. I wonder if Agent Vail ever got ahold of him, or if he was letting all his calls go into voice mail so he could screen them. But why would he want to avoid talking to the police?"

"Because he doesn't have a good alibi. Not really," a voice from the door interjected. "If she reached him on his own cell phone, he could be sitting in his car in the driveway for all we know."

Skye put her hand over her heart. "Nancy, you scared the bejeezus out of me." The magazine writer stood just over the threshold. "Would you like to join us? You're welcome as long as you promise not to tell anyone about our contraband food."

"Thanks. I'd love to." She pulled a chair over to their group and after everyone was introduced said, "Don't worry, I'll never tell. As you know, I have my own illicit supply."

"What are you doing wandering around?" Skye remembered that Nancy hadn't had an alibi for the time of Esmé's death.

She hesitated, then shrugged. "Now it's you-all's turn not to tell, but one of my ways of writing about a place is to poke around when everyone's asleep and can't cover up any problems."

"Aren't you afraid to roam alone with a killer on the loose?" Skye blurted out.

"I would be if the murderer hadn't confessed." She drew her bare legs up under her nightshirt and wrapped her arms around her knees.

"Oh." All eyes turned to Skye, and she finally said, "Right. I guess I forgot." It was a lame answer, but all she could think of. Trying to change the subject, she asked, "Has anyone heard if the spa will go on with its regularly scheduled activities?"

Nancy nodded. "Margot assured me it would, and begged me to stay."

"Don't you all find it depressing that Esmé's death is being treated almost as an afterthought?" May asked as she entered the solarium and pulled up a chair next to Skye.

Loretta trailed the older woman. She was the only one still dressed in street clothes. She closed the circle by adding a chair to the open end.

"What do you mean, Mom?" Skye asked.

"Well." May's face was sober. "A woman died here less than sixteen hours ago, and no one seems to care."

"I doubt that's true, May." Loretta eyed the group thoughtfully. "It's just that none of us knew Esmé. I'm sure Whitney and Margot are upset."

"That's right." Frannie nodded. "Remember, they stayed away from dinner."

"Considering the food, that's not really a sacrifice." Bunny playfully whacked Frannie's upper arm with the back of her hand.

"See." May scowled at the redhead. "*That's* what I mean. People are joking and complaining as if nothing happened. Heck, you're all having a party."

May's shoulders sagged and Skye put her arm around them. "This isn't like you, Mom."

"I know." The lines in May's face were deeper than they had been that morning and she appeared smaller. "But it suddenly struck me that this woman was famous. Millions worshipped her, yet not one person seems to be grieving. Her stepdaughter resented her, and her so-called friend Margot wants the spa to stay open as if nothing has happened."

"You can't blame people for how they feel, Mom, and you can't make them feel the way you think they should." Skye looked at her mother, then at the others. Everyone's expression was somber and Frannie and Trixie seemed ready to cry. Dredging up a lecture she had heard in graduate school, Skye said, "Murder is the ultimate breach of social contract, the very worst crime we can imagine. We feel vulnerable when it touches us, even indirectly. But people who don't know the victim sometimes feel excitement or curiosity. It doesn't make them bad people."

May shrugged, clearly not convinced. There was a moment of silence, then she said, "I suppose you're right, but . . ."

"But what, Mom?" Skye could scarcely wait to hear her mother's description of how things should be.

"But I sure wish we could go back to the time when water balloons were the ultimate weapons."

Another silence, then Trixie snickered, and Frannie giggled. Finally even May was smiling again as she stuffed an Oreo into her mouth.

Nancy had been quiet during May's diatribe, but as the conversation relaxed, she joined in. She fit in well, as she was quick with a quip and able to laugh at herself.

After a while, Skye asked her, "Where are you from, Nancy?"

"California. How about all of you?"

"All of us, except for Bunny and Loretta, are from Scumble River," Skye said.

"I grew up in a small town near here," Bunny explained, "but I lived in Las Vegas for most of my adult life. I've only been back for a year. Are you a California native or were you born somewhere else?"

"Actually, I was born in Chicago. I didn't move out west until after college."

"Will you be able to visit your family while you're here?" Trixie asked.

"Maybe some of my more distant relatives." Nancy's expression was odd. "I was an only child and my parents were killed in a car crash when I was sixteen. My grandfather and a few cousins live in Sacramento. Grandfather took care of me after my parents died, and moved with me when I got my first job out there. I wanted to work in California to be near my cousins." After everyone expressed their sympathy, she continued, looking straight at Skye, "Since I have so little family, the relatives I do have mean a lot to me."

Skye nodded, wondering why Nancy was making such a point of what she was saying about family. Before Skye could figure it out, she yawned, Trixie and Frannie quickly followed suit, and Skye said, "Looks like it's time for bed." She leaned forward and gathered the leftovers into her tote bag, consolidating the debris. She stood and dumped the garbage into the trash. "Anyone else coming?"

The others all got up, said good night, and moved as a group toward the door.

Nancy, last, put a hand on Skye's arm, drawing her back a little from the others, and whispered, "I need to talk to you alone. Can we have breakfast in my room tomorrow at eight?"

Skye nodded, wondering what in the heck Nancy wanted to talk about.

CHAPTER 13

Cast the First
Stone Massage

"Oh, my gosh! No!" Trixie's shout penetrated the water pounding past Skye's ears and sent adrenaline through her veins. Was the murderer about to kill Trixie?

Skye wrestled with the shower curtain, finally peeling it off her body and flinging it aside. As she leapt out of the tub, she slipped on the tile floor, and skidded into the vanity. A jolt of pain shot through her hip, but she barely noticed it as her mind raced. Maybe she and Wally were wrong. Maybe it was a random killer, and Esmé was only the first victim.

Wrapping a towel around herself as she ran, Skye burst into the room prepared to fight off Trixie's attacker with her bare hands. Heart pounding, Skye's gaze searched the area, only to see Trixie safe and sound, chatting on the telephone.

Dang! She had to stop rushing to the rescue when no one needed her help.

"Yes. Keep them in the lobby." Trixie saw Skye and held up one finger. "No. Do not give out room numbers unless the women say it's okay. We'll be right down." She threw the receiver onto its cradle and demanded, "Why aren't you dressed?"

"What's going on?" Skye stood dripping in the middle of the room, trying to figure out who was in the lobby and why it was her problem.

"We're being invaded."

"By the media?"

"By the men."

"What?" Skye wrenched open a drawer and snatched up a pair of panties and a bra. "Why?" After donning the underwear, she jerked on a red T-shirt and black sweatpants and jacket.

"It seems they heard about the murder, and have come to rescue their womenfolk."

"You're kidding." Skye ran back into the bathroom and grabbed her comb.

"No. None of us could call our husbands, boyfriends, et cetera, last night to explain what was happening, but fifteen minutes ago WGN News broke the story, so the rest of the media won't be far behind."

"Shit!" Skye pulled her hair back into a ponytail and slipped on a pair of flip-flops.

"So now the lobby is full of men demanding to see their women." Trixie shook her head. "Margot wants us to do something."

"When did we become her personal protection team?"

"We didn't. She's closed the gates and hired a security firm. They're arriving via helicopter from Chicago so they should be here pretty soon."

"Oh. That's a good idea."

"But the men are already here and she's afraid all the women will leave." Trixie finished tying her sneakers. "And she's convinced if everyone stays and things go smoothly from now on, she can still get a good review from *Spa* magazine."

"Damn. If the men make their women go home, it would ruin Wally's plan. We have to stop them."

"How?" Trixie stood with her hand on the knob.

"I have no idea."

As they descended the main staircase, they saw Rudy, the groundskeeper, Bryan, the bellboy, and Frisco standing shoulder-to-shoulder across the bottom step. Skye and Trixie eased around them and faced the dozen or so men who had gathered in the lobby.

Skye gave a small sigh of semi-relief when she saw that

at least half of the throng were guys connected to her own group. Her father Jed and godfather "Uncle" Charlie Patukas were there to protect her and her mother—both would be relatively easy to persuade to go home. Owen, Trixie's husband, would be no problem for Trixie. Xavier, Frannie's father, and Justin, her boyfriend, were probably there for different reasons—Xavier to take the girl home, Justin to help her investigate the story, since he was the coeditor of the school newspaper.

And then there was Simon. In view of the fact that he was the coroner and had been in charge of removing the body, he knew about the murder yesterday, and Wally had, no doubt, informed him of the confession. So why was he here? To make sure his mother, Bunny, didn't get into trouble—a talent she had demonstrated often in the past?

Still, Skye wished he'd go away. She hadn't seen him since their fight in the bowling alley basement, hadn't even acknowledged an "I'm sorry" gift he'd sent, and she certainly didn't want to talk to him the day after she and Wally had made love for the first time.

Trixie interrupted Skye's rumination by murmuring, "I'll go talk to Owen."

Skye nodded, refocused her thoughts to the problem at hand, and joined her father, the most sensible man in the room, and her Uncle Charlie, the most influential. "Dad, Uncle Charlie, what brings you to Scumble River Spa? I can recommend almost any of the treatments, except for the mud bath."

Jed gave a slight shake of his head, indicating he did not think this was an appropriate time for Skye's sense of humor, but before he could speak, Charlie boomed, "We're here to take you and May home. This was a stupid idea to begin with. Why in blue heaven would you stay here after a murder was committed? Sometimes I wonder about you two."

Charlie was a big man, six feet and over three hundred pounds. He owned the Up A Lazy River Motor Court, and sat on nearly every important town committee. He was in his late seventies and although never married, had a reputation as quite a ladies' man.

Skye glanced at the men standing around; they had all moved closer, figuratively and literally behind Charlie. Whatever Charlie decided, the rest of the men would go along with.

She raised her voice, speaking as much to the crowd as to her godfather. "Yes, there was a murder, but the killer confessed and is in custody. The victim wasn't from here. She had nothing to do with Scumble River. Neither did the murderer. Just two outsiders bringing their problems to our small town." Skye laid it on as thick as she dared, knowing that most Scumble Riverites had an "us versus them" mentality.

"But those protestors"—Charlie gestured with the unlit cigar he held between sausagelike fingers—"those Real Women. They want to run this place out of business. Who's to say they won't keep killing people until the spa closes?"

"Margot has increased security. No one will be able to get past the lobby without showing a key card." Skye made eye contact with several of the men. "The security firm will be here any minute."

"That doesn't answer my question." Charlie stuck the cigar in his mouth and talked around it. "Suppose those Real Women get past the guards?"

"The protestors are only interested in models and such. They want the publicity. Killing one of us won't get them that." Skye crossed her arms. "And by the way, Uncle Charlie, didn't I hear they were staying at your motor court? Why don't you kick them out? Maybe they'd go away if they didn't have a place to stay."

Charlie ran his fingers through his thick white hair, and his face turned red. Finally he said, "It's easier to keep track of them if they're at the motor court."

"Fine. You keep track of them, and then we'll all be safe here, right?"

Several women who had gathered applauded Skye's speech.

Charlie nodded reluctantly. "Right."

Trixie, May, and Frannie had joined Skye and now linked arms.

May said, "We're staying. We'll be fine." She looked at the other Scumble River women. "Are you going to let a bunch of kooks ruin your weekend?"

"No!" they all shouted.

"Are you going to let your husbands and boyfriends tell you what to do?"

"No!"

"Do you want to stay and get all the massages and manicures and such, or go home and cook and clean?"

"Stay here!"

Most of the men retreated like snakes slithering back into their holes, but Xavier, Justin, and Simon stood their ground.

Xavier and Justin flanked Frannie, Xavier trying to persuade the girl to leave, and Justin shooting questions at her about the murder. Skye's first instinct was to go to Frannie's aid, but the memory of her recent superfluous attempts to rescue Trixie kept her rooted to the spot.

After a heated exchange, Xavier threw up his arms and stomped out. It was interesting seeing a teenage girl get the better of a Vietnam veteran, but Frannie had grown up without a mother, and she was her father's daughter through and through—independent and strong willed.

Justin didn't give up; instead he loped over to Skye and begged, "Ms. D., you gotta make them let me stay. It's no fair that Frannie will get the story without me, just because she's a girl."

Frannie glared at her boyfriend. "And how many stories have you gotten just because you're a guy?"

Justin had recently had a growth spurt and now topped six feet, but his weight had not caught up. His hair was military short and he hid his long-lashed brown eyes behind thick glasses.

Still, there was something about him that appealed to a certain type of teenage girl, and he now attempted to use that charm on Frannie. Justin took her hand and drew her a bit away from the others. A moment later Skye heard giggles and whispers.

Turning to leave, Skye spotted Simon having an intense discussion with his mother across the room. Skye edged closer. Even though she didn't want to interact with Simon directly, she did want to hear what they were saying. Where Bunny was concerned, it was a good idea to be prepared.

The wooden staircase banister sat atop a solid marble panel, sweeping dramatically out into the lobby after the steps ended, and Skye concealed herself within that curve. Leaning against the cool stone, she thought of her ex. Simon was tall and lean, with auburn hair and golden hazel eyes. He wore expensive suits as if they were comfortable old blue jeans, and enjoyed the finer things in life. He and his mother had only recently begun to re-form a relationship that had been interrupted twenty years ago.

Although she couldn't see the pair, Skye heard Simon say to Bunny, "If you leave, then Frannie has to go too, and surely you agree that she'd be better off at home than running wild around here."

Skye edged closer and peeked around the banister, barely fitting between the staircase and a large round cherry pedestal table. Simon and Bunny were standing at the foot of the stairs. He was bending forward, trying to get his mother to see his logic. The contrast between his elegance and Bunny's flamboyance was striking.

Bunny answered in her high-pitched voice, "She is not running wild. I'm keeping a close eye on her. She's researching a story." Bunny retied the lime and orange chiffon scarf holding her long red curls back from her face. "She's perfectly safe here."

"How can you say that?" Simon's tone was low and persuasive. "A murder has been committed. Even if the chief thinks he's found the culprit, he could be wrong."

"Oh, poo." Bunny ran a long red nail down the lapel of Simon's taupe suit jacket. "You just want him to be wrong because Skye is dating him now."

Simon's normally pale gold complexion turned burnt orange, and his voice became clipped. "One has nothing to do with the other." His tone forbade any questions or comments. "Skye and I have come to an impasse. I'm not explaining myself to someone who doesn't trust me. What she does now is her own business."

Skye frowned. Clearly Simon's stand hadn't moved an inch since she'd last talked to him.

Simon turned as if to leave, but paused and spoke to someone descending the stairs. "Spike, what in the world are you doing here?"

Spike? Spike Yamaguchi? Simon's college friend from California? The woman he'd had an affair with! From her hidden position, Skye couldn't see whom Simon was addressing, but how many Spikes could Simon know? What in the world was she doing at the Scumble River Spa? Skye crept forward, determined to get a glimpse without revealing her presence; but it was no good. Worse yet, Simon and Spike moved away from the staircase, and now Skye couldn't even hear them.

Sure that she was about to reveal herself, she poked her head around the banister and assessed the situation. Simon had seated himself on one of the sofas in the lobby, and although she couldn't see Spike, Skye could hear the murmurings of a female voice from the cushion next to him.

Bunny bounced over to join Simon and Spike, and Skye strained to hear what was being said. She chewed her lip. How to get over there without being seen? She spotted a housekeeping cart piled with fresh towels in the corner of the room and darted over to it. Using the cart as a shield, she inched it forward until she was behind the couch Simon and Spike were occupying.

Bunny had taken a chair at a right angle to the sofa and Skye heard her say, "I still don't understand. How can you be both Spike Yamaguchi and Nancy Kimbrough? I thought Spike was a college friend of Simon's. You look way too young to have been in college the same time he was."

Nancy was Spike? But Skye liked Nancy. She frowned. The pseudo-reviewer's friendliness must have been an act. Skye moved the cart a little closer, not wanting to miss a word.

Simon's voice became edged with impatience. "Bunny,

I'll explain it all later, once I understand it. How about you give us a little privacy now?"

Nancy's pleasant contralto interjected, "Let her stay, Simon. And Skye might as well join us, too. It can't be comfortable crouched behind the sofa. Besides, she's the reason I'm here."

Simon leapt to his feet and twisted around. "Skye's here, now?"

Skye rose grudgingly to her feet and gave a little wave, feeling stupid, exposed, and curious all at once. She took the chair opposite Bunny, leaving Simon and Spike—AKA Nancy—on the couch between them.

Simon asked Skye, "How long were you there?"

"Since you started talking to Bunny, before Nan . . . er . . . Spike appeared," Skye reluctantly admitted.

"How much did you hear?"

"Nothing since you started talking to Nancy or Spike or whoever she is."

"Call me Spike." Spike ignored Skye's churlishness. "Nancy is the writer who never showed up." Spike turned toward Simon and said, "Let's start over and clear everything up, once and for all."

"If that's what you want, but don't do it for my sake."

"That's what I want."

"Okay." Simon nodded. "Let's start with what you're doing here."

"I came to straighten things out." She shook her head at Simon. "When you told me what had happened between you and Skye after I answered the phone, when you were staying with me in California, I felt like your splitting up was somehow my fault. And I knew you'd never break your promise to me, even if I gave you permission to."

"You don't have to do this," Simon said. "You have a right to your privacy. Besides, I don't think telling everything at this point will fix things."

"Maybe, maybe not, but it's time for everything to come out into the open." Spike's expression was resolute.

"So, you came to Illinois to find Skye and explain?" Simon asked.

"I needed to interview some people in Chicago the first part of this week," Spike clarified, then as an aside said to the two women, "I'm an investigative reporter."

"But how did you get here, at the spa?" Bunny asked.

"When I arrived in Scumble River, everyone told me Skye would be at the spa for the weekend. So, I decided to come here and see if they had any rooms available. When I arrived, Margot mistook me for this magazine lady who was a no-show. I realized right away it was the perfect setup. I could get to know Skye without her prejudging me. And it worked. We were on our way to becoming friends. At which point I would have explained the mix-up concerning Simon and me."

"Mix-up?" Skye yelped. "You call sleeping with my boyfriend a mix-up?"

"No." A tiny smile was trying to break out on Spike's face. "The mix-up was you thinking I was a guy, then when I turned out to be a girl, you thinking Simon and I had a sexual relationship. We don't and never would."

"Why should I believe you?"

"Because I'm his half sister." Spike gazed meaningfully at Bunny as she spoke.

The redhead's face registered total shock; then she lost consciousness, pitched forward, and hit the ground without a sound.

CHAPTER 14

Keep Your Powder Dry

"You know, for a second before she said she was Simon's half sister, I thought she was going to say she was gay." Skye sat with her back to the headboard of her bed, telling Trixie about Spike's bolt from the blue. "Then when Bunny fainted, I thought we had another death on our hands."

"I'm still having trouble putting it all together." Trixie lay on her side across the bottom of the mattress, her head supported on her hand. "How can Spike be Simon's half sister and Bunny not know her?"

"I stayed for the short explanation, but I couldn't really ask questions. I felt like I had to leave the three of them alone to hash things out. After all, I'm not family."

"Which brings up another matter. Now that you know Simon didn't cheat, where does that leave you two, not to mention you and Wally?"

"I'm not going to think about that right now." Skye clutched her head. "First I need to get the whole Spike-as-Simon's-half-sister clear in my mind."

"Okay, tell me what you know."

"Until this morning, I knew Bunny had left Simon's father when Simon was three, then only saw him intermittently until he was fourteen, at which point she disappeared for good."

"That leaves twenty to thirty-one years of her life unaccounted for, depending on how you count."

"Right. Simon never seemed willing to discuss Bunny's past, with her or with me." Skye pursed her lips. "At the time, I thought he didn't want to know what his mother had been up to, but now I'm confused. It's as if I never knew him at all."

"Simon has always been hard to read," Trixie agreed, then asked, "So, what did you find out today?"

"To start at the beginning, when Bunny left Simon's father, she was already sleeping with the owner of the club she was working at."

"And this guy was Asian-American?"

"Right." Skye adjusted the pillow behind her back. "A month or maybe even less later, Bunny discovered she was pregnant."

"Oh, my. Was abortion legal back then?"

"I'm not sure, but that doesn't matter. Despite all of Bunny's faults, she's a practicing Catholic. No divorce. No abortion. She was going to have the baby."

"Did she know who the father was?" Trixie sat up and hugged her knees.

"She told the club owner it was him, but since she wasn't divorced, and I suspect the guy wasn't really sure it was his kid, he arranged for a black-market adoption."

Trixie asked, "How did that turn out?"

"Surprisingly well. He must have been a smart man. He had two couples lined up, one Asian-American, one Irish-American. If the baby looked more like him when it was born, it would go to the Asian-American couple. If it looked like Bunny, it would go to the other couple."

"Did Mr. Reid know she was having a baby?"

"No." Skye shook her head. "Once she started to show, she stopped visiting Simon and didn't go back until she had regained her shape."

"So, Spike was born, had Asian features, and was adopted by the Asian-American couple. Did she know she was adopted?"

"No, she didn't find out until their deaths, when she was sixteen."

"How awful for her." Trixie winced. "In a way, it must have been like losing her parents twice."

"No doubt. It's always a mistake not to tell children they're adopted."

"Yeah, but sometimes it's not the kids the parents are keeping the adoption secret from," Trixie pointed out. "So, let me guess. As soon as Spike found out she was adopted, she tried to track down her birth parents?"

"Right you are. Her birth father was dead—he was quite a bit older than Bunny—and Bunny was somewhere in Las Vegas, moving from apartment to friend's house to motel, depending on her finances, which made her impossible to find."

"On the other hand, Spike's half brother Simon was right here in Illinois," Trixie finished Skye's thought.

"A senior at Northwestern University at the time."

"So Spike tracked him down and told him he had a little sister?"

"Yep. That's why he claimed she was his college friend," Skye explained.

"But why the big secret?" Trixie leaned forward. "Why not tell you he had a half sister and was visiting her? Especially once you heard her voice and accused him of cheating?"

"After Simon told Spike about Bunny, and what she was like, Spike decided she didn't want to know her mother after all. Spike made Simon swear that he would never tell anyone about their relationship, especially Bunny."

"I'm surprised she took Simon's word for it." Trixie made a scornful noise. "What if he had been lying?"

"Look at it this way, she was only sixteen." Skye's face furrowed. "No doubt, part of her was afraid to meet her biological mother, a woman who had already rejected her once. She probably grabbed at what Simon offered her."

"I sure wouldn't have believed a half brother I had never met before. I would have wanted to see for myself."

"It's hard to say what we would or wouldn't have done at sixteen."

Trixie didn't look convinced, but she let go of the subject and asked, "Is Spike staying at the spa or what?"

"She'll explain everything to Margot, and ask if she can stay as a paying guest. Now she wants a chance to get to know Bunny," Skye explained. "And I can't see Margot turning her down, especially since she *is* a part of the media, and while she might not write a review, she could write a favorable feature story about the spa."

Skye and Trixie were silent before Trixie said, "Which brings us back to my original question—does this change things between you and Simon?"

"We're getting together to talk after dinner tonight, but I think this info came a little too late for us."

"As in one day too late?"

"I don't know what you mean." Skye was not ready to reveal her and Wally's lovemaking to anyone yet, not even her best friend.

"Let's just say you were glowing last night, and I don't think it was because of the Oreos."

"It must have been the new face cream I tried." Skye refused to meet her friend's stare.

"Sure." Trixie rolled her eyes. "I believe that almost as much as I believe Michael Jackson never had plastic surgery." They were both quiet again until Trixie said, "Gee, for someone as calm and composed as Simon, he sure has a lot of drama in his past. I wonder how many more siblings he has floating around out there?"

The invasion of the men and Spike's revelation had eaten up most of Friday morning. Skye hadn't been able to talk to any of the people she and Wally had targeted for her to question. Now, she had only the afternoon, all day Saturday, and Sunday morning left to quiz the staff. She had decided the best way to have a casual conversation would be to sign up for a treatment with each of them, so she studied the list of options.

Kipp, Amber, Frisco, and Ustelle were easy, as they were involved in several activities a day, but Margot led only the "Dress for Sexcess" seminar and Dr. Burnett saw only guests for medical procedures such as Botox and collagen injections.

Skye was willing to learn how to dress for "sexcess," but she drew the line at invasive medical procedures. She would need to figure out a different way to grill the good doctor—although maybe she could just let him talk about the treatments.

Glancing at the bedside clock, Skye saw that it was nearly twelve fifty. Margot's class started at two, thus taking the decision of whom to talk to first out of Skye's hands. She picked up the phone and signed up for the seminar, then realized that lunch, what there was of it, ended at one.

She grabbed her fanny pack and a book, dashed out the door, and sprinted down the stairs. She was hoping the dining room would be empty and she could chat with the second waitress, the one she hadn't yet interviewed.

A couple of Scumble River women were just finishing up their meals when Skye entered. They waved, and Skye waved back, but held up her paperback as a silent explanation of why she didn't join them, and then took a seat at a table across the room.

When the waitress appeared, Skye covertly glanced at the girl's name tag. She had recognized her previously as a former student of Scumble River High School, but hadn't been able to place her.

Now that she could identify her, Skye said, "Hi, Farrah. Do you remember me?"

"Like, sort of." The girl wrinkled her brow. "You're, like, Mrs. Frayne's friend? She was, like, my cheerleading sponsor in high school."

"Right. I'm Ms. Denison. You graduated, what, a year and a half ago? What have you been up to since then?"

"I, like, went to JJC, but it was boring." Farrah swished her blond ponytail. "Then I worked as a receptionist for old Doc Zello, but he was, like, obsessed with me being on time, *every single* day. So, when my mother saw the ad for this place, she made me apply?"

Skye put on her counseling face and murmured the occasional, "Mmm," as Farrah continued. JJC—Joliet Junior College—was one of the best community colleges around, but clearly it hadn't been able to break the teen from using "like" every other word or making statements sound as if they were questions. Maybe that had been the boring part. Finally, Skye asked, "How's this job?"

"Like, so far it's okay? Ms. Margot's been talking to me about learning to do manicures and stuff, but my dad wants me to quit because of the murder and all."

"Did you know the police have a confession?"

"Duh. Like, otherwise I wouldn't be here right now." Farrah glanced pointedly at the wall clock. "So, what would you like to eat?"

"Sorry, I didn't realize it was so late. I hate to keep you. What's the easiest thing on the menu?"

"One chopped salad coming up." Farrah wrote it down. "Would you like something to drink?"

"Water will be fine." If she couldn't have Diet Coke, she'd stick to H_2O.

When Farrah returned with lunch, Skye asked, "Can you sit down a minute and keep me company?"

Skye noticed an odd expression in the girl's eyes, but Farrah said, "Okay, but I can't for long."

"Sure." Skye forked some salad into her mouth, chewed, and swallowed. "So, you and the cook were together when the murder took place?"

"Yes. She's teaching me to knit when we have free time, but we need to keep an eye out for Ms. Margot. She doesn't like us to sit around, even when we haven't got anything else to do."

"Did you know Esmé at all?"

"No. She thought she was too good to talk to the help." Farrah absentmindedly started to pile the items from the table onto her tray.

"Are the other guests like that?"

"Not this weekend, since most of you are from town."

Skye nodded, noting the young woman had stopped using the word "like" when she was answering questions. "Have you heard anyone say anything negative about Esmé, either before or after the murder?"

"No." Farrah stood, cleared the rest of the table, and said

as she left, "Now if it had been Ms. Margot, there'd be plenty of suspects. She sure has rubbed a lot of people wrong."

After Farrah left, Skye sat for a moment pondering what the girl had said. Margot's name kept coming up, and Margot and Esmé did look an awful lot alike, especially from the back. Had the killer murdered the wrong woman?

Margot's seminar was held in one of two meeting rooms that had been carved out of the former ballroom. This one could hold up to fifty and the other two hundred, but today there were only seven women present. Two of the attendees surprised Skye—Bunny and Whitney. Skye would have thought family issues would have kept both from attending. On the other hand, perhaps Whitney needed a diversion, and maybe Bunny and Spike needed some time apart to regroup.

Tiny gilt chairs and petite tea tables were set in rows. Bunny sat in the first row, and gestured for Skye to join her. Skye nodded, then excused herself to the already seated women until she reached the front. She gingerly eased into the delicate chair next to Bunny. It was a tight fit, and she was afraid that one false move and the chair would shatter into toothpicks. On the table lay a small notepad and miniature gold pen.

Bunny greeted Skye, but before she could say anything more, Margot came out on a small stage next to a large white screen. The spa owner wore an animal-print skirt with gold sequined trim and a tight white tank top with a sequined sunburst across the chest. Skye frowned. Hadn't she seen Esmé wearing that same outfit at breakfast yesterday? Either Margot had bought the same clothes as her friend, or she was already raiding the dead woman's closet.

Margot waited a few minutes for everyone to get settled, then began, "Good afternoon, ladies. First, I'd like to thank you all for staying. Esmé's death is a tragedy and we are all saddened by the loss, but the police have already apprehended the killer."

She paused for a breath, and Skye scanned the faces in

the room. Most had the solemn look people don when hearing bad news that really doesn't involve them, but Whitney's expression was hard to read. Although Skye would have bet money that Whitney and Esmé didn't have a loving relationship, maybe Whitney didn't like to see her stepmother's death dismissed in a couple of sentences, and then business as usual.

Margot continued, "Just to make you all feel even safer, I've hired a security firm from Chicago to make sure only those authorized will get past the lobby. There's also a man at the gate keeping the media out."

Skye glanced around, wondering why Margot was repeating what everyone already knew—after all, it had been announced that morning to the men. Maybe the spa owner didn't realize just how fast news traveled. Finally, after a minute of silence to remember Esmé, Margot started the class.

Her first question was, "Who here thinks what I'm wearing is sexy?"

Bunny and a couple of the other Scumble River women raised their hands. Skye thought the model looked a little like a hooker on safari and kept her arm down.

Margot shook her finger at those with their hands in the air. "Wrong. Flashy isn't necessarily sexy."

Skye studied the spa owner. Was Margot really cutting down her dead friend's taste in clothes?

Margot pressed a button and a woman's foot appeared on the screen. "Study this shoe and be prepared to tell me what about it is sexy."

Skye examined the shoe as Margot disappeared behind the screen. It was a black sandal with a four-inch heel, and bands across the toe and around the ankle. Gold rings held the straps together and a tassel of gold chains with onyx beads on the ends cascaded from the ankle ring to the sole. She recognized the designer as Gucci, and remembered seeing it in one of those oversized magazines she leafed through when she got her hair cut.

While Margot was gone, Bunny stage whispered to Skye,

"So now that you know that Sonny Boy wasn't cheating on you, are you taking him back?"

"We're discussing it tonight."

"What's to talk about? Either you forgive him or you don't."

Skye didn't want to have this conversation right now, and especially not in public, but ended up saying. "I'm not sure I can trust a man who has a sister he doesn't tell me about. How can I be sure how he feels about me, if he's keeping such huge parts of his life secret?"

"Honey." Bunny shook her head. "Men only have two emotions—hungry and horny. If you see one without an erection, make him a sandwich."

Thankfully, before Skye could respond, Margot reappeared, this time wearing a red and cream patterned dress. It had an empire waist, spaghetti straps, and knee length skirt. Skye thought the outfit was better suited to someone under twenty-five, but maybe that was supposed to be the attraction—women as baby dolls.

As soon as she had everyone's attention, Margot asked, "Who can tell me why the shoe on the screen is sexy?"

Several answers were shouted out. "The high heel makes your leg look longer." "The thin black strap accents your ankle." "It showcases your pedicure."

Margot shook her head. "Anyone else? How about you, Skye?"

Skye raised an eyebrow. "It makes women look helpless, because they can't really move in this kind of shoe."

"Interesting perspective." Margot's voice was icy. "But the real reason is—"

Whitney cut her off. "The real reason is that the shoe cost seven hundred dollars, and spending that kind of money always makes a woman feel sexy."

For a split second, Margot narrowed her eyes, then nodded benignly. "Close, Whitney. It's the confidence engendered by wearing such an exquisite design, not the cost."

After that piece of wisdom, Skye's thoughts drifted off to what she would do about Simon, Wally, and the murderer. Most of the rest of the class was about recognizing and buying designer clothing, nearly all of which was either too tight or too short for Skye's curvaceous figure, even if she had that kind of money to spend on clothes.

Toward the end, a tussle between Bunny and Margot brought Skye's attention back to the front of the room. Bunny jumped out of her seat and stood nose-to-nose with Margot, both women wearing low-cut jeans and a shirt with high heeled sandals. Margot's top was a brown glitter-trimmed camisole that matched the brown suede laces running up the side of her jeans. Bunny wore a black and gold beaded backless camisole held together by ties across her back and black LYCRA jeans woven with gold threads. Bunny was poking Margot's shoulder with her right index finger and shouting, "What do you mean, this isn't a sexy outfit?"

Margot was trying to get away from the irate redhead by inching back and stuttering, "Now, Bunny, you took what I said the wrong way."

Bunny moved forward, "You compared our two outfits and said mine looked cheap."

"Well, what I meant was, ah, less expensive." Margot edged back a little more.

"So, you admit it's a sexy outfit?" Bunny continued to poke the spa owner.

"Well, I'm sure for a certain type of gentleman," Margot stammered, still trying to get away from the gleaming red nail being driven into her shoulder.

"*Most* gentlemen." Bunny emphasized her point with an extra jab. "This mare may have a few years on her, but she can still make nearly any stallion jump over to her side of the fence."

Margot nodded while taking one more step away from Bunny, but it was one too many—she had reached the end of the stage. The last thing Skye saw as the blonde toppled backward, her five-hundred-dollar high heel shoes pointed toward the ceiling, was her designer jeans sliding down, exposing both her derrière and her baby blue La Perla thong.

Bunny turned her back on the fallen star and dusted off her hands. She rested a hand on the hip she had thrust forward, and said to the women gasping in front of her, "People who get too big for their britches are usually exposed in the end."

CHAPTER 15

Survival of the Fitness Class

After Margot's ignominious display at the "Dress for Sexcess" seminar, Skye wasn't surprised that the spa owner refused to talk to her. Margot claimed she had a migraine and couldn't understand why Skye wanted to discuss a murder that had already been solved. Knowing there was no way to force the woman to answer her questions, Skye let Margot go, then whipped out the spa schedule and checked to see which staff member she could see next.

As she skimmed the list, her heart sank. The only activity scheduled for four o'clock that she could get into without an appointment was Frisco's exercise class. It was listed as a "Taste of Fitness" and included a sampling of yoga, dancercise, fuerza, and kick ball. What in the heck was fuerza, and why would a bunch of grown women play kick ball, a game most ten-year-olds found boring?

Skye wasn't exactly a workout neophyte, but her two previous experiences had not proven encouraging. Her mother had forced Skye to go to what was at that time referred to as an exercise salon when she was in sixth grade. The salon was filled with middle-aged women who repeatedly informed Skye that she would never get a boyfriend as long as she was chubby. They scared her so much, she went on a diet of only eight hundred calories a day until she shed the extra pounds.

She suffered this deprivation for over fifteen years, at which time she had an epiphany and decided that celery was rabbit food, JELL-O was a salad not a dessert, and chocolate was one of the seven basic food groups. She still tried to eat healthfully and swim at least five days a week, but her life no longer revolved around how small a size jeans she could squeeze into and still breathe.

Furthermore, the exercise salon ladies had been wrong. Her problem wasn't hooking men, it was figuring out which were the keepers and which she should throw back into the lake.

Skye's second foray into a health club had taken place only two months ago, when she was on the trail of her contractor's killer. This time no one had scared her, but she had become trapped on one of the machines, breaking a fingernail and tearing the knee out of her sweatpants.

Still, maybe the third time would be the charm; she really had no choice. She had to talk to Frisco. She needed to confirm he had seen Whitney at the pool.

Skye looked at her watch and then reread the program. Attendees were asked to wear appropriate exercise clothing and be in the gym fifteen minutes before the session started, which left Skye less than fifteen minutes to get to her room, change, and find the gym.

Housekeeping had been through, and Skye's room was spotless. The beds were made, the bathroom cleaned and restocked with towels, and the trash cans emptied. Such service was one of the few good things about staying at the spa.

While she changed into her tights and leotard, Skye briefly wondered if she could take one of the housekeepers home with her when she left. It would be so nice to return after a long day at school and find her house looking this pristine.

She could certainly understand why Wally would employ Dorothy Snyder. Come to think of it, Simon had a woman who came in twice a week to clean, too. Uncle Charlie hired a cleaning crew for the motor court that took care of his cottage. And May cleaned Vince's apartment once a week.

What was wrong with this picture? Skye stopped, bent

over, one leg halfway inserted into her tights. Why did the single men in town all have household help when Skye had the biggest house and struggled to keep it up herself?

Did the men make more money, even though she was the one with the graduate degree, or did the men value their time more highly than she valued her own? Something to think about after she caught Esmé's killer.

Several women were already at the gym when Skye arrived, including her mother and Spike. Shit! Shit! Shit! Skye hadn't even thought of how May would react to Spike's disclosure. Now that she was forced to consider it, she knew it wouldn't be pretty, at least not from Skye's point of view.

Both Spike and May gestured for her to join them, and Skye couldn't think how to refuse, so she walked over to where they were sitting on a mat.

"This day is full of surprises." May arched an eyebrow at her daughter. "I never thought I'd see you attend an exercise class, at least not voluntarily."

"Hello to you, too, Mother." Skye tried to sound casual. "Just thought I'd check it out." The last thing she wanted was for May to suspect she was investigating or that the murderer hadn't been caught. May was the queen of speedy transmission of near-factual information, also known as gossip.

Spike had been closely watching the exchange between mother and daughter, but wisely remained silent, other than interjecting a quick "Hi" when Skye had joined them.

Now that Skye knew the truth, she could see little bits of Simon and Bunny in the woman.

While Skye was trying to think of something to say to Spike, May exclaimed, "Why didn't you tell me that Nancy was really Spike, and that Spike is Simon's half sister?"

"I only found out a few hours ago." Skye smiled thinly at Spike, then explained to May, "I needed to process the information before I shared it with anyone."

"I'm not anyone, I'm your mother."

Frisco sauntered into the room while Skye was still trying to think of a response to May's statement. He hugged several of the women as he worked his way to the front and gave each huggee a personal welcome. "Glad to see you back." "You must like my classes, you haven't missed one." "I'll miss you when this weekend is over."

Skye heard one of the women Frisco embraced say to her group of friends after he passed by, "His exercise classes make me feel as if I just attended Mass."

Skye's eyebrows rose into her hairline. This was beginning to feel a bit like a cult. She looked to see if May or Spike had heard the woman, but they gave no sign that they were now in a divine presence.

Once he arrived at the front of the gym, Frisco announced in a rah, rah voice, "There's a thin woman in each of you screaming to get out!"

While the women cheered his pronouncement, Skye muttered to Spike, "That may be true, but if I throw her a couple chocolate chip cookies she usually shuts right up."

Spike was still snickering when Frisco continued, "We're going to start with yoga, slide into dancercise, try a little fuerza, and end with a rousing game of kick ball." He pointed to the mats. "Would everyone take a spot an arm's length from each other?"

Skye shrugged out of her robe, throwing it over the back of a chair at the side of the room, then took a step toward where Frisco had indicated.

Without any warning, one of the "cult" members elbowed Skye out of the way, saying sharply, "Newbies in the back."

Spike whispered to Skye as they found places side by side toward the rear of the group, "This is like my club in Sacramento. The Front-Rowers don't allow the rest of us up there. That spot has to be earned by coming to every class the instructor teaches."

At first Skye thought Spike was kidding, but before she could ask, Frisco led them in their first position.

Yoga went pretty well. Skye had a little trouble getting into the third posture, and was slightly out of breath from trying, when May hissed from behind her, "Have you told Wally that you're going back to Simon, now that you know Spike is his half sister?"

"No." May startled Skye so badly that she lost her

concentration and fell out of the pose. "And this is not the time to talk about it, Mom."

May was silent through the rest of yoga, but as the class changed to dancercise, she tried again. "You *are* taking Simon back, right?"

Skye ignored her mother and danced away. Unfortunately, she went in the wrong direction and bumped into a woman who growled when Skye said, "Excuse me." The woman was as thin as a flower stem, and Skye wondered if she was so cranky because she hadn't had lunch . . . ever.

Skye shrugged and twirled in another direction, but ended up next to Spike, who asked, "Will you give Simon another chance?"

Suddenly, Skye felt like the croquet ball in *Alice in Wonderland*, rattling between the talking wickets. She forced a smile. "Simon and I will discuss the situation later." Wanting to change the subject, she asked, "How did Margot take it when you told her you weren't the *Spa* magazine reviewer?"

"I think she was relieved, considering the murder and all." Spike winked. "And she was happy to take my money and let me stay."

After dancercise, Frisco called a ten-minute break and walked into a small office off to the side. Skye followed him, but paused just outside the door when she realized he had picked up the phone and was punching in a number.

The keypad beeping stopped, and he said, "Are we on for tonight?"

Skye missed the next few minutes when two women in the gym started yelling at each other about coming on time for class, but she heard him say, "But, darling, she's been taken care of. Meet me in the garage at eleven."

Skye was still wondering who was taken care of, who Frisco's darling was, and why they were meeting when he came out of his office and started passing out wooden poles. The presence of potentially lethal weapons made Skye focus on the task at hand. The rods turned out to be for fuerza, a strength training exercise done with wooden staffs that looked as if they came from a grade B samurai movie.

Frisco smiled from the safety of the front of the class, then instructed the women to beat the air with the sticks. He joked, "My darlings, pretend you're hitting your ex-husband or cheating boyfriend."

Skye was busy whomping the heck out of all the men who had ever betrayed her when a woman with violet eyes and a black page boy brought her pole down on Skye's arm.

Skye shouted, "Ouch!"

Instead of apologizing, the woman showed her teeth, uttered something that sounded like, "high karate," and spun away, twirling her rod as if it were a baton.

Skye was edging toward the door—enough was enough, she'd wait to talk to Frisco *outside* the gym—when her mother nabbed her.

May had Spike by the other arm, and said, "Let's make sure we're all on the same team for kick ball."

Skye shook herself loose of May's grip. "Why? You know I'm not very good at sports, and you like to be on the winning side. You pout for a week if your bowling team loses."

May beamed at Spike and Skye. "I just think family should stick together."

Spike and Skye both spoke at the same time. "Family?"

May herded the two women toward where the kick ball teams were forming. "I know it's a little soon to be talking about the wedding, but once you and Simon make up, I'm sure things will start to move faster."

"Mom, you're driving without your headlights on again." Skye tried to make a joke of May's comments, afraid Spike would repeat them to Simon.

"Don't be silly." May went on relentlessly. "Just think, you could be a June bride, like I was."

Skye closed her eyes. Nothing she could say, at least not in a public place, would convince May that Skye and Simon were not about to pick out their china pattern. Skye gave Spike a weak smile and shook her head to indicate that May was way off base.

Before May could say anything else, Skye asked Frisco, "Why kick ball?"

"It is, how do you say, to get in touch with your inner child."

Skye muttered to herself, "What happens if our inner children are spoiled brats named Damien?"

Spike sniggered and put an index finger on either side of her head like horns, indicating she had gotten Skye's reference to the devil child in *The Omen*.

Five minutes into the game and Skye was considering faking an injury. She hadn't liked gym activities when she was a student and found they didn't improve with age. She had expected a casual game with lots of laughter as they all made errors, but most of the women were out for blood, her own mother included.

Despite May's machinations, she and Skye had ended up on different teams, and now Skye was sorry. She looked up just in time to see her mother lining up a ferocious kick aimed directly at Skye's middle.

Skye froze, mesmerized by the competitive gleam in May's eyes. She would have taken the hit if Spike hadn't pushed her aside.

After the game was over, May's team winning by a wide margin, Spike said to Skye, "No offense, but your mother is the Cruella De Vil of kickball. Did you see all the people she got out?"

"No offense taken. I agree. I'm thinking of buying her a Dalmatian fur coat." Skye shook her head. "This experience has been an eye-opener for me. The weird forms of exercise, the territoriality of the women, and the competitiveness. Yikes!" She wiped her face with a towel from the stack near the door. "My exercise usually consists of swimming laps, alone."

Spike threw her used towel in an open hamper. "I'm used to it. You should see my gym at home. They have Karaoke Treadmill—sing your way to cardiovascular health; Meditative Aerobics—visualize yourself as a size two; and a dancercise thing called Crumpin'."

"Crimping?" Skye was totally confused.

"No, Crumpin'. I had to look it up on the Internet. It's a dance style that was started in LA by clowns."

"Like Bozo?"

"Right." Spike paused, her hand on the door bar. "You flail your legs and arms around like you're a puppet on a string, and your puppeteer is having a seizure." After imparting that last factoid, Spike left.

Skye waited for the gym to empty out, then went in search of Frisco, who had disappeared as soon as the kick ball game ended. She had a good idea where he had gone, but when she rounded the corner into his office she gasped.

Margot lay on her back on the desk with her skirt bunched up around her waist. Frisco stood between her thighs with his shorts puddled around his ankles.

As Skye backed out of the little room, she wondered if Margot had found a new cure for migraines, and if so, would they be selling it as part of the overall spa package?

CHAPTER 16

Too Many Curling Irons in the Fire

Skye contemplated what she had seen as she made her way back to her room. If Frisco was screwing Margot at this very moment, who was the darling he was meeting in the garage at eleven that night, and who had been taken care of? The obvious answer to the latter was Esmé. But why would Frisco kill Esmé, even if she was only one of the women in his harem?

Unless he was going to keep killing his lovers until he was down to one lucky winner. Did that mean either Margot or his garage girl was his next victim? That just didn't make any sense at all.

When Skye entered their room, Trixie was talking on the phone. "No, I'm sorry, she's still not here."

At the sound of the door opening, Trixie looked up, then said into the receiver, "Wait one second, she just walked in." Trixie handed over the phone. "It's Wally. He's been calling and calling. Didn't you see my notes?"

Skye shook her head—she hadn't been back in the room long enough to notice them—then spoke into the handset. "Hi . . ." She paused. What should she call him? After last night it seemed she should have an endearment for him. Honey? No, too common. Precious? No, too syrupy. Sweetheart didn't feel quite right either.

Before she could come up with the perfect word, his velvety baritone flowed through the wire. "How you doing, sugar? I've been trying to get hold of you all day. Is everything all right?"

Trixie sat on her bed and stared at Skye, not pretending to do anything but listen.

Skye gave her friend an exasperated look and pulled the phone cord as far as it would stretch, ending up just inside the bathroom. "Why didn't you use the radio? I had it with me like you told me to."

"That's for official business." His silky voice held a challenge. "This is strictly pleasure. When can I see you again?"

Skye bit her lip. This would be the tricky part—explaining about Spike and Simon, and why she had to see Simon that night rather than Wally. Maybe she wouldn't have to. Maybe she could offer an alternative, then divert his attention.

"How about tomorrow night? I'm using all of the daylight hours to investigate. Have you found out anything about our suspects?"

"I started background checks on them all, but nothing has come in yet." Wally sighed. "Unfortunately, the papers have picked up the murder."

"All of them?"

"Both the *Trib* and the *Sun* have it, although it's not their headline story. Unfortunately, we weren't as lucky with the *Joliet Herald*, the *Kankakee Journal*, and the Laurel paper."

Skye winced. "Which printed . . . ?"

"Joliet leads with 'Beast Kills Beauty,' Kankakee has 'Deadly Beauty Mud Kills Ex-Model,' and Laurel has 'Cursed Mansion Kills Again.'"

"Ouch."

"Yeah." Wally's voice took on an edge. "It made the TV news this morning, too."

"Yeah, I know. Margot closed the big gates by the road and hired security to keep the reporters out, but it feels like we're under siege. I overheard the cook telling one of the housekeepers that a reporter snuck past the guards and stole the trash bag she put outside the kitchen door."

"It'll only get worse," Wally said. "Tonight one of the

entertainment channels is doing a program called, 'The Passing of a Fashion Icon.'"

"Great. At least there are no television sets at the spa so people here won't get stirred up." Skye wasn't surprised. She knew Esmé had been a big name in her time. And there was nothing like a dead celebrity to bring out the crocodile tears of an industry that declared women over the hill at thirty. Changing the subject, Skye asked, "Did you get the autopsy results yet?"

"The contractual ME's swamped. He said the regular ME should get to her on Monday."

"He gets the weekend off?" Skye knew they were a small county and the medical examiner was also the local pediatrician, but this was ridiculous.

"Our usual ME is away for the holiday, and due to budget constraints, the county only hired this guy for so many hours, which are nearly up."

"How about the state police's ME? I thought they were helping out."

"We have a confession, remember? That means this case goes to the bottom of the priority list." Wally's tone was rueful. "That includes our trace evidence, too."

"Terrific." Skye frowned. She hadn't considered the consequences of the false confession. Then she brightened. "Does that mean Special Agent Vail is off the case?"

"I guess you could say that." Wally's tone grew sheepish. "When I talked to the state police this morning to check on when I could expect their lab results, I asked if she was still available for assistance, and no one had heard of her."

"You're kidding."

"No, they talked to all the supervisors and finally checked the computer. There was never a Special Agent Vail on the state police force."

"That is so odd." Skye leaned against the bathroom door. "And she never showed up at the PD today?"

"No, but her Miata is gone, so she must have picked it up sometime last night. I sure wish I would have gotten the license plate number. If she shows up at the spa, try to keep her there and call me immediately. Impersonating a police officer is against the law."

"Do you think she had anything to do with the murder?"

"Anything's possible. She could be a part of the protest group, or one of the treasure hunters. Anyone with a police scanner could have known there was a murder at the spa and that I had asked the state for backup."

"I thought you kept the murder off the radio to keep the media away for as long as possible." Skye remembered Wally mentioning that fact when they were at his house.

"Only after we realized we were dealing with a celebrity. The initial call went out over the scanners per our normal procedure."

"Oh." Skye's thoughts went back to Ronnie Vail. "Did you see any identification from her?"

The sheepish note in Wally's voice intensified. "No. I made a rookie mistake. Because she walked the walk and talked the talk, I never doubted her."

There was a pause while they both thought of the fake investigator, then Skye said, "Things have been weird around here too." She gave him a brief rundown of everything that had taken place since she had returned to the spa, including the men trying to make the women leave, Margot and Frisco's affair, and Frisco's other dalliance. She ended her report by saying, "Should I stake out the garage, and see who Frisco's other lady friend is?"

"No, I'll do it. If this turns out to be Frisco setting up another murder, I don't want you there armed with only a Taser and pepper spray."

"Okay." Skye didn't want to confront another murderer either. After a slight pause, she said casually, "By the way, one of our suspects is here under a false name. Nancy Kimbrough is really Spike Yamaguchi—yes, it's her real name, she had it legally changed, *and* she's Simon's half sister." Skye went on to explain Spike's revelation.

The silence at the other end of the line was deafening. Finally Wally asked, "Does that change anything between you and Reid?"

"No." Skye hoped she was telling the truth. "But I did

promise to take a ride with him tonight so we could discuss the situation in private. As you know, the walls have ears around here."

"Yes." Wally sounded troubled. "Maybe we could get together afterward?"

"I would love that, but Simon's not coming over until nine. He has a funeral tonight and can't leave until it's over. So, by the time we get back, you'll be staking out the garage."

Wally grunted his agreement.

"How about I call you tomorrow morning, when I get up?" Skye suggested.

"How about we meet when I get finished with my stakeout?" Wally's voice was low and purposely seductive. "Have you ever made love in the back seat of a squad car?"

A bright flare of desire ran through her, but Skye realized that after talking to Simon she wouldn't want to go immediately into Wally's arms. "Can I have a rain check?"

"Any time, any place."

"Then I'll talk to you tomorrow, first thing."

"Bye, darlin'. You be careful tonight."

"I'm not the one staking out a possible murderer," Skye reminded him.

"No, you're spending time alone with an ex-lover. That's a hundred times more dangerous."

Once again, dinner was flavorless and meager. Afterward Margot produced board games and packs of cards and recruited people for various competitions. Trixie and Frannie chose Scrabble, and Bunny and May chose poker.

Bridge attracted Skye. She hadn't played since breaking up with Simon and missed the competition. Margot had set up a two-table progressive, which meant there would be seven rounds and each person would be partners with and play against all other players during the course of the evening.

For the first round, Skye found herself partnered with Spike, against Whitney and Loretta. Skye knew Loretta played, as bridge had been a popular pastime at their sorority house, and she was not surprised that Spike played, since Simon was an avid player, but she was taken aback by Whitney's presence at the table. Bridge took a mathematical and organized mind, not something Whitney had so far displayed.

After the first hand was dealt, the bidding was completed at two no-trump, and Loretta had led a four of spades, Skye asked, "Have you been playing bridge long, Whitney?"

"Since I was twelve." The girl didn't look up from her cards.

"Wow, you were young." Skye as dummy laid down her hand. "I didn't learn until I went to college."

Spike played the six of spades from the board.

Whitney frowned and laid down her nine. "My dad needed a partner for duplicate, and none of his women were smart enough, so he taught me." She dug in her purse, producing a wallet, and flipped it open. "See, this is my dad and me at a tournament."

They all murmured appropriate words of appreciation, then Spike took the hand with a queen and led a seven of clubs.

She looked at Whitney and said, "I thought you told me that your mom and dad divorced only a year ago."

Loretta played her king, and Spike overcame it with the ace from the board.

Whitney threw in a three, her nostrils flaring. "True, but Mom refused to play with Dad because he gets mad when he doesn't win, and, as I said, his girlfriends du jour were too dumb."

Skye made a mental note—Esmé's new husband had a temper and had played around throughout his marriage—then asked, "Did your stepmother play?"

After Spike won another hand with the queen of clubs from the board, and led a seven of diamonds, Whitney answered, "She claimed she did."

Loretta took that hand with her ace and led a two of spades before saying, "Did Esmé play in the duplicate tournaments with your dad?"

Whitney glared at Loretta as Spike won the hand with the

jack from the board. "That was a dumb move. You should have known the queen had already been played."

Loretta shrugged, not responding to the dig.

Skye examined Whitney. She had underestimated the girl. Whitney was either a savant bridge player or a lot smarter than she let the world see.

Spike led a two of clubs from the board and Whitney took the hand with an eight. For the first time, the girl smiled and answered Loretta's previous question. "Esmé was an awful bridge player. My dad wouldn't have gotten any masters points with her." She led the ten of diamonds.

Spike took the hand with the jack, led the king taking another hand, then led a nine of hearts taking a third hand. She needed one more to make the bid. "So, your dad didn't play with her in the tournaments?" she asked before leading a four of clubs from the board.

Whitney shook her head, then smiled triumphantly and took the hand with her jack, then led her king and queen of hearts in quick succession. She paused before laying down her last card, a queen of diamonds. If Spike took the hand she would make her bid; if Whitney and Loretta took it, they would set her.

Grimly Spike threw in her ace of spades and the ten of clubs from the board. Loretta put down her king of spades and Whitney jubilantly pulled in the winning hand.

Skye refused to think of this as a date. She and Simon were just getting together to discuss recent developments. Still, she wanted to look nice, and she had pretty much run out of wardrobe options. Her choices were the jeans she had worn to the spa, a dinner dress, or exercise clothes. A dress might suggest that she considered their get-together more than just a chat, but she had no intention of meeting him in a sweat suit either.

At eight thirty, she asked one of the Scumble River women to sit in for her during the rest of the bridge game, and went upstairs to get ready. After several minutes of agonizing, Skye finally shimmied into the jeans and pulled on a marmalade wrap sweater intended to be paired with a skirt.

After spritzing her hair with water, she used the hot air brush to tame the curls into a smooth curtain. Although she wanted to make sure she was on time for Simon—she had told him to meet her around the side and not to come into the lobby where they might be ambushed by friends and relatives—she took a few minutes to reapply her bronzer and mascara and put on dangling topaz earrings. Marmalade slides with kitten heels added just the right touch of sophistication without looking like she had fussed.

She breathed a sigh of relief when she made it down the stairs and out the side door without being seen. This exit led to the gym and other new additions. Most of the recently constructed buildings were private cottages for those guests who didn't want to mingle with the hoi polloi. The bungalows were scattered along a heavily landscaped pathway, trees and trellises strategically placed to maintain utmost privacy.

As Skye made her way down the path she noticed several recently dug holes—clearly the murder and the security guards had not stopped the treasure hunter. The dense landscaping blocked out the moon, and the small lights edging the concrete sidewalk illuminated only to knee level.

Suddenly Skye felt as if she were being followed. Reaching into her tote bag, she drew out the tiny can of pepper spray attached to her key chain, and whirled around. A small man was jogging toward her.

His gaze fastened on the canister of pepper spray, and he threw his hands in the air. "I'm Jack Novak from *Entertainment*, what can you tell me about Esmé's murder?"

"No comment." Skye aimed the pepper spray at the reporter's eyes. "This is private property. Either leave or I'll spray you."

"All I want to know is how she looked." Novak took a step backward. "Did you see her?"

"I'm spraying on three." Skye followed him. "One."

"Is it true her eyes were gouged out of their sockets?"

"Two."

"She was naked, right? Were her boobs fake?"

"Three."

Skye pressed the button and Novak took off like a rabbit being chased by a greyhound. She nodded in satisfaction, and decided on their way out, she'd ask Simon to stop at the gate so she could tell the guard about the reporter.

Speaking of Simon, where was he? She pressed the stem of her watch and the dial lit up. It was already ten after nine. The wake must have run long. Frowning, she took a few more steps down the path then stopped.

Two of the VIP cottages had lights showing through their windows. They were supposed to be unoccupied during this trial weekend. Who was in them?

All the guests, plus Margot and Dr. Burnett, were playing games, which left the staff. Could Frisco be seeing yet another woman before his eleven o'clock date? Was this where Ustelle went when she disappeared? Maybe it was another reporter or the spa vandal/treasure hunter.

Or was it the murderer?

CHAPTER 17

Still Water Therapy
Runs Deep

S hit! Shit! Shit! What should she do? It would be stupid to approach whoever was in the cottage by herself, not to mention it would be extremely difficult to check out both cottages without being discovered. She had not brought her emergency-equipped fanny pack, and she had emptied her tiny pepper spray on the reporter. But if she left to get help, there was nothing to prevent the people in the cottages from also leaving.

Skye bit her lip. Okay. She would take just a little peek—first the cottage on her right, then the one on her left. No matter what she saw, she would not do anything to reveal her presence. She stepped off the paving stones and the mulch underfoot felt like a sponge. Someone must have just watered the area.

Trying not to disturb any of the newly planted landscape, she tiptoed to one of the illuminated windows. The interior wooden shutters were half open, but tipped down. Drat. All she could see were two pair of feet. One was clad in expensive looking high-heeled sandals and the other in dirty generic tennis shoes. Evidently, Frisco's tryst in the garage was not the only one going on at the spa that night. But who were these participants?

This wasn't getting her anywhere. Maybe one of the other windows would afford a better view. She squished her way around the cottage and peered into that window, but the shutters were completely closed.

As she rounded the third side, she noticed the window was open a crack and over the faint strands of a golden oldie a female voice said, "See, isn't this nicer than going to McDonald's? We can be alone here, listen to good music, and I packed you a little snack."

An adolescent male voice answered, "This is mighty fine, but I want to take you out soes all my friends can see me with you."

"But, sweetie, I'll be fired if Margot finds out about us. We already had one close call."

Skye bit her lip. Good grief! The male speaking was Elvis Doozier, and she was ninety-nine percent sure the female was Amber Ferguson. Did that mean that Amber had been lying about Elvis stalking her? Was the sophisticated technician really dating a country bumpkin?

Skye took another step forward. She was nearly to the open window when a hand came down on her shoulder and she screamed. It was only one sharp squeal, but in the nanosecond it took for her to whirl around, identify the owner of the hand as Simon, and look back, the light in both cottages had been extinguished. Next she heard the music cut off in midbeat, two doors slam, and the sound of running footsteps.

Skye tried to run after at least one of them but Simon grabbed her by the upper arms.

She wiggled. "Let me go."

"First, tell me what's going on."

Tilting her head to look at him, she said, "There were lights in these cottages, and they're supposed to be unoccupied. I was trying to see who was using them."

"Why do you care?"

She thought quickly, and lied, "It could be the vandal and/or treasure hunters." She felt him relax and demanded, "Now, would you please take your hands off me, before they all get away?"

Simon released her, and she ran in the direction one of the sets of footsteps had gone, following the disturbed earth until she came to the path where there was nothing left to track.

She was stamping her feet, mostly to get the dirt off of them, but also in exasperation, when Simon caught up with her. "Sorry about that. I had no idea you were still investigating, since the murderer confessed."

This time she said, "Yeah, what with the murder and all, we sort of forgot the vandal/treasure hunter, but when I saw the lights on in cottages that were supposed to be empty, they reminded me."

"Don't you think the protestors were probably behind the vandal's activities?" Simon plucked a pine needle from Skye's hair.

"I haven't really thought about it." She shrugged. "Like I said, I forgot about the whole vandal/treasure hunter business until I saw the lights just now." Skye glanced down and noticed that Simon's pants legs were muddy. She pointed to them and asked, "How did you get so dirty? It couldn't have been just following me off the path, because only your shoes would be soiled."

"Uh." An embarrassed expression stole across Simon's face. "Well, you see, I thought I had figured out the riddle, so since I got here a little early, I was looking for the hidden jewelry."

"Really? On private property?" Skye didn't think that sounded like the Simon she knew.

"I have Margot and Creighton's permission, as long as I give them half of whatever I find." Simon finished brushing off his pants legs and folded away his handkerchief. "They want the treasure found so that everyone will quit bothering them."

"I can understand their reasoning." Skye finished scraping the muck from her shoes. "Did you find it?"

"No," Simon answered, then asked, "Do you still want to take a ride, or would you rather do this some other time?"

"It's better that we talk sooner rather than later. May is already jumping to conclusions, and Bunny's hopping close behind. She tried to give me advice this afternoon concerning your various 'appetites.'" Skye looked around. "In fact, let's get out of here before someone spots us."

They made it to Simon's Lexus without being intercepted and Simon asked, "Is there any place special you want to go?"

"Are you hungry?" Skye knew that Simon often didn't eat before a funeral, preferring to have dinner after he finished work. "I'm starving, the food at the spa is awful, but it's after ten o'clock and I can't think of anywhere nearby that's open this late."

"There's that truck stop about ten miles north on I-55. Their restaurant is open twenty-four hours. Would that be okay?"

"Fine." Skye could already taste the homemade pie for which that restaurant was locally famous. "We shouldn't run into anyone we know there."

"I wouldn't think so."

Skye gazed at Simon's handsome face, bathed in a golden glow by the moonlight pouring into the car window. She had no idea where to start the conversation they needed to have, and he seemed as much at a loss for words as she was. How had they ever become so estranged?

Before they left, Skye asked Simon to stop at the gate so she could tell the security officers about the reporter and the lights in the cottages. The guards promised to send a patrol to look around the grounds, and Skye relaxed as they exited the estate.

As they drove toward the diner, Skye thought of all that had happened since the summer. Suddenly she remembered the gift Simon had sent at the end of September and said, "Thank you for the book."

He glanced over at her. It was the most intimate action he had committed since picking her up. "You said *Little Women* was your favorite book as a child, so when I saw it in a used book store in California, I thought of you."

"That was sweet."

"I'm not sure that's a good thing." This time his glance lingered, but not long enough to make her uncomfortable. He was a master of the art of making his meaning clear without being direct. "Sweet doesn't seem to be what you want anymore."

Skye didn't respond, and neither of them said anything else until they arrived at the restaurant. Simon walked her to the door with his hand resting lightly on the small of her back. He was smooth, there were no rough edges on Simon, and just maybe that wasn't a good thing either.

Once they were seated, Skye was surprised to see a number of customers present despite the late hour. The waitress brought them menus, glasses of water, and poured coffee in the cups already on the table.

She was a short woman in her late fifties or early sixties, nearly as wide as she was tall, but light on her feet. She had nut-brown, curly hair and wore a pink nylon uniform dress with MASIE embroidered above her left breast. She greeted many of the customers like regulars, and offered a friendly smile and pieces of pie to the others.

After making the rounds, refilling water glasses and coffee cups, she came back to take their order, then Skye and Simon sat in silence.

The stillness grew to an uncomfortable length until finally they both couldn't stand it and tried to talk at once. "Are you—?" "I wonder—"

They both stopped and said, "You first." "No, you."

Skye chuckled uneasily. "I insist. What were you about to say?"

"I just wanted to ask if you were enjoying the spa, despite the murder, of course."

"Not really," Skye confessed. "Some of the treatments are pleasant, and the people are fun, but I'm not really a spa kind of girl."

"This one sounds sort of regimented. Bunny was telling me about the enforced diet. You'd probably like the more resortlike spas better."

Skye nodded.

"What were you going to say?"

"I can't remember." Skye gave a nervous laugh. "As May would say, it must have been a lie."

Masie arrived just then with their Diet Cokes, toasted cheese sandwiches, and bowls of tomato soup.

Skye gazed at the food, then at Simon, remembering that they often seemed to be on the same wavelength, ordering the same food at restaurants. She took a bite of her sandwich, hoping he would start the conversation.

Simon cleared his throat, opened his mouth, then seemed to change his mind. "Pass the pepper, please."

She handed him the shaker and sighed, trying to weigh the whole structure of events and in spite of everything, came up with the same unanswered question. "What I still don't understand is why you couldn't just tell me Spike is your half sister."

"Because I promised her." The corner of his mouth twisted in exasperation. "What's so difficult to understand about that?"

Skye felt a scream of frustration at the back of her throat, but swallowed it. "I'm a psychologist. I'm trained to keep secrets. I would never, ever break confidentiality. You could have told me."

His voice was heavy with sarcasm. "So you get to maintain confidentiality, whereas it's okay for me to tell?" He was normally a careful man, but that veneer was starting to crack.

"Yes." Skye stared into his golden hazel eyes, trying to understand her perplexing gamut of emotions. "I'm not just anyone. At least I thought I wasn't. I thought I was someone special—the other half of your whole. The one person you would never keep any secrets from."

"Everyone has secrets." Simon pushed his plate away. "The relationship you're describing doesn't exist, except maybe in those romance books you like to read. I love you, but I don't delude myself into thinking you're my soul mate."

The cynicism of his statement grated on her. She took a calming breath, afraid she would start crying, and he would think she was weak. "It seems we disagree on the very nature and meaning of love."

"No, we don't." His disparaging stare drilled into her. "If

you really and truly think two people can be meant for each other and no else, how could you start seeing Boyd so quickly once we broke up?"

"Maybe I was wrong about who my soul mate is, but I'm not wrong that there is one person who completes you."

"Then you're saying that even though you know I was innocent, that I didn't cheat on you, that I still love you," his tone was bleak, "you're not willing to give our relationship a second chance?"

"It's too late. You should have told me right away." Skye refused to meet his stare. "You shouldn't have made this a test of my trust for you. That wasn't fair."

"A fair is the place you go to eat too much cotton candy; it has nothing to do with real life."

The few bites of her sandwich and sips of her soup she had taken lay like balls of lead in her stomach. "You don't know how tempted I am to go back and pick up where we left off, but that's because our relationship made me feel comfortable. There weren't real lows, but there weren't real highs either."

"That's why our relationship is worth saving."

"I just don't know how two people can look at the same thing and see something totally different." Skye twisted her napkin. "Now I realize that the reason our relationship was on such an even keel was that you kept secret anything you thought might be bothersome."

"Maybe I did that because you told me too much." His expression hardened. "I heard every word your mom said to you, every detail about your job, what all your friends were doing. Even when Bingo caught a mouse it became part of Skye's six o'clock news."

"I thought you liked to hear my funny stories." She was too stunned by his attack to say more.

"When you first moved back here, you were interested in the world. Now all you talk about is Scumble River. I thought we'd travel the globe, maybe even sell the funeral home at some point and move somewhere exciting. But now, I'm pretty sure you'd never leave, because where else could you run around pretending to be everyone's guardian angel? Why do you need to be the one to right every wrong?"

"You don't like that I share my day with you, that I'm happy living in my hometown, and that I try to help people when I'm able?" His contemptuous tone sparked her anger. "Yet, prior to today, you never even gave me a hint this was how you felt? Is that right?"

"You're twisting what I said." His lips thinned and he narrowed his eyes.

"No, I'm just showing you something you don't want to see," she countered icily.

"Right." Simon's tone was sarcastic. "Or are you making things up because you've already moved on and don't want to repair our relationship? You've always been attracted to Boyd and now you have him. Is the sex enough to make up for everything else?"

"Now you're the one twisting things," she said in a choked voice, guilt swelling inside her, threatening to spill out. "We're not, I mean, that's not . . ." She trailed off, then noticed the look of derision in his eye. She straightened her back and said coldly, "I'm free, way over twenty-one, and have no commitment to you or anyone else. I can do *what* I want with *whom* I please."

"Yes, I guess you can." Simon stood up and threw a twenty-dollar bill on the table. "Maybe when you get tired of playing cops and robbers with Boyd, you'll see what I've been trying to say. And maybe, when you finally come to your senses, I'll still care. Or maybe not."

The shock of his words held her immobile.

He stood there, tall and impatient. "Are you coming?"

"No. Go ahead without me."

"I'm not leaving you stranded here."

"Suit yourself." Skye picked up her spoon and dipped it into her soup bowl. "But I'm not riding with you."

He glared at her, swore, then whirled around and marched out of the diner, his footsteps sounding like firecrackers on the linoleum.

Once he left, she let her spoon drop and sank back in the

booth, her head resting against the wall. She felt an extraordinary emptiness and had no idea what to do next.

What seemed like minutes later, Masie leaned into the booth and whispered, "Miss, Miss, are you okay?"

"Yes." Skye blinked and focused; she'd been replaying every word she'd just exchanged with Simon. "Is there a phone I can use?"

"You need a ride home?" Masie asked sympathetically. When Skye didn't answer right away she added, "I noticed your boyfriend leave in a snit. You should have seen the gravel flying from underneath his tires when he pulled out of the parking lot."

"I'd like to call someone to pick me up," Skye inserted, not wanting to hear anymore about Simon, or what their fight had looked like to other people.

"You live in Scumble River?"

"Yes, but I'm spending the weekend at the new spa."

Masie pointed to the clock on the wall, which read quarter to twelve. "I get off in fifteen minutes and I'm going in that direction. I'll give you a ride."

"No, really, if I can just borrow a phone I'll be fine."

"It's only a mile or so out of my way." Masie winked. "You don't remember me, but last year my grandson got in some trouble for having a box cutter at school. He uses it at his part-time job stocking shelves at the grocery store and forgot to take it out of his pocket. The principal kept yelling about a 'no tolerance' policy, but you stuck up for him and talked the principal out of suspending him. He was a C student at best, and if he would have been suspended he wouldn't have graduated on time and would probably have just quit. Because of you, he got his diploma and was able to get a good job at the power plant."

"Thank you for telling me that, and thank you for your kindness." Skye smiled for the first time in hours. Simon may think she was an interfering busybody, but at least something she did had had a positive effect. "I would love a ride home." She scooped up the twenty Simon had dropped on the table and handed it to Masie. "This is for our bill and you keep the rest. Is it all right if I meet you by the door? I need to go to the restroom and freshen up."

Masie nodded and Skye scooted out of the booth and walked to the back of the restaurant. She used the facilities and was splashing her face with cold water when two forty-something women came into the ladies' room and headed into adjoining stalls. Both wore jeans and sweatshirts advertising the local casino boat.

The brunette yelled through the partition to the blonde, "I'm calling the police in the morning. That so-called Magic Mud is a fraud. I had my neighbor, the one who teaches chemistry at the high school, check it out. It's nothing but dirt they dug up from their backyard."

Skye frowned. Was the spa selling a phony product? No, the spa's mud was called Miracle, not Magic. She combed her hair, playing for time until the brunette came out of the cubicle and started washing her hands.

Skye tapped the woman on the shoulder. "Were you talking about the mud the Scumble River Spa is selling?"

"No." The woman reddened slightly. "We bought ours from this roadside stand. It was a quarter of the price the spa wanted."

Ah, the pieces were falling into place. "Was this stand on Cattail Path?"

"Why, yes. A heavily made-up woman was doing the selling." The blonde added helpfully, "I think her name was Glinda, like the good witch in *The Wizard of Oz*."

"Thanks." Skye backed out of the bathroom, muttering under her breath, "Good witch my eye. The only way Glenda Doozier is a good witch is if a B is substituted for the W."

CHAPTER 18

Beauty Is Only
Skin Deep

Every muscle in Skye's body throbbed, and she felt light-headed. The muscle aches were probably due to the unaccustomed exercise, and maybe the dizziness was from lack of rest since it was only six a.m. Masie had dropped her off at twelve thirty, but she hadn't been able to fall asleep for hours, alternately crying over lost love and seething over Simon's unreasonableness.

She might also be woozy from lack of nourishment. After sharing the supplies she'd brought back Thursday night, she had run out of food by lunchtime yesterday.

Or maybe, she was coming down with something. She'd gotten a flu shot, but in her profession she was constantly exposed to germs that even regular hand washing and water-less cleansers couldn't completely eradicate.

Holding her head, Skye eased upright. The room spun a couple of times, then righted itself. She made it to the bathroom, and after a shower, felt somewhat better.

Trixie continued to snore softly from the other bed as Skye threw on jeans and a sweatshirt, then scooped the daily activity list from the floor. She still needed to talk to Amber, Ustelle, and Kipp, as well as Dr. Burnett.

Taking a seat at the desk, Skye plotted her day. Should she have the treatments first, then run home for clothes and food and to check out the Dooziers? No, it would be easier to make appointments for the afternoon and take care of the non-spa stuff right away.

Skye took a sheet of stationery from the desk drawer and wrote:

> 7:00 A.M.—CALL FOR SPA APPOINTMENTS/BORROW TRIXIE'S CAR
> 7:30 A.M.—HOME: GET MORE CLOTHES AND FOOD
> 8:00 A.M.—BREAKFAST WITH WALLY
> 9:30 A.M.—CHECK OUT DOOZIERS
> 11:00 A.M.—FACIAL WITH USTELLE
> LUNCH
> 1:00 P.M.—MANICURE AND PEDICURE WITH AMBER
> 2:00 P.M.—HAIR WITH KIPP
> 4:00 P.M.—CONSULTATION WITH DR. BURNETT
> 5:00 P.M.—MEET WITH WALLY RE EXCHANGE OF INFO
> DON'T FORGET VANDAL/TREASURE HUNTER!

As soon as the second hand of her watch clicked onto the twelve, Skye picked up the phone and hit the appointment button.

Her call was answered immediately by the receptionist. "Good morning, how may I help you?"

Skye made all of her arrangements, thanked Barb, and hung up, then walked over to where Trixie slept.

She shook her shoulder gently. "Trixie, can I borrow your car?"

Trixie turned her head away, mumbling, "Sure, fine, whatever."

"Where're your keys?" Skye kept her voice low.

Trixie muttered, "Purse," then pulled the covers up over her head.

Skye found the keys, stuffed her dirty clothes into her suitcase, wrote Trixie a note since she didn't think her friend would remember their conversation, and hurried out of the spa. She waved at the few people who were already up and about, but kept moving, refusing to be waylaid by casual conversation.

The bellboy wasn't on duty, but Skye had no trouble finding Trixie's car in the back lot. Luckily it wasn't blocked in, and she could drive away with no problem. Heading home, she was tempted to check out the Dooziers, but realized they were better left until she had a full stomach, a clearer head, and had conferred with Wally.

Bingo greeted Skye ecstatically as she came through the door, purring and rubbing against her legs. This affectionate welcome lasted precisely a minute and a half, then some internal feline signal sounded and he herded her toward the kitchen. A bowl of water and another of diet cat food sat untouched near the counter, but his Fancy Feast dish was licked clean and pushed into the center of the room.

Skye shook her head. The vet didn't want her to give Bingo canned food, but the cat refused to eat the dry food if the moist one was withheld. The last time she had tried to follow the vet's orders, Bingo had gone for three days without eating before Skye caved in and gave him what he wanted. It was pretty sad that her cat had more willpower than she did.

After she spooned the pungent-smelling grilled tuna into his bowl, she grabbed a brown sugar cinnamon Pop-Tart for herself—her own form of Fancy Feast—and the cordless phone, then went upstairs.

As she changed into black jeans and a leopard patterned long-sleeved T-shirt, she phoned Wally. He was on the other line so she left him a message to meet her at eight for breakfast at the Feed Bag, the only real restaurant Scumble River could claim. Their other choice was McDonald's, and that would be filled with kids and families.

Quickly she dumped the dirty clothes from the suitcase into the hamper, then packed a few clean outfits. She left the rest of the luggage space for the food she planned on getting from the grocery store.

Skye had made record time, and it was only a few minutes after eight when she pulled into the Feed Bag. There was no sign of a squad car in the parking lot, but as Skye swung Trixie's Civic into a spot by the entrance, Wally's cruiser turned in.

Skye waited on the sidewalk, watching Wally as he strode

toward her. His powerful, well-muscled body moved with an easy grace, and as he came nearer, she could see his broad shoulders straining against his navy uniform shirt.

There was a look of contentment on his ruggedly handsome face that she didn't remember seeing before. And when he reached her a sensual gleam lit his brown eyes. "Darlin', what a wonderful surprise." He gathered her into his arms. "I thought I wouldn't get to see you until tonight." His mouth covered hers hungrily.

Carried away by her own response, she forgot they were in a very public place until Wally released her, and she found herself looking straight into the eyes of Father Burns, the Catholic priest from her church.

As her cheeks reddened, she managed to stammer, "Good morning, Father."

The priest murmured, "Good morning," back, but hurried past them to his car, his brow wrinkled.

"He usually stops to chat," Skye said to Wally.

"Maybe he was late for an appointment."

"Maybe." Skye wondered if the priest was upset she was dating Wally, a divorced non-Catholic. Or maybe it was just their public act of affection he disapproved of—though he usually wasn't the officious type.

Wally seemed unaware of Skye's concern. He took her hand and began kissing her fingers.

"We need to be more discreet. People will talk if we . . ." She trailed off, trying to stifle the dizzying electricity caused by Wally's lips on her skin.

"If we what?" He swung her into the circle of his arms. "Hug?" His mouth swooped down to capture hers. "Kiss?"

"Yes." Her voice was breathless. "Either. Both." She tried to move away.

"Then let them." He kept his arm around her waist, not letting her go. "We don't have anything to keep secret or be embarrassed about. I'm proud to let everyone in Scumble River see that we're together."

"It's just that . . ." Skye hesitated; she had almost said that Simon always said they should be circumspect. "We both have jobs where our public image is important."

Wally scowled. "That sounds like Reid talking."

"Well, maybe, but you see his point."

"No. He's just a tight ass." Wally grinned, then turned serious. "Look, I'm not saying we make love in the middle of the parking lot, but a kiss or a hug is not out of line for two people involved with each other. We don't have to hide our relationship and I don't want to. Are you ashamed to be seen with me?"

Skye looked into his warm brown eyes and shook her head. "Never."

"Good." He took her hand and led her into the restaurant. It had been redecorated in 1984, with lots of mauve and brass. Twenty years later, time was catching up with the interior. Rips in the vinyl seats had been repaired with duct tape, and smudges on the walls had been dabbed with a color that didn't quite match the original paint.

After they were settled into the back corner booth Wally had requested, Skye asked, "How did your stakeout go last night?"

"Interesting." Wally glanced at the menu, then closed it and put it aside. "You witnessed Frisco's affair with Margot, were told about his affair with Amber, and from what you overheard, there's also a chance he was sleeping with Esmé. Well, Whitney met him in the garage."

"So much for her period of mourning."

Wally's eyes glinted with amusement. "Yeah, her grief seems to be as real as her eyelashes."

"Did they . . . ?"

"Let's just say your mother may want to spray the backseat of her Olds with Lysol as soon as she gets home."

"They used my mother's car! Why?"

"It was one of the oldest parked there, which means it's got the biggest backseat. Plus she never locks it."

Skye smirked. "I can't wait to hear her reaction when you tell her that."

"I'm not the one who's going to tell her."

She opened her mouth to protest, but the waitress interrupted. Without thinking, Skye ordered the farmhand special: two eggs, two pieces of bacon, two sausage patties, hash browns, and two buttermilk pancakes. Immediately she felt embarrassed and chuckled weakly. "Guess I'm a lot hungrier than usual. They don't feed us much at the spa. I don't eat like this all the time."

Wally asked for biscuits and gravy, then waited for the waitress to fill their coffee cups and leave before saying, "You can eat anything you want. I promise I'm not judging you. It's not like I ordered the diet plate."

"No, but you're not . . ."

"Not as gorgeous as you are?" Wally captured her hand, and caressed it. "Why are you suddenly so insecure? Is it because we made love?"

Skye shrugged. She didn't know what had come over her. A few years back she had gotten off the diet roller coaster and decided to accept herself the way she was, and she had. Why was she suddenly having second thoughts?

"Maybe it's the spa. There certainly is an expectation there that everyone will do whatever it takes to be perfect—including but not limited to starvation and surgery."

Wally looked thoughtful. "But who gets to decide what's perfect? And is a perfect outside any guarantee of a perfect inside?"

"I know you're right, it's just hard to resist the propaganda. I hope Frannie doesn't succumb to it. Good thing we'll only be there one more day."

Wally nodded. "Except, of course, that only gives us one more day to find the real killer. Ms. Blossom still insists she did it, and her lawyer doesn't seem inclined to talk her out of her confession. I did speak to the ME again, and he said the dissection and tox screens definitely won't be done until Monday, but when he completed the external examination he found several injection sites between the eyebrows."

"That's probably from a Botox treatment. Margot mentioned that Esmé got them." Skye pressed her fingers against her temples, trying to remember all she wanted to tell Wally. "I'm not doing much better with my investigation. Although I did spot several more indications of digging, and I was waylaid by a reporter, so people are getting past the guards.

Simon claimed responsibility for one of the holes, but I saw at least three.

"Also, Amber and Elvis are definitely an item. I saw them together last night in one of the VIP cottages. She must have lied about him stalking her because of Margot's rules. And there was a light in another cottage, too."

"I'll stop by and ask the guards to tighten up the perimeter." Wally took a sip of coffee. "What are your plans for the rest of the day?"

"I have appointments with Ustelle, Kipp, Amber, and Dr. Burnett this afternoon."

"Good. Keep that fanny pack I gave you with you at all times and be careful."

"Yes, sir." Skye gave a mock salute.

They were silent as their food was served and they ate, but toward the end of the meal, Wally finally said, "You mentioned that Reid was treasure hunting? That doesn't seem like him."

"He's good with riddles and he got permission from Margot."

"Oh." Wally kept his gaze on his plate. "So, how did it go with Reid last night?"

Skye hesitated, torn by conflicting emotions. She hated discussing Simon with Wally, yet he had a right to know where he stood. Heaven knows she had made him wait long enough for her decision.

As she stalled for time by adding Sweet'N Low and cream to her freshly refilled coffee, an angry voice rose from the restaurant's entrance. "What do you mean you can't seat me immediately? I see at least three empty tables."

Skye saw a man in his late forties arguing with the Feed Bag's owner/hostess, Tomi Jackson. She was a tiny woman, although her platinum-blond beehive added several inches to her height, and although she seemed ageless, she had to be at least in her sixties, since she'd run the restaurant for as long as Skye could remember.

Tomi's voice was firm. "Those are for my regulars. It'll only be a short wait until one of the other tables is vacated."

Wally, who was facing the door, tensed, then as the angry

customer continued getting more and more abusive, he slid out of the booth.

Skye watched as he approached the man, who looked somewhat familiar. Next to Wally's six-foot plus height, the troublemaker appeared short, but his open shirt revealed a muscular chest covered with curly brown hair.

She couldn't hear Wally's words, spoken in a low soothing tone, but she heard the man's high-pitched reply as he poked Wally in the chest. "Take that badge off and step outside, and we'll see who leaves this dump and who gets to have breakfast with the chubby cutie in the back booth."

In a move too fast for Skye to really see, the troublemaker's hands were cuffed behind his back and Wally was marching him outside. The city police might need to wait until someone broke a law to handcuff him, but in Scumble River, an ounce of prevention was considered just fine on the scales of justice. No judge in Stanley County would ever convict a police officer of harassment for taking such a precaution.

Several minutes went by, and Skye was about to make sure everything was all right, when Wally rejoined her. There wasn't a mark on him. "What happened?" she asked.

"He decided to eat somewhere else."

"Did you arrest him?

Wally shook his head. "The only thing I could charge him with would be ignorance, and, unfortunately, that isn't against the law. I told him if he caused any more trouble in Scumble River, I'd throw his ass in jail and forget where I put the key."

While Wally was talking, Skye was thinking. Where had she seen that guy before? Finally it came to her. "You know, Whitney showed us a picture of her dad last night, and I think that might have been Rex Quinn."

"Shit."

"Sorry, I should have figured out who he was earlier." Skye bit her lip. "But he certainly didn't seem grief stricken."

"No. I think he was lining you up as wife number three," Wally teased.

"Yeah. I'm sure he'd go for a 'chubby cutie' after having a *Cosmo* cover girl."

"Maybe he's seen the error of his ways."

"Right." Skye changed the subject. "He must have just gotten in from Europe, if he was telling the truth about where he was when Esmé was killed."

"Great. Now I have to find him for questioning."

Skye grinned. "My guess is he'll go to the spa to pick up his daughter." She paused. "That is, as soon as he finds another place to have breakfast."

"Then I better be at the spa to greet him when he arrives." Wally stood up. "Are you going back too?"

"Not right away. First I'm stopping at the grocery store. I've got a good business going in black-market food. Though from what I've overheard, someone on the staff may be competing with me. I'd lower my prices, but no one's paying me to begin with."

Wally chuckled. "You can't make people stick to a diet like the one you've described if they don't want to."

"I think Margot and Dr. Burnett will have to rethink their mandatory diet if they want the spa to succeed."

"Where are you going after the grocery store?"

"To the Dooziers'." Skye followed Wally to the register. "The Elvis and Amber relationship bothers me. I just know she's going to hurt him. And to top it all off, rumor has it the Doozier clan has started their own Scumble River beauty mud business."

CHAPTER 19

In Hot Water

The Dooziers were hard to describe to anyone who hadn't grown up knowing what and who the Red Raggers were. The best comparison Skye could come up with was a group of wild dogs, intensely loyal to their pack but with no empathy toward outsiders. They weren't known for being the sharpest knives in the drawer, but they did have a certain instinct for finding and taking advantage of those people whose blades were even duller.

Earl Doozier, Elvis's older brother, was the patriarch of the Red Raggers. He and his clan always seemed to turn up whenever there was trouble. They didn't necessarily make the first move, but they never missed an opportunity to contribute to the commotion.

Skye had established a good relationship with Earl through working with his many children, sisters, brothers, nieces, and nephews in her job as a school psychologist, but for the most part the Dooziers kept to themselves—except when they were running some con on the out-of-towners.

As Skye drove north on Kinsman, she was surprised to see orange traffic cones blocking off the street. She hadn't heard of any road work going on, and usually if one of the major thoroughfares leading to I-55 was going to be closed, the story made both the paper and the local radio.

Once Skye saw that the cones were rerouting traffic directly to the Dooziers' dirt driveway, understanding dawned. How else would the Dooziers get customers? They didn't exactly live in the middle of town or on a busy street. In fact, they often took down the street signs so people couldn't find their house, which was probably for the best.

The Dooziers' property was almost as hard to describe as its owners. Dried-up weeds lined the cracked sidewalk, and dead grass showed between the carcasses of junked cars and shells of old appliances littering the yard.

The house's color was indeterminate. It might have been white at one time, but now the siding resembled the interior sections of a cardboard box. Long years of neglect made it seem about as stable as a house made of playing cards.

A barking dog was nowhere in sight, but the odor of the canine's recent visit to the front lawn hovered in the air.

Only one thing had changed since Skye's last visit. A crooked and misspelled sign painted on the back of a flattened carton read:

MAGIC MUD
GAURANTEED TO STOP THE SIGNS OF AGING
YOUR VERY OWN FONTANE OF YOUTH
$5.00 FOR ONE JAR/TWO FOR $10.00

Skye appeared to be the only customer. She had barely gotten out of the Civic when Earl rushed out of the house, letting the front door slam shut in his haste. He was wearing sweats and a flannel shirt with the arms cut off above the elbow. Even though it was November, temperatures remained in the seventies.

Earl was skinny, except for the bowling-ball-sized potbelly that hung over the elastic waist of his pants. His greasy brown hair formed a horseshoe around the back of his head, leaving a cereal-bowl-sized bald spot.

As he loped toward Skye, a wide smile appeared on his face, revealing several stumps and missing teeth. "Miz Skye. What're you doin' here? I heared you were spending the weekend at that fancy new spa."

"I am, but I heard you had better mud than they do, so I

came to check it out." Skye allowed herself to be hugged, trying not to make contact with any of the many tattoos covering his bare arms. They had a scaly feeling that reminded her of handling a snake. She knew tattoos usually felt smooth, but Earl's were as different as he was.

"Maybe you could sell it for us. Instead of bein' an Avon Lady, you could be a Doozier Doll." A crafty look appeared in Earl's brown eyes. "You know what they say. Strike while the bug is close."

"Gee, thanks, Earl." As Skye tried to sort out his meaning, remove herself from his embrace, and not agree to go door-to-door with Magic Mud, all at the same time she flashbacked to Wednesday morning when she had agreed to go to the spa in hopes of meeting a prince or a duke or an earl. *Earl* Doozier had not been what she'd had in mind. "But you know how busy I am fixing up my new house."

"Sure. Sure. But why do you want to see our mud? You don't got no wrinkles."

A high-pitched voice suggestive of someone who had sucked on a helium balloon screeched, "Earl Doozier, if brains were taxed, you'd get a refund."

Striding toward them, carrying a box of clinking mason jars, was Glenda Doozier, the family matriarch. From her grimy feet shod in gold stiletto-sandals, to her dyed blond hair with two-inch black roots and eyes heavily framed in black eyeliner and false lashes, she was the embodiment of an ideal Red Ragger woman.

Earl rushed over and took the box from his wife's hands. "Now, honey pie, how can you say that? You know we don't pay no taxes."

She ignored her husband and glared at Skye. "We ain't doing nothin' illegal. You just get off our property."

"Why, Glenda, I never said you were," Skye assured the volatile woman. Dealing with Glenda was like handling a snake; you never knew when it would bite.

"If rich city women want to spend their money on mud, there ain't no reason it can't be our mud instead of that fancy pants place at the edge of town."

"Except," Skye paused to carefully word what she had to

say. "Except, the spa mud is actually sterilized before they use it on people. Do you do that?"

As quick as a boa attacking a hapless bunny, Glenda grabbed a bottle from the box Earl was holding, twisted open the lid, scooped out a handful, and smeared it on Skye's cheek. "See, ours is just as good as theirs. We may not have special silver colored towels and a fancy bathtub, or a private underground room, but nobody's died in our mud bath."

Skye was only half listening to Glenda's sale pitch as she rummaged around in her purse for a tissue, but the last part of the woman's spiel caught Skye's attention.

Wary after already having mud spread on one side of her face, Skye asked, "You have an actual mud bath? You don't just sell the jars?" This she had to see.

"Sure, Miz Skye." Earl plunked the box he was holding down on the ground and took her arm. "Come on. I'll show you. It's out back."

In the many times Skye had visited the Dooziers she had never been in their backyard, and she was a little nervous of breaking that precedent, but she followed Earl. Glenda trailed behind, muttering.

They rounded the corner, pausing as Earl unlatched the metal gate. Another hand-lettered sign read:

> $25 FOR 1 HOUR
> TOWEL EXTREE
> DON'T PET THE DOG!!!

Earl led them across the backyard toward a small metal shed—the type used to store lawn mowers and snowblowers. As they neared, a dog started to bark. Skye looked in the direction of the yapping and saw a hound dog standing in a pen baying at them.

"Don't pay Lady no mind. She's just sayin' howdy." Earl kept hold of Skye's arm, not stopping until they stood in front of the shed. Skye had a bad feeling, but forced herself not to turn on her heel and run away. Earl would never hurt her, of course, but Glenda was another story.

With a flourish worthy of Ralph Lauren at the beginning of a fashion show, Earl flung open the metal door, yelling, "Ta da!"

The lighting was dim, provided by a single Coleman lantern, but Skye could make out a children's inflatable pool filled with watery mud resting on a rough plywood floor. Off to the side was a pile of thin, gray-white towels and an eight-track player on an old plastic picnic table.

Glenda finally caught up with them, having been hampered by her four-inch heels sinking into the lawn, and declared breathlessly, "See. We mighten have snazzy tile floors and deluxe marble tubs, but we got everything they got that's important. Even music."

"Yes, you do." Skye nodded and stepped away, determined to make it back to the car without ending up in the pool of mud. "I can see you've worked really hard." As she hurried across the yard, she asked over her shoulder, "Has anyone taken one of your mud baths yet?"

Earl trotted up to her and undid the gate's latch. "Nah. We can't figure out why nobody wants to give it a whirl."

"Well," Skye shrugged, relieved to be on the other side of the fence, "you know what they say. You can lead a horse to water—"

Earl interrupted her, "But how?"

She shrugged again. "That's a good question." She kept on walking until she arrived at her Civic. She was anxious to leave, but had one last thing to take care of. "I saw Elvis working at the spa. Did he get a job with a construction company?"

"Not full-time. They just calls him when they needs him."

"Oh. Uh, did he mention liking a girl who works at the spa?" Skye had no idea where she was going with this, but the train had left the station and she was on board—with or without a ticket.

"Yeah, name of Amber." Earl wrinkled his brow. "What you gettin' at, Miz Skye?"

"Well, she's a lot older than Elvis, at least five or six years, and she's sort of, uh . . ." Skye couldn't exactly come out and say that Amber was richer, more sophisticated, and smarter.

"Ain't she good enough for Elvis?"

"That's not it. It's just that . . . you know how the city folks come out here to hunt, but they just leave the animal they shot. They don't skin it or dress the meat. They only do it for the thrill of the pursuit, not to take it home to eat. Understand?"

Earl's gaze went flat. "You're sayin' this girl is playin' with Elvis and she's goin' break his heart?"

Skye nodded. "That would be my guess."

"Gotcha. I'll talk to Elvis tonight."

"Good." Skye put her hand on the car door handle, ready to make her escape.

But Earl said, "Before you go, could you look at somethin' for me?"

Skye glanced longingly at the driver's seat, so close yet so far, then said, "What's that, Earl? I really don't know much about the spa business."

"This is for school." Earl dug in his pants pocket and pulled out a crumpled sheet of paper. "Junior and Cletus missed school on Monday, and when they went back on Tuesday they were told they need a written excuse. I been workin' on it all weekend, but I'm not much on writin', so would you look at it and see if it's okay?"

"Sure." Skye held out her hand. "Let me see it."

Earl smoothed out the blue-lined notebook paper and handed it to Skye.

She read:

Deer Techer,
*   Please exkuse Junior and Cletus for missing skool.*
We forgot to get the Sunday paper off the porch, and
when we found it Monday, we thought it was Sunday
and went back to bed.
*   Earl Doozier*

Skye bit the inside of her cheek to keep from giggling, but quickly sobered when she saw Earl's serious expression.

Should she let the boys turn in this excuse, or was there a
way to write one for Earl without insulting him?

Before she could come up with a graceful way to suggest
he let her write the note, Earl said, "You know, if you don't
mind, Miz Skye, it might be best if you just wrote it and let
me sign the paper. After all, I don't want to embarrass the
boys."

"I don't mind at all." Skye whipped out a pad of paper
from her purse. "I'm sure your note would be fine, but better safe than—"

Earl interrupted her again, "Than punched in the nose."

Skye nodded, wrote the note, then made her escape,
knowing she had learned something important, but unable to
put her finger on what it was.

CHAPTER 20

Pour Body Oil on Troubled Waters

It was quarter to eleven when Skye arrived back at the mansion. Getting past the reporters and TV cameras at the gate was a hair-raising experience. There had been only a few reporters gathered when she left the spa early that morning, but now they were three or four deep, and as aggressive as alligators at feeding time.

As soon as she walked into the lobby hauling her suitcase full of prohibited goodies, one of the new security guards checked her room key, then offered to carry her bag. Although it was incredibly heavy, and she would have loved to have him haul it up the steps for her, she declined, afraid he would hear the clinking of the cans or smell the freshly baked bread.

Her morning dizziness had gone away as soon as she had eaten breakfast, but her muscles continued to ache, even more so after carrying fifty pounds of groceries up a long flight of stairs. Panting, she collapsed on the bed and thought about the weekend. She really hadn't seen that much of May, Loretta, Bunny, Frannie, or even Trixie since the first night. Of course, it had only been seventy-one hours, but with all that had happened, it felt as if she'd been at the spa for a month.

She was just as happy not to have to talk to May and Bunny yet; neither would be happy to learn how things had turned out between her and Simon. However, she missed talking to Trixie and Loretta, and she was vaguely worried about Frannie.

Skye knew the teen was looking for a story, but where was she keeping herself and who was she with? Skye hoped it wasn't with Whitney. On one hand, it would be natural for the two girls to hang out together; they were the youngest guests at the spa. But even though they were only a few years apart chronologically, Whitney was decades older than Frannie in worldly experience. Besides, Skye didn't get a good vibe from the poor little rich girl.

Noting that it was now nearly eleven, Skye stowed the forbidden fruits of her shopping trip under the bed, changed into sweats and a T-shirt, and twisted her hair into ponytail. Then, after putting on Wally's fanny pack and making sure the door locked behind her, she ran to her appointment.

Ustelle was waiting for her with a surprise. The Nordic beauty waved Skye excitedly from next door to the facial room. "Miss, I have arranged a special treat for you." Ustelle ushered Skye into the room. "Because I was late for you on your first day, and then you had to miss your mud bath, I ask Miss Margot if I can give you an Aqua Float massage along with your facial."

"Oh." Skye looked suspiciously at the concrete coffin-sized box in the middle of the room. "Why is it so special?"

"It's brand new. No one else is trained to use it, but I was taught in my last job, since that salon had one."

"Where was that?" Skye touched the thick pad covering the top of the box. It was firm. Where did the aqua or the float part fit into it?

"Miami," Ustelle said over her shoulder as she lined up bottles and tubes. "I'll step out of the room, while you take off your T-shirt and shoes."

"That's all?" Skye still had no idea how the Aqua Float worked.

Ustelle nodded and disappeared out the door. Skye took off her shirt and Keds and waited. Ustelle was back in a few seconds, and helped Skye lie down on the pad covering the Aqua Float apparatus. Ustelle pulled a sheet, blanket, and heavy pad over Skye, covering her from her feet to the tops of her breasts.

Skye started to feel claustrophobic. "How does this work?"

"Just lie back and enjoy." Ustelle spread a thin, cool layer of exfoliate on Skye's face, neck, and upper chest. "This needs to stay on for ten minutes. Would you like some music?"

"No, thanks." Skye wanted to talk, not rumba. "Did you like Miami?"

"Very much." Ustelle smiled widely, revealing perfect teeth.

"Why did you leave?"

"The spa I was working for closed down." Ustelle was silent until she wiped the exfoliate from Skye's face with a cotton ball, then applied a light mask.

"Oh, why was that?"

"There's lots of competition, especially among the day spas." Ustelle looked at her watch. "Ten minutes for this step as well."

"Was that your first job in the U.S.?"

"Yes. I had only been finished with my training a few months when Carlos comes to the place I'm working and hires me on the spot." Ustelle wiped away the mask with more cotton balls, then said, "Now for the eye mask."

"Are you still in touch with Mr. er . . . ?" Skye trailed off, hoping Ustelle would feel obligated to fill in the blanks.

The masseuse hesitated, then supplied, "LaFever. He's still in Miami." Ustelle spread a thin layer of clear gel under Skye's eyes and over the lids.

"So he was just your employer, not your boyfriend?" Skye asked.

"Who knows with men, but we need to work where the pay is best. You understand?" Ustelle spoke in a "that's all I'm going to say" tone of voice. "Now I'll switch on the Aqua Float, and you relax while your eye mask gets rid of all your little lines and dark circles."

Lines! Circles! Wait a minute, what did Ustelle mean by that? Skye seethed as the pad she was lying on was lowered into the concrete box. *Was she implying that I have wrinkles?* Suddenly the mat began to gently pitch and sway. The motion felt wonderful, and Skye almost fell asleep pondering what she had learned. She needed to write everything down before she forgot something important. She knew there were clues in what she had been told, but what were they?

Ustelle hadn't sounded confident when she said Carlos's last name. Could she be lying about that, and about still being in touch with him? Maybe he was the one she was calling all the time. Skye understood being in love, but making multiple calls to a lover while you were working was a bit much.

For once Ustelle reappeared all too soon, shutting off the Aqua Float and wiping the mask from Skye's eyes. Before she finished, she tried to sell Skye the products that had been used, but the three-hundred-dollar tab for the three tubes made it easy to say no, thanks.

On her way out, Skye asked, "By the way, what CD did you have set for Ms. Gates's mud bath?"

Ustelle tilted her head. "None. There is supposed to be complete silence. The whole point of the bath is to feel as if you've gone back to the womb. No CD players are allowed in that treatment area."

Back in her room, Skye phoned Wally's office and left a message on his voice mail asking him to check out Carlos LaFever of Miami. She also reported that the CD player she had heard at the crime scene was not a normal part of the mud bath setup. Since Ustelle said Esmé hadn't been carrying a CD player when she walked into the treatment room, the killer must have set it up to cover any noise Esmé might make when she was being held under the mud.

Taking all this into consideration, Skye had two questions for Wally: did the player have any fingerprints, and what was the name of the CD?

It was close to noon after she finished her call, and Skye didn't want to waste time by pretending to eat in the dining room. Instead, she pulled the suitcase out from under the bed and filled a large tote bag with lunch from her stash, top-ping the food with a pad of paper and pen. Earlier she had filled a thermal carrier with ice from the bucket and stored the items that needed to be kept cool in that. Now she grabbed the thermal bag in one hand and the tote in another and hurried to the solarium.

Sun shone through the new glass, and Skye was im-pressed that Margot had managed to find someone to replace the shattered window during the holiday weekend. She must have offered top dollar to entice someone from their turkey dinners and football games.

Skye headed toward her favorite spot, but tensed as she heard the faint sound of music. Taking a step forward, she relaxed as she spotted Loretta sitting on a couch with an iPod hanging around her neck and food spread out on the table. The lawyer wore a bright orange crop-style sweat suit that Skye had seen in last month's *Vogue*. Her skin was makeup free, but as smooth and glowing as an ebony statue. She was bent over a legal pad, scribbling furiously.

When she paused to read what she had written, she no-ticed Skye, turned off the iPod, and said, "If it isn't my friend, the famous disappearing detective."

"Very funny." Skye punched her lightly on the arm, plopped herself in a chair, and reached into her bag. "In case you've missed it, a lot's been happening in my life."

"A lot is always happening in your life. That's what makes you interesting." Loretta snatched the loaf of fresh bakery bread before Skye even got it onto the table. "Where and when did you get this?"

"From the local grocery store, this morning just before coming here."

Loretta used the knife Skye produced to cut off four pieces and gave Skye two. "Why were you in town?"

"I needed clothes, food, and to check out the Dooziers." Skye took out a plastic squeeze bottle of mustard and a package of deli ham from the thermal bag.

"I bet you saw Wally, too."

"Well . . ." Skye bit into her sandwich and chewed, giv-ing herself a little time to think before replying. She couldn't claim to be working with him on the investigation since the murderer had already confessed. Maybe Wally was right. It was time to stop trying to hide their relationship. "You'd win that wager."

"Spill." Loretta wiped her fingers and added, "I never got to talk to you after the big Spike revelation, but I want to hear now."

Skye filled her in, up to the moment at the truck stop when she had refused to let Simon drive her home.

"How did you get back?" Loretta took a sip from her can of Coke. "Why didn't you call me?"

"No offense, but you're sharing a room with my mother. You would have been the last person I called." Skye ate a chip. "And don't you dare tell her any of this."

"I swear." Loretta crossed her heart. "Believe me, I don't want to be the one to inform May that you are turning down Mr. Perfect for Mr. Hot. That is what's happening, isn't it?"

"That's how it seems, but I just don't know." Without thinking, Skye unwrapped a Hostess Ding Dong from Loretta's stash. She never ate so much junk food at home. Great! She would be the only one in history who went to a spa and gained weight. "Up until last night, I thought maybe Simon and I could get back what we had, but his stance hasn't changed one iota. He was so arrogant and stubborn, and still insisting I should just trust him."

"And let's face it, the sexual chemistry between you and Wally is off the charts."

"I thought it was just physical attraction between us, too, but now that I'm spending more time with Wally, there's a lot more to it." Skye popped open a can of Diet Coke and poured it into the glass of ice she had prepared in her room. "I like not having to be *so* smart and *so* sophisticated all the time. And I like that Wally considers me an intellectual equal, and that he isn't always perfect."

"Sounds a lot like what I love about Vince." Loretta peeled open a Kit Kat bar and broke off a piece. "He's easy to be with. I can relax. He knows I'm smart, so I don't have to always be proving it. And . . ."

Skye lifted an eyebrow. "And?"

"And he's fantastic in bed."

Skye put her fingers in her ears. "I don't want to hear about my brother having sex."

"Okay." Loretta licked the chocolate from the wafer. "Then tell me about you and Wally having sex."

"No. Some things are not meant to be shared."

"Then you *have* been to bed with him. Trixie was right."

Skye wrinkled her brow. "Since when did you and Trixie become such good friends?"

"Since you haven't been around this weekend. What did you think we were going to do? Sit in our rooms and contemplate our navels?" Loretta looked at her watch and started to pack up the food. "I like Trixie and Frannie."

"Really?" Skye asked. "And have you bonded with May? How about Bunny?"

"May is great as long as the topic of weddings and grand-children can be avoided. And Bunny is a hoot."

"So Scumble Riverites aren't as bad as you thought they'd be?" Skye remembered when she had first discovered that her brother and Loretta were dating, but keeping it a secret because Loretta was convinced the town would never accept a biracial relationship.

"Well . . ." Loretta finished putting the food away and started wiping the tabletop with a napkin. "I'm sure not everyone will be as nice as your friends."

"That's true anywhere. Admit it. You were wrong."

"Maybe." As the two women finished cleaning up their trash, Loretta asked, "Don't you find it odd that the staff doesn't seem to be lacking energy, if they're eating only the spa sanctioned food?"

"I noticed that." Skye thought about it some more. "I did hear a couple of them complaining that someone was gauging them and they were sick of forking over so much money. Maybe someone's selling Little Debbie snack cakes."

"There is definitely something odd going on around here." Loretta got up and deposited the debris into a trash can. "I was scheduled for a seaweed wrap like the one you got the first day, and Ustelle was so late I went looking for her."

"And I bet she was on the phone."

"Yes, she was having a whispered conversation in Spanish, yet earlier, I heard her tell Frisco she doesn't speak the language."

"Well, she could have said that just to get rid of Frisco." Skye wiped crumbs off the table with a paper napkin. "I know he's a hunk, but he flirts with anything that moves, and I'll bet that can get pretty tiresome if you're a fellow employee and stuck around him all the time."

"Someone needs to smack him upside the head." Loretta shook her head, then asked, "So, who do you think Ustelle was talking to?"

"I'd say the media, but she was making mysterious calls even before the murder, and since she was speaking Spanish, it was probably Carlos."

As they both started toward the door, Loretta said, "So how did you get back to the spa last night?"

"The waitress ended up giving me a ride. And as it turned out, I'm glad I waited around because I heard two out-of-towners talking about Magic Mud."

"Miracle Mud," Loretta corrected.

"Nope. Magic. And guess who's selling it?"

Loretta tapped her chin with a perfectly manicured fingernail, then shrugged. "I have no idea."

"The Dooziers."

"The Dooziers?"

Skye understood Loretta wasn't asking who they were— the attorney was well acquainted with the clan—so she explained about the mud, then described her visit to their mud bath and how the shed was arranged. She ended with, "So Glenda sticks her fake boobs in my face and says, 'Except for those stupid silver towels, we got everything that fancy pants spa has, even music.' And she points to an eight-track player." Skye was laughing so hard it took her a few minutes to notice that Loretta had her attorney face on. "What? You don't think that was funny?"

"Yeah. Hysterical. But how did the Dooziers know enough about the spa's mud bath treatment room to duplicate it . . . even in their own oddball style?"

Skye opened her mouth to reply, but realized she had no idea. Even if Elvis had worked on the construction of the room, how would he know about the silvery towels? They had to be one of the last touches Margot put out just before the guests arrived.

CHAPTER 21

Fight Tooth
and Nail Polish

Skye mulled over Loretta's observation as she walked to her next treatment. Not only did the Dooziers know about the towels, they also knew about the music. Ustelle had been emphatic that the CD player was not a regular feature of that room, which meant it had been put out only minutes before the murder was committed.

It wasn't that Skye didn't believe one of the Doozier clan could kill someone; she just thought they'd do it in a much less subtle fashion. A blast from a shotgun would be more their style.

When Skye neared Amber's treatment room, she heard Amber's shrill soprano followed by Frannie's deeper alto. Skye frowned. She had been worried about Frannie hanging out with Whitney, but she didn't think Amber was any better. She definitely had to speak to Frannie about hanging around with either of those two. She hoped Frannie was just spending time with both Amber and Whitney in order to investigate her story for the school newspaper, but she needed to make sure.

As Skye paused, thinking about Frannie's motives, she heard Amber talking. "So I get this really cool La Perla bra, and I put it on and say to her, 'How does it look?' And she says, 'Just like it did on the hanger.'"

Frannie's reply was full of sympathy. "No matter how

you look, someone always manages to say something mean."

"Why did I even ask my stepmother's opinion?" Amber's tone was angry. "I knew what she was like."

"I guess you hoped you were wrong."

There was a silence, and Skye decided it was a good time to go in. Amber was sitting slumped on a black leather director's chair. This treatment room was a bit larger than the others Skye had been in—more the size of a spacious bedroom than a walk-in closet. Two chairs with foot basins were positioned side by side, and two with small glass tables in front of them were located across the room. One entire wall was covered with shelving that contained small bottles filled with every imaginable color, from the palest cream to the darkest black.

Sitting in one of the pedicure chairs, her legs calf-deep in water, was Frannie.

She waved when Skye came in and said, "Amber, this is Ms. D., my *counselor*. The one I was telling you about."

Amber swished her strawberry blond ponytail and said with a small huff, "I know Miss Denison, Frannie. She interviewed me after Esmé was murdered."

"Hi, Frannie, Amber." Skye looked between both girls, wondering what was going on. Why had Frannie emphasized that Skye was her counselor? And wasn't it interesting that Amber was so competitive that she had to claim knowing Skye even as a murder suspect, rather than letting Frannie be one up on her?

Amber pointed to the other pedicure chair. "Ma'am, if you'll take a seat, I'll get you started soaking while I do Frannie's polish."

"Sure." Skye climbed carefully into the slightly elevated seat and eased her feet into the hot, soapy water. "Ah, this feels heavenly."

"Yes, a lot of the ladies have said this is the best part of the spa." Amber pulled up a low stool until she sat directly in front of Skye, dipped her hand into a jar, and worked the lime salt wash into her feet and up to her knees.

The smell was delicious, and Skye joked, "This makes me want a margarita."

Amber's tongue swept her lips. "Too bad there's no alcohol allowed at the spa."

"Among other things." Skye laughed. "Like chocolate and bread and soda and coffee."

Frannie shot Skye a glance that clearly said, "Liar, liar, pants on fire."

"Don't forget sex." Amber giggled. "It's banned, too, except during the coed weekends, and then it's allowed only among the guests."

Skye almost reminded Amber of her own tryst with Elvis the night before, but decided it was none of her business. She had spoken to Earl, and the Elvis/Amber situation was now in his hands.

Amber rinsed Skye's feet and legs, rolled her stool back, and took a pair of terrycloth booties from a steam cabinet. She slid Skye's foot into a bootie. "Is that too hot?"

"No, it feels great." After the second bootie was put on, Skye leaned back and closed her eyes, hoping the girls would forget she was there and talk freely.

Beneath her lashes, Skye saw Amber wheel her stool over to Frannie and take the teen's feet from the water. She quickly dried them and put them on a rolled towel, then got up to empty the basin of water.

Skye felt a light touch on her hand and looked down. Frannie had slipped a tiny piece of paper into her palm. She checked out Amber's location—the manicurist was washing out the tub—so Skye opened the small square. On it Frannie had printed:

Don't mention the school newspaper.

Skye slipped the paper into her pocket and nodded slightly to Frannie. She felt a bit relieved. She had figured that Frannie was investigating her story, going undercover rather than actually befriending Amber or Whitney, but it was good to know for sure.

Amber turned from the sink and pointed to the wall of polish. "Have you decided on a color?"

"I was thinking Ballet Pink."

Amber shrugged. "That's so yesterday."

"What would you pick?"

"Bahamas Mama is hot right now." Amber held up a small bottle of orangey red.

"Okay. I'll take that one."

"Good choice." Amber nodded approvingly. "Men love this one."

"Uh, good." Frannie's tone was doubtful.

Skye tried to imagine Frannie's boyfriend Justin noticing what color the girl's toenails were, but couldn't quite tune in that picture. She watched as Amber expertly painted three of Frannie's toenails, then jump slightly when the wall phone buzzed. Amber jerked to her feet and hurried to pick it up. "Yes?"

Her voice and mannerisms changed from brash to apprehensive. "No. I can't. No. No. Well, okay, but only for a few minutes." She turned back to Frannie and Skye. "Sorry, I'll be right back."

After she left, Skye said, "I sure wish I knew who she was meeting." If Amber hadn't appeared so uneasy, Skye would have thought the call was from Elvis.

"Yeah, it's not as if either one of us could follow her without leaving a trail." Frannie scrunched up her face. "I could see if Miss Bunny is in our room. If she is, she could try and find Amber."

"No." Skye shook her head.

Frannie's expression was unreadable. "I thought you liked Miss Bunny."

"Bunny's good at a lot of things, but subtlety is not one of them."

"Maybe being open is better." Frannie seemed unwilling to let go of the subject.

"Sometimes it is." Skye suddenly became conscious that Frannie wasn't relating to her the way she usually did.

"Like if Simon had told you the truth about Spike right away?"

"Right." Skye wasn't naïve enough to ask Frannie how she knew about Skye's personal life. Somehow everyone in town had heard the story almost as soon as Simon returned from California last August. And since Frannie and Bunny were rooming together, no doubt Bunny had immediately shared the whole Spike revelation with Frannie.

"Why aren't you taking Simon back, since you know Spike's his sister?" The teen's words rushed out in a single breath.

Skye was momentarily surprised that Frannie knew she wasn't getting back together with Simon, but she quickly figured out that Simon had probably told his mother, and Bunny had told Frannie. Now the only question was how much of her personal life was appropriate to share with the teen. Finally, she said, "It's just too late."

"Why?"

She knew Frannie was extremely close to Simon—her dad worked for him and Simon treated Frannie like a little sister—so she didn't want to say anything negative about him. "There are some junctures in our lives when everything has to be right. The right person, the right time, the right place, and if one of those pieces doesn't fit, the moment passes. When Simon didn't explain about Spike to me right away, our moment—the one when we could have been together—moved on."

Frannie was silent for quite a while, then she asked, "Can you ever get to that moment again?"

Skye shrugged. "I wish I knew."

"I like Chief Boyd."

"Good," Skye answered cautiously, leery of where Frannie might be going with the conversation.

"But he's not the right guy for you."

"Why?"

Frannie shrugged. "I just know."

Relieved to let the subject drop, Skye nodded, then said, "So, how's your story coming along?"

Frannie glanced at the door. There was still no sign of the manicurist. "I'm not telling anyone that I'm the coeditor of the school newspaper, so please don't say anything."

Skye put up her hand in the traditional Girl Scout pledge. "I swear." She nudged Frannie. "Now you swear to come to me right away if you find something. No investigating anything dangerous by yourself."

"Okay." Frannie held her middle three fingers together and promised. "Besides, the killer is in jail. I'm just trying to figure out where the treasure's hidden."

Skye felt bad letting everyone think the murderer had confessed. She'd be happy once the weekend was over and she could tell them the truth. And she'd be really happy if she could figure out the true killer's identity before then.

"What's your take on Amber and Whitney?" Skye asked. "Are they friends, or not? Whitney seems to think Amber isn't rich enough to be her friend anymore, but isn't her dad giving her presents again?"

"Yeah, but an occasional pair of designer jeans or even a car is not the same as a trust fund or a twenty-thousand-dollar-a-month allowance." Frannie twirled a strand of hair. "Plus when Amber's father left, and she and her mom had to move, Amber and Whitney didn't keep in touch."

"Right, four years apart is a long time."

"That's just it." Frannie leaned down and patted her toenails. When no polish came off on her finger she got up. "They just got back in contact over the Internet a few months ago. Now they meet again in person, and instead of being equals, one is an employee."

"Right."

"But Amber seems to have the upper hand. Isn't that weird?"

"It could be that Amber's been on her own, and feels more like an adult than Whitney, who still lives at home," Skye offered. "Or maybe she has something on Whitney that she's holding over the girl."

"What girl?" Amber dashed into the treatment room, flushed, frenetic, and much chattier than before she left. "What are we talking about?"

"A girl in my class who seems to be able to make everyone do what she wants," Frannie blurted out.

"Ah, a queen bee, like I was." As she finished Frannie's

pedicure, Amber talked about her high school triumphs. "I had the cutest little BMW convertible. I only let the cool girls ride in it. If I wore something, then everyone wanted it, but I made sure whatever I picked was really expensive and hard to find."

Frannie's face was expressionless, but her gaze kept searching out Skye, asking silently what was up. Finally she blurted, "Didn't you care that you were hurting other girls' feelings?"

"Nope." Amber shook her head. "High school was the best time in my life."

Skye requested Razzle Dazzle Rose for both her finger-nails and toenails, and while Amber was working on her asked, "How long have you been doing this?"

"Not long." Amber stroked a second coat of polish on Skye's toenails. "My dad refused to pay my college tuition. Would you believe he suggested I go to junior college? But I said I'd rather flip burgers at McDonalds."

"What did you do?" Skye asked.

"This and that. I finally found a job as a go-fer. My em-ployer knew Miss Margot and asked her to help me. She arranged for me to take the classes I needed to become a makeup artist, which, if I had to work, I thought would at least be a cool job."

"That was nice of her," Frannie commented.

"She didn't do it out of the goodness of her heart." Amber stripped the terrycloth gloves from Skye's hands and worked lotion into them. "I had to sign a contract that says I'll work here for seven years."

"Seven years!" Frannie exclaimed. "That's forever."

"Yes, it is. I'll be old by then, nearly thirty."

Skye forced herself not to slap the girl. Imagine thinking thirty was old. Instead she asked, "So you do makeup, wax-ing, manicures, and pedicures? That seems like a lot."

"Well, Kipp also does makeup, and Ustelle also does waxes, so we can help each other out, but then we all have something only we do. I'm the only one who does manis and pedis. No one but Kipp does hair, and only Ustelle does the wraps and massages."

"How do you like working here so far?" Skye asked.

"It's okay. But what I really want to do is work with models and actresses."

"Margot hopes to attract those sorts of people to the spa, doesn't she?" Skye said.

"Maybe." Amber shrugged. "But I can't see really famous people coming here. Just the has-beens like Esmé."

"What happens if the spa doesn't make it and they close down?" Skye asked.

"Then my contract is null and void, and I'm free."

Skye glanced at Frannie, who lifted an eyebrow. Amber had a lot to gain if the spa went bust. Could she be behind the pre-opening vandalism? Was she trying to shut down the business? Had she gotten desperate when that didn't work, and tried to gain her freedom by killing the owner, only to murder poor Esmé by mistake?

CHAPTER 22

Strike While the Curling Iron Is Hot

Due to Amber's mysterious fifteen-minute disappearance, Skye was late for her hair appointment with Kipp Gardner. Of the spa's professional staff, he was the one she'd had the least contact with. She had seen him only once—the day Esmé was murdered, when all he could do was scream.

The salon was located in one of the new buildings next to the gym, and built to look like a stand-alone hair salon. Picture windows bracketed the glass door and a silver green awning jutted over the front entrance.

Hating to be late, Skye approached the salon at a jog, then skidded to a stop when she heard voices. The door was propped open—it was another surprisingly warm day for November—and she paused to listen, thinking how easy it was to eavesdrop around the spa. People didn't bother to lower their voices or close their doors. Inhibitions seemed to peel away like exfoliated skin.

She cocked her head. Who was in there with Kipp? The high-pitched voice sounded somehow false. The conversation seemed strangely similar to the ones she'd been having with the other professional employees.

"Where did you work before coming here?"

Kipp's tenor answered, "Here, there, and everywhere. I don't like to be tied down, that is unless there's a bed and a whip involved."

"Oh, you naughty boy." The voice sounded almost like an alto trying to speak like a soprano. "Did you know Margot and her husband before coming here?"

"No. One of my clients was a friend of hers and recommended me." Kipp paused, then said, "Look up. I want to get your bottom lashes."

"I heard that there were quite a few problems that might have delayed the spa's opening. Who do you think was behind them?"

"This is an old building. There are bound to be spirits who aren't happy with new occupants." Kipp's answer sounded rehearsed.

"Do you think there really is a hidden treasure?"

"I've had a look and didn't find anything, but I was never very good at riddles," Kipp answered, then directed, "Okay, close your eyes, and I'll give you a quick spritz of setting spray so your makeup will last longer."

"Phew. It's so hot in here, I think it'll melt off before I even leave."

"Sorry. The heat is on and I can't get it off. Margot assures me they're working on it. Just one of those glitches. Shall I open the door wider?"

Skye took that as her cue to go in. As she stepped over the threshold she gasped. She was looking straight into the eye-shadowed and mascaraed gaze of Justin Boward, Frannie's boyfriend and the coeditor of the high school newspaper. Skye knew he was a relentless reporter, but she would have never guessed he would go as far as putting on a dress to pursue a story.

Justin sat in the slightly reclined salon chair, holding on to the arms as if he were about to be shot into space. He was wearing a shoulder-length blond wig, pink silk blouse, and a pink and green paisley skirt. On his feet were the biggest pair of pink ballet flats Skye had ever seen, and she wore size nine herself.

Before Skye could react, Kipp turned and asked, "Do you two know each other?"

Skye hastily found her voice. "I thought so at first, but I must have been mistaken." She held out her hand. "Hi,

I'm Ms. Denison. I work at Scumble River High. Do you attend?"

"Yes. It's nice to finally meet you. I'm Justine, Justin Boward's sister. He's told me how nice and understanding you are."

"How sweet of Justin to say so. He's usually not so full of compliments." Skye bit her lip to stop the giggles that were threatening to burst out. "I haven't seen you around the spa this weekend, Justine. Are you a guest?"

"Uh, not exactly. But my friend, Frannie, told me how wonderful everything was, and I decided to see if I could get an appointment." Justin stared at Skye, daring her to comment. "I have a special date and I wanted to have my makeup done by an expert."

"Right," Kipp interrupted. "And since I had an opening, the receptionist snuck her in. Don't tell Margot. She doesn't want to accept day appointments. But I think it's better than sitting around with nothing to do."

"No problem." Skye winked at Kipp, then turned to Justin/Justine. "By the way, I just love your skirt. Liz Claiborne?"

"No." Justin look startled. "It's mine. I bought it at Sears." He adjusted the ruffle down the front of his blouse. "This, too. The saleswoman said they were an outfit."

Justin had clearly gone overboard in his pursuit of breasts, and the ruffle nearly met his chin as it stretched between the two huge mounds. What in the heck had he used for his fake boobs? Coconuts? He looked as if he had just gotten off the set of *South Pacific*.

Skye turned her giggles into a coughing fit, and determinedly did not meet the eyes of either Kipp or Justin. Once she regained control, she said to Kipp, "Are you all finished with Justine?"

Kipp nodded and held out his hand. "All but . . ."

Justin picked up a dainty pink purse from the floor and clumsily undid the gold clasp. He reached inside, pulled out a fifty-dollar bill, and handed it to Kipp.

"Thanks." Kipp stuck it in his pocket and started to straighten the makeup tray.

Justin stood with his hand out, clearly expecting change, but Kipp was just as obviously well practiced at not noticing.

Before Justin could say anything, Skye stepped over to him and gripped his arm. "I need to have a word with you, outside."

His expression said no way did he want to talk to Skye alone, but he answered, "Yes, ma'am."

They started out the salon, Justin's six feet towering over Skye's five-seven, but Skye turned back to Kipp and said, "I won't be long."

"Sure. You're my last appointment. I'll start cleaning up while I wait for you."

As soon as they were outside, Justin said, "He didn't give me my change. It was supposed to cost forty-two dollars."

"He probably thought the remaining eight was his tip, since it's close to twenty percent."

"Tip! He gets a tip after charging over forty bucks for half an hour's work?" Justin scowled. "Man, what a rip-off."

"Welcome to a woman's world." Skye put her finger to her lips and directed Justin toward the empty gym. "I take it you're here dressed like Doris Day in order to get a story for the newspaper?"

"Who's Doris Day?"

"A nineteen-fifties movie star best known for her renewable virginity."

"Huh?" Justin jumped as if poked by an electric cattle prod, his face turned red, and he tested the gym door to make sure it was closed.

"Never mind." Skye shook her head. Justin and Frannie never failed to amaze her. He had the guts to dress as a girl and sneak into a spa, but the word virginity freaked him out. "Are you here for a story, or have you just discovered your true sexuality?"

"Ms. D! Don't even kid about that." Justin frowned. "You know I couldn't let Frannie scoop me on the hidden treasure story. She'd never let me forget it."

"Granted, but you do realize someone from town is bound to notice you? Most of the ladies here for the weekend live in Scumble River and have kids your age. If you stick around looking like that, I'll give you odds that someone snaps a picture of you, which will go through school faster than a flu germ."

He blanched, but remained stubbornly silent, staring at her as only a teenager could.

Skye was unfazed. She'd been dealing with Justin since he was in eighth grade, and had learned that he used silence like a weapon. "Why did you have Kipp do your makeup, of all things?"

"He was the only one willing to break the rules and take a day appointment." Justin gave her an "are you stupid" look and said, "My other choice was to have him do my hair, and I figured he'd notice I was wearing a wig."

Skye nodded. "So you're not booked anywhere else?"

"No. That was just to get past the guards. Now I'm going to take a look around."

Skye knew she should stop him, but how? Tie him up with his pink and green silk scarf? She had already made Kipp wait fifteen minutes; making him wait any longer would be just too rude. "Justin, be careful. There's already been one murder. Let's not add another to the list."

"Don't worry, Ms. D. I'm not investigating the murder. I just want to write a story about the treasure."

Skye walked back into the salon, troubled by Justin's reassurance. It sounded like the famous last words spoken in every teen movie, just before the villain's ax came down on the speaker's head.

Kipp was sitting in the client chair reading a copy of *W* when Skye reentered. He was a short, slim man of indeterminate age—somewhere between thirty and fifty. His face was unwrinkled, his hands baby smooth, but both his attitude and his eyes seemed to indicate he was older.

His khaki pants were perfectly pressed, and the spa's regulation silvery green polo shirt with his name stitched discreetly above the breast pocket was neatly tucked in. His tasseled loafers were polished, but he wore no socks.

As soon as he noticed Skye, he closed the magazine and got up. "All ready?"

"Yes. Thank you so much for your patience."

"No problem. I assume you straightened out our friend Justin."

"You knew she was really a he?" Skye wasn't surprised. Justin did not make a believable girl.

"Yep. The Adam's apple always gives them away."

"Them?" Skye sat down in the styling chair.

"Transvestites." Kipp whipped a cape around her neck. "Though I'm a little surprised to see one so young out in public in such a small town."

Skye smirked. "Oh; we're pretty open-minded in Scumble River." She couldn't wait to tell Justin that Kipp not only saw through his disguise, but thought the boy was a cross-dresser.

"Well, that's a relief." He ran his fingers through her hair. "Now, what would you like done?"

"I'd like to go blond."

"No."

"Why?" Skye was surprised. She'd always wanted to see what it would be like to be blond, plus it would take a while, giving her a chance to pump Kipp for information.

"Wrong complexion." Kipp wound a strand of her chestnut hair around his finger. "Besides, this is a beautiful color."

"How about some highlights?"

"That would work, especially with a new style." Kipp stepped back and studied her. "We should take off about two inches, do a side part, and just a hint of bangs."

"No bangs and only an inch off." Skye wore her hair all one length, just past her shoulders. She liked to keep it long enough to put in a ponytail or braid. "Let's try the side part."

"I'll dry it straight and use the flatiron to turn the ends under just a smidgeon."

"Perfect." Skye beamed. "So, how did you end up in Scumble River?"

An hour later, Skye hadn't learned anything new, but her hair looked terrific. Kipp stuck to his story. He grew up as an army brat, living all over the world. When he graduated from hair styling school he worked in various salons, day spas, and cruise ships. This was his first experience at an overnight spa.

Kipp handed Skye a mirror and twirled her around so she could look at the back of her hair.

"It's perfect." Skye got up and as she watched Kipp sweep up the bits of hair littering the floor, she said, "It must be hard to be stuck in Scumble River after traveling the world."

"For days off, Chicago's only an hour away." Kipp kept sweeping. "Otherwise we aren't supposed to leave the spa grounds."

"That sounds confining."

"It's the same as if I were working on a ship." Kipp still didn't look up.

"But at least when you get a day off on a ship, you're at some exciting port like St. Thomas or Acapulco. Here you're always at Scumble River."

"Sometimes it's nice to have a little bit of the same old, same old."

"True." She gathered her things and walked to the door. "Sorry I made you wait."

"Not a problem." Kipp waved good-bye.

As Skye walked down the brick path, she considered what she had learned from the hairstylist. Putting it all together, she was beginning to believe he really didn't know anyone at the spa before interviewing for the job. Still, there was something furtive about him. She had a feeling he was hiding something.

Lost in thought, it wasn't until she got to her room and reached for her key card that she discovered she had left her tote bag at the hair salon. Turning on her heel she hurried back, hoping Kipp hadn't locked up and left already.

The salon was dark when she reached it, the door closed and the lights off. Still, Skye thought she could hear something, so she knocked on the glass. Nothing. Maybe there was a storeroom in back where the hairstylist was working. She walked around the side and saw a door propped open. Good. Kipp must still be around.

Skye listened intently. She could hear music playing and

a rustling sound. She raised her hand to knock, and as soon as her knuckles touched the steel door it swung open on well-oiled hinges.

On a lounge chair that he'd obviously "borrowed" from the pool, one hand thrust deeply into a bag of nachos and the other holding a full margarita glass, sat Kipp Gardner. He was surrounded by shelves filled with bags of snacks, boxes of cookies, and sacks of candy.

Skye had stumbled on the Scumble River Spa black market. Had Esmé discovered the same illicit activity and threatened to expose Kipp? Would someone kill over a chocolate bar?

CHAPTER 23

That Puts a New Wrinkle on It

"So then he says, 'Five days a week my body is a temple. The other two, it's Disneyland.'" Skye finished putting on her makeup. She had a half hour before meeting with Dr. Burnett, and she wanted to look good for her appointment.

Trixie laughed so hard she fell off her bed. Still giggling, she picked herself up and asked, "What did you say?"

"What could I say? It's not like I exactly follow the FDA-approved food pyramid myself."

"Did Kipp admit to selling the forbidden food to the staff and clients?"

"Sort of. It was almost as if he thought I was taping him." Skye held up a pink tweed jacket with fringe trim and raised a questioning eyebrow at Trixie.

"That would look great with that pink long-sleeve T you just bought—the one with the lace around the bottom." Trixie peeled off her sweat suit. "Do you think Kipp killed Esmé because she discovered his undercover business?" She disappeared into the bathroom, leaving the door open so they could continue their conversation.

"No." Skye pulled on a pair of black slacks. "He didn't seem all that upset that I had discovered his secret." She slipped the T-shirt over her head, careful not to mess up her new hairstyle. "If he killed her for finding out, he would have tried to kill me too."

"So we can cross him off the suspect list." Trixie's voice rose above the sound of her shower. "How about the list of suspected treasure hunters?"

"He's still on that." Skye put on gold and pink chandelier earrings. "He admitted to Justin, AKA Justine, that he had looked for the jewelry, and obviously he likes making money."

Trixie came out of the bathroom wrapped in a towel and whistled. "You look terrific. I really like the highlights Kipp put in your hair. I wonder if I can get an appointment with him tomorrow before we leave."

"Go for it." Skye stepped into black loafers and grabbed her fanny pack. "Okay. I'm off to 'consult' with Dr. Burnett, then I'm meeting Wally so we can exchange information."

"Right. Exchange body fluids, maybe."

"Trixie!"

"And you'd better be careful with Dr. Frankenstein or you'll end up with a new nose, or humongous breasts, or lips so full of collagen you'll look like a blowfish."

"Mmm. Maybe he can get rid of this wrinkle between my eyebrows," Skye teased as she walked out and closed the door behind her.

Dr. Burnett's office was in a part of the mansion Skye hadn't yet visited, located just before the private suite of rooms he and Margot occupied.

Skye arrived precisely on time and knocked on the massive carved oak door.

An intercom buzzed to life. "Yes?"

"Hi. I have a four o'clock appointment with Dr. Burnett. It's Skye Denison."

"Come in."

A lock clicked open and she turned the knob. It felt like she was entering the Wizard of Oz's castle. The doctor sat behind an enormous desk. A gorgeous Tiffany lamp provided soft lighting—no harsh fluorescents in this doctor's office.

The room was huge, and a couch and two chairs formed a sitting area separate from the desk. Classical music was playing, and the aroma of sugar cookies floated in the air.

Skye took a big sniff. "Wow. It smells heavenly in here. Just like my grandmother's kitchen when she's baking."

"Aroma-Oxygen." Dr. Burnett got up and walked over to the sitting area, indicating Skye should follow him. She sat on the burgundy leather sofa and he chose a matching wing chair. "It takes away cravings for the real food."

Skye didn't comment, thinking the only thing that would substitute for a real sugar cookie would be a chocolate chip cookie or maybe a brownie.

After they were settled, Dr. Burnett asked, "What don't you like about yourself, my dear?" He reached out and gripped her chin with his thumb and index finger, then turned it first to the right, then to the left. "Mmm. Good skin tone, no acne scarring or deep wrinkles. No bags under the eyes."

"Thank you." Skye ignored his question and asked one of her own. "How long have you been a plastic surgeon?"

"Well, I'm not a plastic surgeon, per se." He fingered his silver mustache. "How would you like to try something brand new, a LifeWave Energy Patch?"

"A what?"

"It's like a nicotine patch, but instead of helping you to stop smoking, it revs up your body's flow of energy, which helps burn fat."

"No, I'm not really one to test products out." Skye tried to steer the conversation back to what she wanted to find out. "If you're not a plastic surgeon, what is your specialty?"

Dr. Burnett's answer was clipped. "Nutrition." His tall, lean body tightened and his smile was forced. "I know what would be perfect for you. How about a cell invigoration treatment? No medication or surgery required. You just lie in an infrared capsule."

"Sorry, I'll have to pass on that, too." Skye had heard of nutritionists, but never heard of a medical doctor specializing in nutrition. "Where did you practice before opening your spa?"

"Chicago." Dr. Burnett's long, thin fingers drummed on the arm of the chair. "Permanent eyeliner. The tattooing only takes moments, and saves you lots of time the rest of your life. I have hundreds of colors to choose from."

"Gee. That sounds terrific. But I have so many allergies, I'd be afraid of the dye." Skye answered in a rush, half afraid he would whip a needle from the pocket of his Italian silk suit. "Did you work from a hospital or your own office in Chicago?"

"I had my own clinic." Irritation was starting to crack Dr. Burnett's smooth façade. "I'm afraid I don't do the more involved surgery such as liposuction or tummy tucks, but I could recommend a colleague."

"Uh, no, thanks." Skye knew she was running out of time. "Was Esmé one of your patients at your Chicago clinic?"

"No."

"Oh, that first night at dinner, I thought she said that you had saved her by helping her with her diet."

"She didn't actually come to the clinic for that." Dr. Burnett hesitated a beat, then said, "It was one of those cases where someone corners you at a cocktail party for advice. As a psychologist, you must get that sort of thing all the time."

"Yes, I do." Skye nodded, although she was more likely to be cornered in the produce department at Walter's Supermarket than at a swanky party.

Dr. Burnett stood and Skye realized she couldn't squeeze in many more questions before he showed her out the door. "Do you have any theories about who was vandalizing the spa before it opened?"

"It was just someone's idea of a joke." Dr. Burnett herded Skye toward the door. "Or more probably, someone looking for that damn treasure. We're still getting fresh holes every day."

That wasn't what he had said when he demanded to see Esmé's body, claiming he feared it was really Margot who had been killed. "How about all the missing items the guests are complaining about?"

"Probably the housekeepers. I've told them if the thefts don't stop I'm firing them all."

"Maybe the vandalism is connected to Esmé's murder."

Skye watched as the good doctor's hand tightened on the knob.

"Of course not. The killer confessed. Unless you think those protestors were around before the opening day."

"Couldn't the vandalism and the treasure hunting be a cover for the real motive behind the murder?" Skye asked as the door opened.

"Anything's possible."

Burnett's hand on the small of her back was gently but firmly propelling her out. She could fit in only one or two more questions; she'd better make them good ones. "Margot mentioned that Esmé had gotten Botox injections in the past. Were you still giving them to her?"

"No, she had a bad reaction to the last ones, so when she arrived for this weekend, I told her I couldn't give her anymore."

Ah, huh! She had just caught him in a lie. Skye gripped the door jamb to stop her forward motion. "But you just said Esmé wasn't your patient, that you gave her diet advice at a cocktail party. So, when did you give her the shots?"

"My dear, you have obviously had little contact with the rich and famous." Burnett's tone was even, but his eyes indicated his irritation. "They do not go to clinics. Procedures such as Botox injections are given in their home or during a girls' night out get-together."

"Oh." Skye stumbled a bit as Burnett succeeded in pushing her over the threshold. "When you refused to give her the shots this weekend, did she say she would go to someone else for them?"

"Yes. And no, she didn't tell me who." As he closed the door, he said, "The offer for the LifeWave Energy Patch is still open. You could drop twenty pounds in a week."

Skye stopped herself from blowing a raspberry and forced herself to say, "No, but thanks for the offer."

It was a few minutes after five, so Skye hurried past the stairway, through the lobby, and out the front entrance. Wally's personal car, a blue Thunderbird convertible, was parked at the end of the sidewalk, and as soon as he spotted her, he got out and hurried around to open the passenger side door.

Skye kissed him on the cheek, hopped in, and said, "Let's get out of here."

He closed her door, jogged around the hood, and slid in beside her. With a questioning look, he put the car in gear and drove away.

She sighed and leaned her head back, not speaking until they had cleared the front gate, which was still mobbed by reporters being held back by security. Finally, she said, "They are all crazy back there."

Wally smiled and took her hand. "Tell me all about it." He turned toward I-55 and added, "I thought you'd probably feel like taking a break and getting out of town, so I made a reservation at the country club for dinner, okay?"

"Sure. Are you a member?" Skye forced herself not to sound surprised. She associated Simon with martinis at the country club and Wally with a six-pack on the lake at the recreation club.

"Yep, but I don't get there much."

Mmm. Skye worried her bottom lip. First the fancy car, then the new furniture, a housekeeper, and now a membership at the country club. Wasn't all that too much money for a cop's salary? Could he be on the take? No! She had jumped to conclusions about Simon; she wouldn't do the same with Wally. She knew the car was a gift from his father. Maybe the rest was, too.

Wally squeezed her hand. "You're awfully quiet. I thought you were going to tell me about all the crazy people at the spa."

"Just trying to get my thoughts in order. I know I got some good clues today, if I could separate them from the useless information." She smiled at him and squeezed back. "One thing I am worried about is Justin. You won't believe what he did."

"I bet I would."

After Skye finished describing her encounter with Justine, she said, "I meant to check and make sure he didn't get into any trouble investigating, but I ran out of time."

"No need to worry." Wally chuckled. "I thought that was him dressed in drag being tossed out by the security guards when I pulled in the front gate."

"Why didn't you make sure he was okay?" Skye had visions of the guards beating him up.

"The boy's got to learn the consequences of his actions. If he's going to be a journalist, he'll get thrown out of a lot of places." Wally must have noticed Skye's narrowed eyes because he added, "He was fine. His wig was hanging from his ear, he had lost a shoe, and I doubt the grass stains will come out of his skirt—which we hope he won't be wearing again anyway. Otherwise he was intact."

"Okay." Skye sighed. "Now if I could just think of what else I've forgotten."

"Take your time." Wally let go of her hand and turned on the CD player. "Maybe some music will help."

Wally was a golden oldies fan, and Skye let the familiar melodies roll over her as she processed what she had learned. When a new song started her eyes popped open. "That's it!" she shouted.

"You know who the murderer is?" Wally sounded incredulous.

"No, sorry, but I do know which song was playing on the CD when I found Esmé's body."

"This one?"

"Yes, 'The Great Pretender'." Skye hit herself on the forehead. "And that reminds me, the CD player was hot pink. I remember thinking it clashed with the restful decor."

"Which reminds me, I talked to the crime techs this afternoon," Wally picked up from where Skye left off. "They fingerprinted the CD player at the murder scene, but didn't collect it as evidence, so I came a little early tonight to pick it up. But it was gone."

"Crap!" Skye massaged her temples. "We just can't get a break."

"Maybe not, or maybe this is our break." Wally turned the car into the long drive that led to the country club. "Maybe the killer took it, not to get rid of it but because he—but I'm thinking now it's probably a she since the player is pink—feels safe enough to want it back. After all, no one but you and I know that the CD player was brought in by the murderer."

"I bet you're right. Now, we just need to check out everyone's rooms." Skye's tone turned sour. "But no search warrant because they already have a confession, right?"

"True, but the player's probably in plain sight so if someone happens to catch a glance . . ." He trailed off as he maneuvered the car into a tricky parking spot.

The clubhouse was cream-colored brick, and sported huge floor-to-ceiling windows. Inside, the golf shop and offices ran the length of the right wing; the opposite area consisted of several small rooms whose dividers could be opened to form one large space. Tonight the folding walls were all pushed back, and the restaurant was full.

Skye and Wally were shown to a table in a back corner against a window overlooking the eighteenth hole of the golf course. The hostess handed them menus, asked what they wanted to drink, and disappeared. A few minutes later, a waitress brought Wally his beer and Skye her frozen margarita, took their dinner order, and left them alone.

As soon as the server went away, Skye asked, "Did you ever find Rex Quinn?"

"Yes. You were right, he showed up at the spa looking for Whitney."

"Anything?"

"It was a touching reunion." Wally took a healthy swallow of beer. "A lot of crying, and Daddy telling Whitney she was his best girl, and it was just going to be the two of them from now on."

"It doesn't sound as if you believed their grief."

"You were more upset the time Bingo disappeared than these two are over Esmé's death. To be fair, Quinn seemed pretty broken up at first, but Whitney was faking it."

Skye nodded, then asked, "Did Mr. Quinn have proof he'd been out of the country?"

"He showed me his airline ticket stubs and hotel receipt, and gave me the names of people who can vouch they were with him the day of the murder."

"That's what I figured. It wouldn't make much sense for him to kill her. They'd been married only a year, and before that had been waiting for his divorce for a long time." Skye rummaged in her purse for a sheaf of yellow papers. "Did he take Whitney home?"

"No. He said he was exhausted from traveling and was afraid he'd fall asleep at the wheel, and Whitney can't drive a stick shift, so he got a room at the motor court and they're leaving for Hinsdale tomorrow. He moved there from Kenilworth after his divorce." The waitress served their salads and Wally speared a forkful of lettuce. "He said he's got a business call at eleven a.m. so they'll probably hit the road around one. He's got a huge, fancy funeral all planned for the day after. I told him the ME may not have released the body in time for that."

"I'll bet he didn't take that well."

"He said his attorney would take care of it. I didn't bother to argue. The ME won't let the body go until he's finished and no lawyer will change that."

"Right." She was used to the demands and threats of parents. It seemed as if everyone thought their attorneys could solve all their problems.

"Anything on your end?"

Skye scanned her notes, then filled Wally in on Amber's seven-year contract, Kipp's black-market business in forbidden foods, and the fact that Dr. Burnett claimed he hadn't given Esmé any Botox injections since her arrival at the spa.

Wally finished the last of his salad before saying, "Interesting. So unless he's lying, those injection sites the ME found were something else. Maybe some sort of sedative to cause her to lose consciousness and make her easier to hold under the mud."

"But why would Esmé allow someone to repeatedly stick a needle between her eyes?" Skye asked, then answered her own question. "Because she thought it *was* Botox."

"That makes sense."

"I've read a little about Botox. Doctors are *supposed* to administer the injections, but they often merely supervise others. Which means, Esmé might not have thought there was anything odd about a non-physician doing it, especially if she really wanted it and had been turned down by Dr. Burnett."

Wally broke off a piece of roll and buttered it. "We'll keep that in mind. Did you find out anything when you visited the Dooziers this morning?"

"Other than that they're trying to get people to pay for a mud bath in a children's swimming pool set up next to the lawn mower in their utility shed, you mean?"

He chuckled, popped the bread into his mouth, and made a go ahead gesture with his hand.

Skye started to say she hadn't learned anything else, then stopped suddenly and snapped her fingers. "I just realized that the Dooziers, as the leaders of the Red Raggers, have a widespread network they can tap into for information. Think about it. The few Red Raggers who actually do work for a living work in the service industries—cleaning, waiting on tables, and cutting grass. And a lot of the guys, like Elvis, pick up jobs here and there with construction companies."

"So?"

"So, that means they know about the treasure and there's a good chance they're the ones digging holes all over the place and causing all the vandalism. In fact, remember I mentioned seeing Elvis around the spa on several occasions?" Skye took a sip of her margarita. "Did I tell you they knew all about the mud bath treatment room, even down to the fact music was played?"

"No. But what's that got to do with the murder? Do you think a Doozier killed Esmé because of the treasure?"

"A Doozier would scam you for the treasure but not kill for it. No." Skye was silent for a minute, processing all the information, then nodded to herself. "What I do think is that for them to know something that only occurred during a short period of time, maybe an hour at most, there must be another way into that section of the spa."

"Wouldn't Margot or her husband have mentioned that? Unless you think one of them is the killer?"

"Not really. I can't come up with a motive for either of them, and you're right, they would have mentioned an alternative entrance to Trixie and me when Margot first asked us to catch the spa vandal."

"I'd forgotten she originally wanted you and Trixie to help her with that." Wally ran his fingers through his hair. "So, yeah, I agree she would have told you about another entrance."

"The more I think about it, the more I'm convinced that when the addition was built, the construction crew included several Red Raggers. We already know about Elvis, and there were probably others I wouldn't recognize. Together they added some sort of secret entrance into the main building without anyone knowing." Skye tapped her finger on the table. "To them it would be like opening a bank account. As long as the spa attracted a wealthy clientele, they could make frequent withdrawals."

She was silent for a moment, then added, "You know, now that we're talking about it, I've heard about several missing items—Whitney's cell phone, Bunny's watch, Dr. Burnett's cuff link, and another guest was complaining about losing a pair of earrings. Burnett blamed it on the housekeepers, but I bet it was the Dooziers."

"Sounds like you're on to something. Which means we need to convince the Dooziers to tell us where the entrance is and who else knows about it." Wally chugged the rest of his beer and stared morosely at the bottom of the glass. "Shit. How am I going to get Earl to come clean?"

"Maybe if you tell him how important this is and that he won't get into trouble for his treasure hunting . . ."

Wally shook his head. "There are a million things that influence Earl Doozier's decision to do anything, but reality is rarely one of them."

CHAPTER 24

Two Facials Are
Better Than One

"Let me see if I've got this straight." Trixie was sitting cross-legged on her bed, eating leftovers out of the doggie bag Skye had brought from the country club. "You've narrowed the killer down to a woman because the CD player is pink. You think she used a secret tunnel the Dooziers built for themselves so they could hunt for the hidden treasure and steal things from the guests. And whoever did it has access to a syringe and some sort of medication that will put a person to sleep. Is that right?"

"Right, except it doesn't have to be a tunnel, just another way into the spa's mud treatment suite." Skye finished putting on her pajamas and crawled into bed.

"Okay, that moves Dr. Burnett and Frisco down to the bottom of the suspect list, but Kipp seems to be the type of guy who might think a pink CD player was cool."

"True, but when I discovered him yesterday with his hand in the cookie jar, so to speak, I noticed his CD player was the normal black color. I'd be surprised if he has another one in pink back in his room. People with live-in jobs like this tend to travel light."

"Okay." Trixie finished off a chicken leg and licked her fingers. "So, all we need to do is look in everyone's room for a pink CD player, a CD with 'The Great Pretender' on it, and a syringe."

"Right. And we need to do it without a search warrant, so we need to have a legitimate reason for being in their room." Skye sat up and pulled a slip of paper from her PJ pocket. "Here's who we need to check out: Ustelle and Amber, Whitney and Margot. Also, the waitress and housekeeper who didn't have alibis, and Spike."

"Spike? You don't seriously think she's the murderer? What would be her motive?"

"Who knows? We know very little about her. Same goes for the housekeeper and waitress. Probably not, but maybe they knew Esmé years ago, and she did something to them."

"Bunny and Frannie didn't have alibis either," Trixie badgered. "How about them?"

"Very funny." Skye slid down and pulled the covers over her shoulders. "I'll put them on the top of my list."

Nearly everyone had made it to the eight o'clock breakfast. Even Skye had gotten up early, borrowed Trixie's car, and gone to the early Mass so she'd be back in time.

Now she sipped tea, and looked over the people scattered throughout the dining room. The spa's professional staff—Ustelle, Kipp, Amber, and Frisco—all shared a table, but ignored one another.

The Scumble River women sat together discussing the pros and cons of taking Frisco's nine o'clock water aerobics class versus Margot's Dress for Sexcess class. They had until noon to use the facilities, then an hour to change into their street clothes, and after that their spa weekend was officially over.

Skye ticked off in her mind where everyone else was headed. May was going to get a seaweed wrap with Ustelle, Bunny was having a manicure and pedicure from Amber, and Frannie was getting her hair done by Kipp. Loretta had opted for Margot's class and Spike for Frisco's. Margot had announced that Dr. Burnett was unavailable for appointments because he was away from the spa all morning. Whitney was unaccounted for.

Speaking of unaccounted for, where was Trixie? She

should have been down to breakfast by now. Had the first
step of their plan gone wrong?

Skye's gaze worriedly swept the dining room entrance.
Instead of seeing her friend coming in, as she hoped, she
saw Frannie and Elvis Doozier in an intense discussion.
Skye half rose from her seat to see what they were talking
about, when Frannie grinned like the Big Bad Wolf con-
fronting Red Riding Hood, and kissed Elvis on the cheek.
He stood frozen for a moment, then stumbled back, watching as Frannie rushed way.

Before Skye could decide which one to follow, Trixie
hurried into the dining room, dropped into the chair next to
Skye, and whispered, "Mission accomplished."

"You talked Margot into hiring us as temporary housekeepers?" Immediately, all thoughts of Frannie and Elvis
fled from Skye's mind.

"No problem." Trixie held up a key card. "I told her we
had narrowed the treasure hunter/vandal/thief down to half a
dozen guests and staff, and we wanted a legitimate reason to
look around their rooms."

"You're a genius. A scary genius, but still a genius." Skye
paused, then added, "Did she ask whose rooms we were
going to search?"

"Yes, but I managed to divert her attention without answering. I also had Margot tell the other housekeepers we
would be cleaning some of the rooms, and then I waited
until Margot walked away before I told Ruth and her partner
which rooms we wanted to clean."

"Excellent." Skye rubbed her hands together. "We'll start
as soon as everyone finishes breakfast and goes to their first
appointments. That way all of our suspects will be out of our
way while we search their rooms."

They waited until the dining room was empty, then gave
everyone ten more minutes to get to where they were going.
Finally, Skye scooted her chair back and got up, her
emergency-equipped fanny pack clanking. "Whitney is the
only suspect unaccounted for, so we need to be careful when
we get to her room."

"What's Wally doing while we snoop around here?" Trixie bounced up from her seat.

"He'll be looking around those empty guest cottages, especially the ones where I saw the lights on the other night. Elvis and Amber were using one, but I didn't get a chance to check out the other." Skye drank the last of her tea and put down the cup.

Trixie grabbed it and sniffed. "This is Earl Grey. How come the tag says Chamomile?"

"I knew I would have to eat down here this morning, so I switched tags on a couple of tea bags. I can cope with nothing edible, but I need my Earl Grey."

"You can cope with nothing edible because you've managed to avoid most of the meals. I, on the other hand, have not been so lucky. When I get home Owen won't recognize me. I'm nothing but skin and bones."

"Whose idea was it to come to this spa to begin with?" Skye demanded.

Trixie opened her mouth, then closed it. Finally she said, "Do you want to talk about the past or solve this murder?"

"Okay. Prepare to launch Plan B." Skye shook her head. "Let's hope it isn't the disaster Plan A turned out to be," she muttered under her breath, remembering that plan resulted in them capturing five treasure hunters instead of the one vandal they were really after.

Skye and Trixie had decided to start with the owner's suite, knowing Margot's class was the shortest activity on the schedule. After knocking several times to make sure the suite was empty, Skye and Trixie used their housekeeper's passkey card to let themselves into the sitting room. It was beautifully decorated but impersonal. There was no hint of the characters of the people who used it.

Skye whispered to Trixie, "You check out the sitting room, I'll take the bedrooms."

Trixie nodded and started looking through the desk.

The first bedroom Skye entered was clearly Margot's. Expensive perfume scented the air and the dresser was covered with jewelry and scarves. Skye quickly searched. No CD player, no CD, and no syringes.

She duplicated her search in Dr. Burnett's room and again found nothing. Trixie came up equally empty in the sitting room. After they finished their search, they hurriedly cleaned the suite, hoping Margot and Dr. Burnett wouldn't notice that the cleaning wasn't up to the usual standards.

Skye and Trixie repeated this procedure with each of their guest suspect's rooms, finally heading up a second flight of stairs to the staff's rooms, first searching and cleaning Ustelle's, then Kipp's, and finally Frisco's. They found nothing in any of them.

When they broke for lunch, Skye and Trixie went to the solarium for one last picnic lunch.

"It's a shame that the unalibied waitress lives off property, and that the housekeepers clean their own rooms," Skye said as she finished unpacking what was left of the food she had brought to the spa.

"I did find out that they've both lived in Scumble River their whole lives, so it's highly unlikely they had any chance to run into Esmé before this week. I think it's safe to scratch them off our suspect list." Trixie sat forward and made herself a sandwich using the last of the bread and lunch meat. "The real problem is that both Whitney and Amber had DO NOT DISTURB signs on their knobs, and we weren't sure if they were in the room or not, so we couldn't risk going in to search them."

"Why do you want to get into Amber and Whitney's rooms?" Frannie flung herself into one of the chairs drawn up to the coffee table and claimed the nearly empty bag of chips.

Skye and Trixie looked at each other. Skye gave a small shrug. In another hour, Wally would release the information that he didn't believe Rose Blossom was the real murderer, and everyone would know the investigation was still open. They might as well tell Frannie now.

Trixie gestured to Skye, who explained.

Frannie listened, then exclaimed, "I knew it! I just knew you two were up to something." She huffed and sat back on her chair. "I'm not a baby. If you had told me, I could have helped."

"Wally swore us to secrecy. Only Mrs. Frayne and I knew, she didn't even tell her husband," Skye soothed the teen. "You're the first one we've told."

"Weeellll." Frannie drew out the word in a manner only teenagers are capable of. "In that case, I've been in both Amber and Whitney's rooms. What were you looking for?"

Skye hesitated; should she tell Frannie? "Before we go any further, you must promise not to try and investigate on your own, and to stick with us until you and Bunny leave the spa. And you can't tell Whitney or Amber anything we've said."

"Duh. As if I would." Frannie swished her ponytail. "You know I'm only hanging around them to gather facts for my story." She wrinkled her nose as if she smelled rotten eggs. "They're not the type of friends I'd want."

"Right." Skye nodded. "I apologize. I was just worried about your safety."

Frannie shook her head. "Those two are so into themselves, I don't think they'd even notice if I searched their room right in front of them."

"But you won't," Skye warned.

"Don't be silly."

Skye was still unsure whether they should involve Frannie, and before she decided she had one more question. "What were you talking to Elvis about this morning?"

"I promised not to tell anyone." Frannie looked stubborn.

Trixie made an impatient sound. "Did it have anything to do with the murder?" When Frannie shook her head, Trixie said, "Fine. Now let's get back to something important. We're looking for three things—a hot pink CD player, a CD with 'The Great Pretender' on it, and a syringe."

"Okay, let me think." Frannie leaned back in her chair and closed her eyes. After a minute or so she said, "No syringes."

Skye leaned forward, hanging on the teen's every word. "What about the other stuff?"

"Yes, definitely a pink CD player. I don't remember seeing a CD disc, but I do remember hearing that song a couple of times. They both like oldies."

"Which one had the CD player?" Trixie asked impatiently.

"The problem is they share things, so I really don't know which one owns what." Frannie bit her lip. "I saw the CD player in both rooms."

"Shit!"

"Ms. D!" Frannie sounded shocked. "I've never heard you swear before."

"I rarely do, and never at school." Skye felt color creep into her cheeks. "I'm just so frustrated."

"Maybe there's something else that would help you decide which one did it," Frannie suggested.

"I'm leaning toward Whitney. Even though Amber doesn't have an alibi, I can't think of any motive for her, but Whitney clearly hated her stepmother." Skye rubbed her hand across her eyes. "And with Esmé dead, she gets her daddy back all to herself."

"But she had an alibi," Trixie reminded Skye.

"Unless Frisco lied for her." Skye chewed her bottom lip. "Wally did see them having sex in the garage Friday night." She ran her fingers through her hair. "But then, Frisco seems to be having sex with several women, so I'm not sure that would buy her his loyalty."

"On the other hand," Frannie jabbed her finger in the air, "by alibiing Whitney, Frisco provides an alibi for himself. That's his motivation for lying about Whitney being at the pool."

"Why would he need an alibi if he isn't the killer?" Trixie asked.

"Maybe he's the killer's partner," Frannie offered.

Trixie bounced off her chair. "That's it. It must be Whitney, and Frisco is covering for her. She has motive and opportunity. All we have to figure out is what she injected her stepmother with, then make Frisco admit he lied."

Skye pressed her fingers against her temples. Something was wrong with that logic, but she couldn't figure out what it was. "Frannie, you've got a great memory, right?" The teen nodded. "Okay, start with Whitney's room and describe everything you saw."

Frannie sat up straight and stared at the ceiling. "It was a mess, clothes and toiletries everywhere." She continued, ending with, "And this really cool black lace over white nylon tunic. Do you think I could find one in my size?"

Skye nodded absentmindedly. She hadn't heard anything that would help them, but she said, "That was great, Frannie. Can you do the same thing with Amber's room?"

"Sure." Frannie's voice was confident. "We spent more time there because she had a fridge and . . ." Her words skittered to a stop and she looked up at both adults with wide eyes. "And she had some vials in it, like the kind you see at the doctor's that he sticks the needles into before he gives you a shot."

Skye's mind leaped back to the first night and she smacked her knee. "Trixie, do you remember at dinner on Wednesday, Margot mentioned that Amber is diabetic?"

"Oh, my gosh, you're right." Trixie's words spurted out. "A diabetic needs insulin, but giving insulin to someone who isn't a diabetic will produce insulin shock, which eventually results in a coma."

Skye cut in when Trixie took a breath. "And since Amber is working here as a makeup artist, I'll bet Esmé would trust her to give her Botox injections, especially after Dr. Burnett turned her down. And Botox treatments involve several injections, so Amber could have given Esmé a massive dose of insulin, which along with Esmé being extremely thin and probably not having eaten much of anything—I didn't see her at breakfast that morning—would work really quickly."

"But why didn't Ustelle or Kipp spot Amber?"

"Amber probably injected Esmé with the insulin before Esmé went down in the mud bath treatment room. Then Amber waited for her opportunity, knowing that Ustelle nearly always left her clients if there was any chance to get away. Once Ustelle left, Amber checked, found Esmé unconscious from insulin shock, and pushed her under the mud."

"But why did she bring her CD player?" Frannie frowned. "Did she want music to commit murder by?"

"Because she wasn't sure that the insulin would render Esmé completely unconscious, and she wanted something that would cover up any noise her victim might make," Skye answered, then added, "Which is why Amber didn't just let her die from insulin shock, it was too iffy. Someone might find her in time to revive her."

Trixie screwed up her face. "Granted, Amber had means and opportunity, but what's her motive?"

They were all silent as they considered Trixie's question until Frannie mused out loud, "Now if it were Amber's stepmother, I'd understand. Amber hated Sheila's guts, especially after she got pregnant."

Skye's gaze fastened on Frannie and she demanded, "Say that again."

"What?" Frannie's expression was puzzled. "If Amber's stepmother had been the one murdered, Amber'd definitely be the killer?"

"Yes. That's got to be it." Skye jumped to her feet. "I'm ninety-nine percent sure."

"Sure of what?" Trixie urged.

"Do you remember that first dinner we had, when Margot mentioned that Whitney and Amber had been reunited around the time that Amber's stepmother died?"

"Yes." Trixie drew her brows together. "So? Are you saying Amber killed her?"

"No. Whitney did it for Amber." Skye's tone was confident. "And in return, Amber killed Esmé for Whitney. That way neither had a motive for the murder they actually committed."

"Strangers on a Train," Trixie murmured.

"Huh?" Apparently Frannie was not a Hitchcock fan.

"It's a movie made in the fifties, where two men each agree to kill off someone the other wants dead."

Frannie nodded excitedly. "That makes sense. Amber and Whitney love old movies."

"That's what's been bothering me." Skye smacked her knee. "Whitney claimed she wasn't really friendly with Amber, and we, the adults, never saw them together socially at the spa. But because Frannie was closer to their age, and made a point of hanging out with one or the other, she did. Frannie just told us they were often in each other's rooms and shared their stuff to the extent that Frannie didn't even know what belonged to Amber and what belonged to Whitney."

"That's right." Trixie nodded. "Why deny a friendship unless it was important that people not associate you with the other person?"

Skye felt galvanized. "Okay, here's the plan. I need to find Wally, so he can check how Amber's stepmother died. And let's hope he can get a search warrant for her room."

"Why wouldn't he be able to?" Frannie asked.

"I don't know if we have enough evidence to convince a judge to issue one," Skye answered distractedly, then said to Trixie, "Can you go get our suitcases and check us out?"

"Sure."

"Frannie, you absolutely cannot tell anyone about this conversation until I've spoken to Wally. I want you to go get your stuff and Miss Bunny, and meet Trixie at the reception desk. Okay?"

Frannie nodded, but made a face. "I know not to tell anyone. I wish you'd stop treating me like a baby."

"Sorry." Skye was too distracted to take the time to deal with Frannie's resentment, but she made a mental note to try to smooth things out later. As she hurried toward the door, she flung over her shoulder, "Trixie, make sure Mom and Loretta check out, too. I'll meet you all in the lobby. Everyone needs to be safely gone if Wally comes back with the search warrant."

"Will do."

Skye ran down the hallway and out the rear door toward the cottages, hoping Wally would still be there. When she arrived he was nowhere to be seen. Suddenly, she remembered the police radio in her fanny pack. Feeling like an idiot for having forgotten it, and wasted time, she took a deep breath and glanced around.

It looked all clear, so she took the radio out and keyed the mike. "Wally, this is Skye. Are you there?"

A few seconds later Wally's voice echoed thinly, "Go ahead."

"I have some urgent information."

"Not over the radio. Are you okay? Where are you?"

"I'm fine," Skye answered. "I'm on the path between the VIP cottages."

"Stay put. Be there in ten. I'm back at the police department."

She found an out-of-the-way bench and sat down. While she waited, Skye went over everything in her head. She was sure she was right. Amber was the killer.

Time ticked by slowly, with Skye checking her watch every few minutes. Finally, at exactly one o'clock, she saw Wally hurrying down the path. She sprang up, and grabbed his hand, dragging him back to her secluded bench.

She checked to make sure they were alone, then told him the whole story, concluding with, "So, when Frannie mentioned the insulin vials in Amber's fridge, everything snapped into place."

"It makes an awful kind of sense." Wally leaned forward, resting his elbows on his knees and staring into space. "I'll find out how Amber's stepmother died, and if it's at all suspicious, I should be able to convince a judge to give me a warrant. I wish Whitney wasn't leaving, but at least Amber's staying right here."

They got up, and she said, "What I can't quite grasp is what would make two girls want their stepmothers dead that badly? It's not as if they were children and had to live at home, or that the stepmothers were beating them."

"We've both seen worse." Wally gave her a quick kiss, then turned toward the parking lot. "Luckily, we usually see better."

As she rushed toward the lobby, Skye smiled, happy that Wally was still optimistic after all his years in law enforcement. So many police officers shown on TV were burnt-out. It was a relief to know that the real-life cop she was involved with wasn't like that.

When Skye got to the lobby it was empty except for Trixie pacing frantically with the telephone receiver in her hand. Skye asked, "Who are you calling?"

"Wally, but the dispatcher put me on hold before I could tell her it was an emergency."

"What emergency and where is everyone?" Skye asked, alarmed.

"The mass exodus took place about ten minutes ago. I sent your mom, Loretta, Bunny, and Spike along with the rest of them."

"What about Frannie?"

"She never showed up. Bunny said she came to their room, gave Bunny your message about checking out, and asked Bunny to take her suitcase downstairs."

"No one's seen her since then?" Skye's alarm intensified.

"No. As soon as I realized she was missing, I called the police. I've been waiting on hold ever since."

Skye tried the police radio, but got no response. "We'd better go look for her ourselves. We can ask a security guard to come with us."

Trixie made a face. "Good idea, but as of one o'clock, Margot gave everyone the rest of the day off. The staff poured out of here like water over Niagara Falls. They were gone before most of the guests."

"Shit!" Skye ran up the stairs with Trixie close behind. "Did you see Whitney and Amber leave?"

"No, but Whitney could have left with her dad earlier, and Amber could have used another exit." Trixie looked right, then left. "Which way?"

Skye paused for a nanosecond, then said, "Amber's room."

They sprinted up the attic stairs. The staff floor was decorated very differently than the public and guest areas of the spa. Instead of rich wallpaper, industrial off-white paint covered the walls. The floors were linoleum instead of marble, and the light fixtures utilitarian rather than elegant.

Skye could imagine how unhappy Amber would be in this environment after having grown up in a Kenilworth mansion. Skye shivered. It seemed colder up here, too, as if the furnace had been shut off, or maybe the hallway wasn't heated.

The door to Amber's room was shut, but they could hear Frannie clearly through the cheap plywood. "I really need to go now. Miss Bunny will be waiting for me, and she's not the patient type."

"But I thought you wanted to know about my poor step-mother's tragic death." Amber's tone was mocking and they heard the rattle of a newspaper. "It's just like they reported in the *Trib*, the paper I caught you stealing from my closet. Sheila committed suicide by overdosing on her own sleeping pills after drinking too much vodka."

"Oh, I see. Well, that's that then." Frannie's voice was slightly unsteady. "Gotta go. Can't miss my ride."

"Not just yet. What did Elvis say to you this morning at breakfast?"

"Elvis? The dead singer? You think he talks to me?" Frannie's voice sounded strained.

"Don't try to be cute." Amber's words were like knives, intent on causing damage. "You're too fat to pull it off. Elvis Doozier. What were you two talking about in the dining room this morning?"

"I promised not to tell."

"Why? Did he let you in on a big secret?"

"I can't say." Frannie's footsteps came toward the door.

"Since you're so interested in our business, if you tell us what Elvis told you, we'll tell you the real story of my step-mother's death."

"That sounds like an interesting story, but I don't have time right now. Maybe we could e-mail." Frannie sounded as if she were right on the other side of the door. "Miss Bunny will be wondering what's happened to me."

"It's good that you have adults who worry about you." Whitney's tone was wistful. "At least someone will be sad when you turn up missing."

"Why would I be missing?" Frannie's voice was even shakier this time.

"Because we know what Elvis told you, and we can't let you tell anyone else."

"Too late." Frannie's bravado sounded near the breaking point. "I already told Ms. D and Mrs. Frayne when we had lunch together today."

There was a sudden hush, then a low buzz of conversation that Skye couldn't hear. Did Elvis know that Amber had killed Esmé, and if so how had he found out?

Finally, Amber said, "We don't believe you. If you had told those two nosy bitches the police would already be here."

"Chief Boyd is getting a warrant as we spe—"

Amber's scream cut Frannie off in midword, "Bullshit!" Skye heard Amber take a deep breath, then say, "But just in case you're telling the truth, we'd better hurry this up." Her voice rang out like a judge sentencing a criminal to the electric chair.

At that moment, Skye knew Amber and Whitney were going to kill Frannie. She wished she could see what was happening inside the room; she'd give anything for an old-fashioned keyhole right now. She reached out and gingerly tried the knob and was surprised when it turned easily in her hand. She gave Trixie a look that said, "Ready?"

Trixie nodded, reached into her purse, and pulled out the mace. Skye took out her own can. She already had her fanny pack open and the police radio keyed to transmit. She only hoped Wally was hearing all this. They positioned themselves on either side of the frame, like they had seen on every cop show, and pushed in the door.

The three girls wheeled around. "How long have you been there?" Amber demanded.

"Long enough to hear you threatening Frannie." Skye held up her police radio. "And I've had this on the whole time, so all of Scumble River heard you. You might as well turn yourself in." Skye tried to sound confident.

"Oh, I don't think so." Abruptly, Amber grabbed Frannie and put her arm around the teen's throat; her other hand pressed a pair of hairstyling shears just below Frannie's eye. "Throw down the mace or I'll cut her so bad she'll never see again, and have to wear a veil for the rest of her life." She dragged Frannie toward the door, Whitney crowding close behind.

Suddenly, Frannie stopped and slumped to the floor. Frannie's heavier weight pulled the lighter girl off balance and Skye saw her chance. She leaped on Amber, spraying the mace directly in her eyes.

Trixie grabbed Whitney's arm and commanded, "Stand still, or I'll give you some of the same."

Amber had dropped the scissors and was clawing at her eyes. Skye was distracted by a moan from the floor and she bent down to see if Frannie was all right. As soon as she took her eyes off Amber, the girl ran from the room.

Trixie renewed her hold on Whitney and barked, "Don't even think of it."

Skye hesitated, but Frannie said, "I'm fine, go ahead."

Even with her eyes burning, Amber was younger and in better shape than Skye—she was nowhere in sight. Skye cautiously tried the doors down the hall; all were locked. That meant Amber had to have gone down the stairs.

The second floor guest rooms were all locked, too, so Skye ran down to the lobby. A vase was smashed on the floor, having been swept off a table that was overturned, and the entrance door stood wide open. Skye ran through in time to see Wally chase Amber across the drive and grab her in just a few strides.

"Let me go!" She wiggled free, darting a few steps. "We just wanted revenge against the women who had stolen our fathers. Is that so wrong?"

"That's for a judge and jury to decide." Wally grabbed her again and hauled her back to the squad car, positioning her face down across the hood. "Take your hands off the car, and I'll make sure your birth certificate is a worthless document."

Skye grinned. It was good to see Amber getting a lesson in reality.

That's a Wrap

It was hard to believe that only five days earlier Frannie had been held at scissor-point by the Scumble River Spa Slayers—at least that's what the newspapers were calling Amber and Whitney. Tonight Frannie looked radiant, surrounded by her friends and family, celebrating her seventeenth birthday.

Skye and Wally had argued about attending Frannie's surprise party, which Xavier, Simon, and Bunny were throwing for her at the bowling alley. Skye thought she should go alone, while Wally wanted to come as the "and guest" on her invitation.

It wasn't that she didn't want to spend the evening with Wally, or be seen in public with him. It just seemed a bit of a slap in the face to Simon and his mother. That, and she was afraid that the two men would get into a fight and ruin Frannie's special evening. Wally had finally agreed with Skye, but he insisted on dropping her off at the party and picking her up when she was ready to leave. Was this a jealous side of Wally she had never noticed before?

She could understand him not wanting her to spend time with an ex-boyfriend. She'd feel the same way about Wally's ex-wife, and she secretly found a little jealousy attractive. But his possessiveness would get old quickly if he acted that way about all the men she came in contact with.

Skye's thoughts were interrupted as Bunny clanked two martini glasses down on the table and dropped into a chair. With a grunt, she adjusted the cleavage created by her pink crocheted halter top, tugged down the matching miniskirt, and pushed her crocheted cowboy hat out of her eyes.

Skye was struck speechless by Bunny's outfit. The red-head looked like a walking doily dyed in Pepto-Bismol.

Bunny finally looked up and said, "You and the police chief have a fight?"

"No."

"Then why isn't he here?" The redhead shoved one of the glasses in front of Skye. "Try this."

"I thought it was inappropriate to bring him to a party that Simon was paying for." Skye looked around. "By the way, where is Simon?"

"He called and said he'd be a little late, but he wouldn't tell me why." Bunny raised an eyebrow. "Maybe his date wasn't ready on time."

"He's bringing a date?" Skye hadn't thought of that possibility, and wondered how she felt about seeing Simon with another woman.

"Who knows?" Bunny threw a pointed look at Skye. "He's free to, right?"

"Certainly." Skye knew she'd better change the subject, so she sniffed the concoction in front of her—it was the same color as Bunny's outfit—and asked, "What's this?"

"Cosmopolitan à la Bunny."

Skye took a mouthful. "Hey, this is good. Thanks."

"Of course it is." Bunny smirked. "I made it myself."

The two women sipped in companionable silence until Skye asked, "Has Spike gone home? I wanted to say goodbye, but with school starting back up, this past week has been a blur."

"She left last night." Bunny's usually ebullient personality seemed a bit dampened. "I'm glad she agreed to stay with me for a couple of days so we could talk."

"Is everything okay between you two?"

"As good as I have a right to expect, after tossing her away."

"Giving her up for adoption is not the same thing as tossing her away." Skye frowned. "You made sure she had a good family when you knew you couldn't take care of her."

"It seemed like the right thing to do at the time. But now I don't know."

Skye was puzzled. "You've never shown much remorse for deserting Simon for twenty years. What's the difference between what you did with him and what you did with Spike?"

"He was with his father, and I kept tabs on him through friends—they even sent me pictures. But Spike was with strangers."

"They weren't strangers to her, they were her family. Do you see the difference?"

Bunny nodded, tears in her brown eyes.

They were silent again until Frannie and Justin joined them.

Frannie held out her left hand. "Look what Justin got me for my birthday." A tiny diamond chip in the center of a gold heart sparkled on her finger. "Isn't it beautiful?"

Before Skye could form the words, Bunny, who seemed back to her usual self, demanded, "Is that an engagement ring?"

Justin, who had been taking a swallow from his can of Coke, choked and Frannie giggled.

"No, silly, it's a promise ring. We're going steady."

Skye felt a huge sense of relief—sixteen and seventeen were way too young to be thinking about marriage. Besides, if Frannie got engaged before Skye did, May would have an aneurism.

As if Skye had conjured up her mother, May appeared beside her and sat down. "What are you guys looking at?"

As Frannie showed off her ring and explained its significance, Trixie and Owen pulled up chairs. They were all admiring Justin's gift to Frannie when the doors to the bowling alley swished open, and Simon strode in. His auburn hair was windblown, his pants legs and shoes were caked with mud, and he wasn't wearing the jacket to his suit.

Skye had never seen Simon in such dishabille. What in heaven's name had happened?

He stopped at the table and dropped wearily into the remaining chair. Up close, Skye could see that his cheeks were flushed and the tip of his nose was red.

Bunny demanded, "What in the world happened to you?"

He put up a finger, indicating he needed a second, then grabbed his mother's martini glass and drained the contents. Smacking the glass back on the table, he grinned. "I found the Bruefeld Treasure."

Everyone started talking at once, but May made herself heard above the others, "Wow. Now you must be really rich."

"Not exactly." Simon chuckled. "First, I agreed to give Margot and Creighton half, and second, I suspect the jewelry is fake."

"What?" Again, the whole table exploded in questions.

Simon finally quieted everyone down and explained. "My guess is that Mr. Bruefeld exchanged the real jewelry for phony pieces when he first started losing money, but never told his wife he had made the switch. Good replicas were often made back then so the real jewels wouldn't be stolen."

"All that trouble and they're worthless," Trixie grumbled.

"Not quite. They're nice costume pieces, collectibles. They're probably worth a couple of thousand dollars."

"So how did you solve the riddle?" Frannie asked.

"The riddle was: THE MAN WHO INVENTED ME DOESN'T WANT ME. THE MAN WHO BUYS ME DOESN'T NEED ME. THE MAN WHO NEEDS ME DOESN'T KNOW IT." Simon paused, as if waiting to see if anyone else could get the answer. When no one did, he continued, "So, I had a little head start because of my profession."

"How does being a funeral director help you solve it?" Justin drew his brows together.

"The 'it' referred to is a casket," Simon explained. "Once I realized that, I went to the family cemetery with a metal detector, and after eliminating metal coffins by their size, I found the spot, dug, and there was the jewelry box."

"Very clever," Skye finally said. She wasn't sure how to treat Simon after their awful encounter at the diner, but felt her silence was growing noticeable.

"Thank you." Simon dipped his head in acknowledgment, then said, "I have a question for you." He smiled back. "Did you ever figure out who were in the cottages the night I startled you?"

"Amber and Elvis were in the one I was peeking into, but I knew that. It's the other one that I didn't get a chance to check out, but Wally thinks he's figured it out." Skye faltered when she saw Simon wince at Wally's name, then went on quickly. "He found a wig, colored contact lenses, a theatrical makeup kit, and a navy pantsuit with a badge pinned to the jacket pocket."

"Special Agent Vail," May shouted out.

"Yep, that's what he thinks." Skye nodded. "For some reason this woman impersonated a police officer for a day, then must have hung out in the cottage for a while watching everyone."

"Any idea who she really was or why she did it?" Justin asked with a reporter's gleam in his eye.

"None at all," Skye answered, trying not to let the teen see that she was still troubled by that issue herself. She had a feeling they hadn't seen the last of Veronica Vail or whomever she was, and that when she reappeared she'd bring her own brand of evil with her.

"Since we're asking questions, I have a few myself." Bunny folded her arms. "For instance, why did Ustelle keep disappearing? Why was Kipp so jumpy? And what was the deal with Frisco?"

"Ustelle and her boyfriend Carlos want to open their own spa, so she was trying to discover the secret ingredient in Miracle Mud," Skye explained. "Kipp was selling contraband food and afraid Margot would find out and fire him, and Frisco was sleeping with anything female and trying to keep them all from finding out about each other."

"What I want to know is, how did Wally get Amber and Whitney to confess?" Frannie asked. "If they would have kept their mouths shut, they might have gotten away with it."

"Maybe." Skye shook her head. "But I doubt it. Once the police knew what had really happened, they would have been able to round up the forensic evidence, such as the needle Amber used on Esmé, to support their case. That, along with Elvis's testimony, would have been enough to put Amber away. Then they would have reopened Amber's stepmother's case."

"Is that why they confessed, they knew the jig was up?" Bunny asked.

"No. Wally tricked them. He told both Amber and Whitney that the other had confessed and blamed both murders on her partner," Skye reported. "Amber held out for a while, but Whitney was the weaker link, and she confessed the whole plan in exchange for a lighter sentence."

"That's not fair." Frannie smacked the table. "They were both murderers."

"True, but sometimes that's the only way to insure the guilty parties come to justice." Skye patted the teen's hand. "And both Amber's and Whitney's fathers are refusing to give them money for their defense."

The group was silent until Bunny whined, "I still don't understand how they did it, or where the Dooziers' secret entrance was."

"Yeah," Frannie chimed in. "How did Whitney get close enough to put pills in Amber's stepmother's booze? Why did Amber take the job at the spa once her stepmother was dead and her dad had taken her back? And, last, why didn't Amber and Whitney just alibi each other?"

Skye combed her fingers through her hair. "About the time Whitney and Amber reconnected online, Esmé started to talk about getting pregnant. Amber warned Whitney what would happen if her father thought he would have a new little girl. Amber's own stepmother was expecting, which had made Amber's father pay even less attention to her. As a result of the perceived neglect, Amber and Whitney concocted their plan to kill each other's stepmothers. Amber's stepmother had to be killed first, before she had the baby. Whitney took a job as Amber's stepmother's social secretary under an assumed name, which made access to the alcohol bottles easy."

"Okay, I can see that, but how about Amber's spa job?"

"Even though the spa just opened, Margot lined up her staff nearly a year ago. Amber signed the contract for the job before her father became a widower and started showering her with presents again. The two girls decided that if Whitney could persuade her father to give her and Esmé the spa trip as a gift, it would be the perfect opportunity for Amber to kill Esmé."

"So why didn't they alibi each other?"

"Because they thought it would look too suspicious, and they didn't want the police to link the two of them so closely. They decided it was more important for Whitney to have an alibi since Amber had no motive. They were careful not to let anyone notice them spending time together, but," Skye nodded at Frannie, "they couldn't hide it from you because you hung around with one or the other of them so much."

Trixie reached over and took a sip of Skye's drink, then said, "What I don't understand is why they panicked when they found Frannie in Amber's room. If they had just played it cool, they might have gotten away with the murders."

"Ah." Skye snatched her glass back and finished off the pink liquid. "It all goes back to the Dooziers."

Bunny scratched her head. "What did they have to do with anything?"

"As it turns out, several of the clan worked on the construction crew that Margot hired to remodel the spa. I noticed Elvis the first day, and the contractor confirmed the others when Wally asked him. Anyway, since they figured the spa would attract a lot of rich people, they added a hidden entrance to the new mud treatment room addition so they could do a little stealing now and then. Remember the floor-to-ceiling windows overlooking the river? Well, one of them opens like a French door."

Skye waited until everyone understood, then added, "The Dooziers also wanted an easier way to hunt for the treasure. They were behind all the pre-opening vandalism. They wanted to delay the spa from being ready for guests until they found the jewelry."

"So Amber used the hidden door?" Justin asked.

"No. That was Elvis." Skye glanced around and saw confusion on most faces. "Unfortunately, he fell in love with Amber and when she didn't return his affection, he turned to stalking her, using the hidden door to gain access to the spa."

"He saw her commit the murder, right?" Trixie guessed.

"Yep, he watched her go into the treatment room after Ustelle left, then come out covered in mud. After the news of the murder came out, he must have figured out what had happened and he threatened her with exposure if she didn't date him." Skye turned to Frannie. "It was him on the phone the day we were getting manicures and Amber had to leave."

Frannie hit her head. "So, that was why Amber was so freaked out about me talking to him. She thought he had told me about her being the murderer."

"Exactly." Skye nodded, then asked, "What *did* he tell you?"

Frannie hesitated, then answered, "He told me he knew where the treasure was, and I could be there when he dug it up to write a story about him. I guess he didn't really know since Simon found it and not him."

Justin shook his head. "Up to that point, those girls were really smart, weren't they?"

"Maybe." Skye made a face. "But like I saw on a T-shirt the other day, the difference between genius and stupidity is that genius has its limits."

School psychologist Skye Denison had endured the situation for as long as she could. Improvements on the outside were well and good, but they didn't make her feel any better about the ugliness on the inside. It was time to put an end to her suffering.

She ignored the ringing telephone. There really wasn't anyone she wanted to talk to badly enough to untie the rope, climb down from the ladder, and find the phone in the mess she had created in her dining room. She sighed with relief when the ringing stopped, but let out a small scream of frustration when it started right up again.

Evidently, whoever was calling knew that her answering machine picked up on the fourth ring and was hanging up after the third. This meant it was someone who called her on a regular basis. Skye paused as she tightened the knot. Who would be so determined to reach her that they would keep punching the redial button again and again?

It wasn't her boyfriend, Wally Boyd, chief of the Scumble River police department. He had phoned earlier canceling their date for that night with the lame excuse that "something had come up." His call had been the start of her bad day.

Another possibility was her best friend, Trixie Frayne, school librarian and Skye's co-sponsor of the school newspaper, but they had already spoken. Trixie had called to tell Skye that one of the parents was suing *The Scoop* for slander, and Trixie and Skye were scheduled to meet with the district's lawyer at seven a.m. on Monday. Homer Knapik, the high school principal, would have a cow when he heard the news—then make Skye and Trixie shovel the manure.

A quick glance at her watch and Skye knew it couldn't be her brother, Vince. Saturday morning was the busiest time at his hair salon. And Skye's godfather, Charlie Patukas, the owner of the Up a Lazy River Motor Court, wouldn't bother with repeated calls; he'd just jump in his Caddy and come over. After all, there were few places in Scumble River, Illinois, that were more than a five- or ten-minute drive.

Shoot! That left only one person, and she would never stop dialing until Skye answered. Moaning in surrender, Skye made sure the rope holding the chandelier up out of the way was tied tightly, and reluctantly climbed down the ladder. She waited for the next group of rings to help locate the phone, then picked up the edge of the tarp she had put down to protect the hardwood floor, and grabbed the receiver.

"It's about time you answered." The voice of May Denison pounded into Skye's ear. "There's a family emergency. Get over here right away."

Skye growled in aggravation as her mother hung up without further explanation. Then her mother's words penetrated the fog of her bad mood. *Emergency!* Had something happened to Skye's father? Her grandmother? One of her countless aunts, uncles, or cousins?

A busy signal greeted Skye's repeated attempts to call back. No doubt May had taken the phone off the hook to force Skye to come over as ordered, rather than phone and ask questions.

Catching her reflection as she hurried past the foyer mirror, Skye hesitated. Her chestnut curls were scraped back into a bushy ponytail, the only paint on her face was the Tiffany blue she was using on her dining room walls, which did nothing for her green eyes, and the orange sweat suit she had put on to work in made her look like a big, round pumpkin.

Shaking her head, she decided it would take too much time to transform herself into a presentable human being, and instead grabbed her jacket, purse, and keys from the coat stand. She ran out of the house and leapt into the 1957 Bel Air convertible her father and godfather had restored for her a few years ago after several unfortunate incidents that left her previous cars undrivable.

The Chevy was a boat of a car, which made it hard to lay rubber, but Skye stomped on the accelerator and the Bel Air flew down the blacktop, white vapor pouring out of the tailpipe in the below-zero temperature. Seven-and-a-half minutes later Skye wheeled into her parent's driveway and skidded to a halt on the icy film covering the gravel.

Where were all the vehicles? If there was a family emergency, the driveway should be packed with cars and trucks. Did her mom need a ride to the emergency? No, May's white Olds was parked in the garage. What the heck was going on?

Skye flung herself out of the Bel Air, jogged up the sidewalk, and across the small patio to the back door. She spared a glance at the concrete goose squatting at the corner. Except for the holidays, when it was dressed as anything from a Halloween witch to an Easter Bunny, its costume was usually a good barometer for May's mood. Given that it was January 10, too late for New Year's and too early for Valentine's Day, the fact that it was wearing an apron and a tiny chef's hat, and had a rolling pin clutched in its wing, must mean something, but darned if Skye had a clue as to what.

Shrugging, she continued into the house, calling, "Mom, what's going on? What's the emergency?"

Silence greeted her as she dashed through the utility room's swinging doors and into the kitchen. Still no sign of her mother, but Skye slid to a stop as her gaze swept past the counter peninsula and reached the dinette.

Skye felt all the blood drain from her head and the room start to sway as she stared at the table. She sank to her knees and closed her eyes, hoping she was dreaming or having a hallucination, but when she opened her eyes again the wedding cake was still sitting there—three layers of pristine white frosting with delicate pink roses and a vine of ivy trailing down its side.

Surely, even May, a women desperate for her daughter to get married and produce grandkids, wouldn't throw an emergency wedding.